SHADOWLANDS SECTOR

THREE

MILA YOUNG

CONTENTS

SHADOWLANDS SERIES

SHADOWLANDS SECTOR THREE

There is no more running…

…this time, I'm willing to fight to the death. Mine and theirs.

Because of me, my three mates have been captured by our enemy, and once again I am all alone.

But I can't let the enemy's treachery be their fate. Not for me, not for the future we thought we had.

My only option is to take this fight to him. Let embrace the monster inside me I have feared my whole life.

The enemy thinks I'm the key to his biggest problem…

The undead.

I can't be that key. I must return. I must save my men. No matter the cost.

I'm running out of time. My life for the alphas.

I have one choice. That's an easy decision. And my monster

agrees. We're out for blood, and this time I'm not leaving until the enemy pays.

Shadowlands Sector is the final book in this trilogy. The spin-off series, Savage Sector, is set in the same world and is coming out soon. Find an exclusive first look at chapter one at the end of this novel.

CHAPTER 1

MEIRA

*F*ear strangles my chest.

I step back, using all four paws easily, which is strange in itself.

I'm a freaking wolf with tawny, reddish fur. No longer the girl I was a year ago… or even the girl I was yesterday. We live in a brutal world and it changes you. Both mentally and physically in my case.

My gaze whips to my three men, three Alphas… three mates who've claimed me. And it kills me to see them lying on the ground, knocked out by Mad's men to get to me. And all I can remember is them being attacked, the terror in Dušan's eyes as he fell. Then I transformed.

These men who've attacked us inch toward me, a semi-circle of half a dozen.

I want them to pay with every fibre of my being, but I'm not even sure how to control my new wolf body.

My wolf is her own entity and it's like there's two of

us in my body fighting for dominance. Is that how the other wolves feel?

She shoves against my insides, and I stumble on my feet to grasp onto any semblance of normality.

Involuntarily tilting my head back, I raise my chin and unleash a shattering howl.

A shiver flares over me, my mind fluttering between sanity and the savagery of my wolf. She's so strong I can barely hold her back.

Hunger and revenge course through me, the emotions rip at me. She craves death, unlike anything I've ever imagined.

Pure addictive ferocity, and I'm salivating at the thought. Except that's not me, is it?

Mad and his assholes approach me in slow motion in a semi-circle to trap me. Still, fear swims in their gazes and I smell it in their air like sour perspiration.

The syringe draws my attention to Mad's fist.

A tall brute lunges toward me, roaring more like a bear than a wolf. Something flashes over my thoughts, like a spark of energy.

Next thing, I'm darting toward the man threatening me, my head in two places at once. I scream on the inside as I crash into his middle, and bring him down fast. While my wolf snarls with satisfaction, panic frantically chills my bones that she has control over me. That I am the one in the backseat of this relationship.

Faster than lightning, she snaps back to his face, teeth sinking into his neck. She rips out his throat so fast, the man has no chance to scream.

Terror latches onto me, and I'm backpedaling, grappling to draw her back. My mind drowns in images of her completely dominating me.

I cling onto that semblance of control as she pulls against me.

If I truly let go and my wolf were to take charge, will I ever find myself again?

Mad smirks, not even caring that his man is gurgling on his own blood at his feet.

I growl, lips peeled back, the back of my neck bristling with fur. The white haired Alpha had captured me in the woods so long ago to trade me. He's going to pay for ambushing his true Alpha, Dušan, and betraying him.

One of his fighters, a barrel of a man, comes at me, a snarl on his lips. Another charges my way too, already in animal form. A gray wolf with a huge head.

Instinct jolts through me, and my wolf snaps into action, taking charge. Except, I hold on and am there with her, both of us pressed together in the driver's seat. Shoulder to shoulder, we shove each other while battling the real enemy outside.

I leap at the first man, suddenly feeling like I'm flying from the strength in my body. I crash into him, headfirst into his gut. He groans, but still lands a punch to my back. My knees wobble, but I never cower away.

My body tingles, and I pivot around and lunge up to bite deep into his shoulder, ripping away flesh to the bone, blood gushing free, splattering the dead leaves around us. The coppery taste is like dirt across my tongue, my body trembling with uncontrollable fury. The need to rip them all apart soars through me.

Something white flashes behind my eyes, an unsatisfiable rage, blinding me.

Another attacker smacks into my side hard, throwing me off my feet and to the ground with a thud. I'm shaking violently, my head still spinning.

His weight presses down on me, and footfalls close in around me.

But I won't be caught, not ever again.

I fucking won't.

I buck against the idiot and snap my head around, ripping my teeth into his arm. Tearing away with skin and fabric, I don't relent as he cries out.

Heat lashes over me, and I scramble to my feet, growling. I recoil from the four approaching monsters. Mad strides forward, his white hair blown off his face from the wind, the bastard looking older, more exhausted than when I last saw him. But a fuckhead is still a fuckhead. His twisted expression is one of a man who is disgusted by what he sees; me standing up for myself.

I can't look away from the syringe he grasps. They already jabbed me once in the neck, and it forced me into a transformation. I somehow doubt that was their intention, or that they expected me to put up such a battle.

My legs tremble beneath me, and adrenaline pumps through my veins, keeping me going. Except, my wolf suddenly drives me aside, and I refuse to stop her. I'm stumbling on my feet, snarling at myself until I crash into a tree.

"What the fuck's wrong with her?" someone asks.

"Stop fighting," Mad's voice cuts through the madness in my head. "I can take care of you. Protect you."

I growl in response. Liar!

"Your choice, Meira." He lifts the syringe. "Come with us calmly and I promise to release my stepbrother and his two men. Keep fighting and we'll take you by force. And with that, I can guarantee I will kill them."

He suddenly pauses as do his men, each of them glaring at me like I'm nothing but a means to an end. I know exactly what he wants from me… my blood. They think I am the cure to a zombie infection. Sad fucks have no idea how wrong they are.

My heart pounds in my ears, my wolf growling in my chest shuddering with violent need, but it's four against one. Even I'm not that foolish to believe I'll win. Another reason I need to pull back my wolf. Especially now that a wounded wolf is climbing to his feet.

I swallow hard as my breaths speed up.

Mad's expression darkens, and underneath the storm in his eyes, there is desperation—one I've seen on power-hungry Alphas before. He'll do anything, kill anyone to get what he wants.

Really, I have one option: get to Mad first and tear him apart while not losing myself to my wolf.

Easier said than done.

Electricity hums over my skin just as it had when my wolf first pushed out of me. She had my skin ripping, forcing herself to come out. The pain is gone now, knitting my wolf and me as one soul, one being, yet she fights me. This can't be right.

I recoil, my sight never leaving Mad's. This isn't the time to stumble. I step back, bumping into a tree, and I shudder.

My wolf growls her threat at me. She doesn't back away... well I fucking do.

They close in. All five of them. Three are in human form, and two have taken wolf form.

Dread taps fast in my chest. I frantically look around for a way out, for anything. Looking down to my men, they don't stir, and worry sinks through me. What had been in the injections to knock them out so fast?

Tension leaks in the air, while rage bubbles to the surface inside me, bringing with it a lick of fire down my back.

I loathe Mad. Wrath rises through me at what these men deserve.

But pain stings my side from where the bastard slammed into me earlier, pulsing across my ribs.

"Get her!" Mad bellows, and my gut reaction kicks in this time.

I twist and lunge away, ignoring the sensation like I'm trying to turn back around. My wolf's betraying me. Running isn't a sign of weakness, it's knowing when you're outnumbered and working out a way to take out the leader.

I dodge trees and dart deeper into the dense forest, scrambling for escape. Shadows seem brighter now, my vision sharper and crisper. Glancing over my shoulder, the five of them give chase. But it's Mad I need to get... chop off the head and the monster dies.

Swinging forward, I charge when an army of shadows emerge from the woods ahead of me.

Fear rattles me instantly. Have more Alphas surrounded me? I startle and skid to a stop by a massive pine tree, stiffening and swing my head in every direction for a way out.

A raspy groan comes from the woods, followed by more noises, and the clatter of teeth or bones follows.

My skin crawls as the first zombie emerges from the darkness.

I recoil. Will they attack me now that I've transformed? I step against the tree and glance back to the wolves' fear-stricken expressions at seeing who's arrived.

The zombie leading the charge has one missing ear and only a thin layer of hair over a spotty, pale head. Torn clothes hang off his bony frame. Another that comes forward has a mangled arm, others broken limbs.

Then the mass follows like a broken dam. They spill out from the woods, staggering, lurching, groaning. Others are licking the air as if already tasting the blood from the earlier wolves I've bitten and killed. That's what drew them here.

Even more undead stumble out of the woods. There has to be close to thirty.

The leader snaps its jaws and reels forward.

I hastily turn, needing to get out, except... fuck!

Dušan, Lucien, and Bardhyl are still on the ground, lying, waiting to be eaten. Are they covered in blood? I don't remember. Wracking my brain, I can't think straight when the undead approaches.

I dive away to escape, unsure if I'm their food or not.

Leukemia had made me immune to the zombies. A fact I learned recently, and everyone knows when a wolf transforms, all human illnesses heal. That means, I would be a meal for the undead now.

I sprint after Mad and his men who dart out of here, my wolf salivating as she thinks this is a chase. They are already so much farther ahead than me, having taken off the second they saw the Shadow Monsters.

Two more creatures suddenly appear at my right, so fast and unexpected, I do a double-take. My paw hooks under a tree root, and I'm tumbling forward and over my head before I can make sense of what just happened. I smack the ground hard and scramble to my feet.

Panic slams into me, feeling vulnerable and open.

Shadows crowd in around me, seeming to come from every direction.

Teeth gnashing, they close in, and I shuffle backward, ice filling my lungs that they're coming for me.

The creatures stumble forward, and I shudder. But then they dart right past me without pause.

Startled, I can't believe my eyes at first, and I study them flowing right past me. They don't notice or touch me!

It takes me moments to come to terms that I'm safe… and it's my wolf that takes charge and growls, warning them.

With their sloppy gait, they approach regardless.

One of them brushes right past me, and I flinch away. But they don't stop. Moaning, they stumble after Mad and his men. These monsters that should attack me don't. Skin peeling away, jaws dislocated, dried blood around their faces, they don't see me.

I'm invisible to them.

My head spins at first, trying to make sense of why they didn't attack me.

Am I still sick? I blink, watching them move away.

But reality catches up with me too, and I need to get my men to safety. I throw myself into the herd and shove them aside to get ahead.

Leaping over logs and dodging zombies, I burst out in front and into the small clearing where Mad and his men ambushed us.

Except, no one's there.

Not the wolves. Not Mad. And not my men.

Sickness churns in my gut that I'm too late. The bastard took them. I should be happy he saved them from the undead, but it doesn't make my men safe for long.

I'm also livid that he took them from me to ensure he has a bargaining tool to get what he wants. Snarls roll over my chest, and I unleash a pent up howl, desperate to chase them down and take back my wolves.

Seething, I catapult toward the Ash Wolves pack compound to catch up to them. To stop them.

The Shadow Monsters hurry to the spots on the ground where the bloody corpses of my victims lie. Falling to their hands and knees, the disgusting things lick up the remains.

My stomach turns.

I keep going, only trees in my view, as Dušan had said earlier we weren't far from his pack home.

It isn't long before I spot figures ahead, darting deeper in the forest, and a few look like they are carrying someone over their shoulders.

My pulse spikes, and I dart forward when a cry draws my attention to my left. My wolf seems to have pulled back. Did I just have to take control of her? Is that all it took?

I stop running and get a better look. A girl is tied to a tree, a gag over her mouth and she's thrashing for escape.

Jae!

What the heck is she doing here? I bumped into her in the woods days ago when she was like now, tied to a tree by a psycho Alpha. Perhaps Mad and his wolves caught her while they searched for us.

I glance back to Mad and his crew, almost vanishing in the woods from sight. My gut tightens.

Groans grow louder behind me, and I whip around.

Crap! Those damn zombies are making their way toward Jae.

Her eyes widen with fear and she cries frantically, writhing against the bonds keeping her tied to the tree. Mad and the others are moving further ahead, but how the hell am I meant to follow them now? If I do, I'm sending Jae to her death.

Frustration worms through me. But I can't waste time, so I throw myself toward her, scampering over the dried foliage and evergreens covering the land. Trampling anything in my way.

She squirms and draws away from me as much as she can, but I growl at her, then I swing to move behind the tree. Biting into the rope securing her to the trunk, I gnaw on them, tugging, and chewing.

I hear Jae sniffing the air then she glances back over her shoulder, down at me. "Meira is that you?"

My snarl is the only response as I wrestle with the rope.

"Please hurry, they're really close," she cries, making whimpering sounds. I inhale her perspiration and fear.

I wrench at the rope and my teeth bite right through it, releasing it.

She's quick to pull free and toss the bonds aside, then swings toward me. "Let's get out of here!"

And I freeze at first, unsure where to take her. Behind her, half a dozen zombies have noticed the commotion and are coming over.

It doesn't take long for the bastards. They are like the sharks of the land. Smell of blood or any sound that sounds like trouble and they appear to investigate. Just in case it's a meal.

"Meira," Jae calls out and is running in the opposite direction to the compound and away from the zombies.

I want to scream after her that we must get closer to the pack. There are snipers on the gate that will shoot the creatures on site. But all that comes out is a guttural growl.

Because I'm a wolf, and it's only now that it hits me, I don't know how to transform back into a human.

A Shadow Monster slips right past me and runs after Jae.

I lunge after the fiend, crash tackling it, bringing it to the ground. It bucks against me, not staying still, never staying down. Fury billows inside me as three others already pass me.

Jae is bouncing deeper into the woods.

Having had enough, I bite down into the back of its neck. It has a massive, healed scar across his bald head which looks painful, if this man was alive. Something suddenly cracks in its body. Please let that slow it down. I don't wait to find out and sprint after the girl.

Putrid blood taints my tongue, and panic flares that I'd made a terrible mistake. Taking their blood into my body might tip me into becoming one of them or... I don't really know because these creatures ignore me like I am still immune. But the notion still freaks me out. Nothing about what's going on with me follows any rules.

Seconds pass and nothing happens to me. No change or urgent need to kill the living. But I don't have time for this. Not now.

I'm running after Jae, attacking the next three zombies, biting deep into their sides and legs to cause damage, to toss them aside. Anything to slow them down. They don't even react, it's as if I'm invisible to them.

I lose sight of Jae, and I look left and right, I sniff the air to catch her faint scent—powdery and earthy.

In seconds, I am on her heels again. She screams at my approach, until she looks back to see it's only me. "I really hope that is Meira inside there," she says nervously.

Glancing behind me, she realizes we've left the creatures way behind us.

She pauses, resting against a tree, breathing fast.

I inhale raspy breaths, then my tongue dangles out, and more than anything, I need to transform back. Looking up at Jae, she stares at me, tilting her head.

Making a whiny sound, I sit in front of her, unsure how to communicate that I'm stuck.

"Why aren't you changing?" she asks, worry coating her words. "I don't really know this area too well, but there are caves farther up the hill behind me I passed days ago. We can go hide there?" She's breathing heavy and talking quickly.

I nudge my head against her thigh, then start moving toward the mountain so she knows I agree with her plan. Another glance behind us and no sign of the undead following. My attention sweeps over in the direction of the compound, where I want to be heading, not away from it.

But first, I need to get Jae out of harm's way.

She steps up alongside me and we're marching through the shadowy woods. She's talking, but I'm not listening at first. Instead, I scan the woods, smell scents, listen for sounds. Then I look up at Jae.

"Meira, please don't tell me you don't know how to change back from wolf form. I once heard of a wolf who got trapped and stayed in her animal form her whole life."

My heart jackhammers at her words. Is she serious? I don't hear another word she says when panic replaces everything else I feel with a dreadful sinking feeling.

I can't be stuck in my wolf form. Please, no!

CHAPTER 2

DUŠAN

a hard fist connects to my back, driving me into the dingy prison cell. Fire burns through my veins as I whip back around to the door made of iron bars slamming shut with a thunderous clang, locking me inside.

The whole room feels like it tilts on its axis, the dark stone walls, the floor covered in dirt and stinking of urine, and I stumble, crashing into the wall, losing my balance. Whatever the fuck they injected into me knocked me out cold. Even when I came to, moments before reaching the cell, I could barely stand, let alone think straight.

I shake my head to clear the fog in my mind. When I glance up, I meet Mad's gaze. He leans against the wall outside my cell in a wide stance, hands deep in his pockets. Shadows gather under his eyes and his mouth splits into a smirk, revealing yellowed teeth.

There's no sign of Lucien or Bardhyl, and only when I look around do I note I'm in the deepest prison, my underground prison. I have two floors of cells since I also use them to help Ash Wolves struggling on full moons. I once put Mad in here when his wolf had lost control on a blue moon. And now the bastard stuck me in here as a lesson, as torment, I have no doubt.

"You asshole!" A growl rolls over my throat as I push myself to stand upright. Every inch of me hurts while my thoughts lock on Meira and the last time I saw her. Mad's wolves injected her, then she experienced her first transformation. My fists curl and I want to slam Mad's head into the wall for touching her. I don't even know if she survived the change, and the thought brings a stabbing pain deep in my chest. I might have lost her.

I have to believe she's alive, or why else would my asshole stepbrother be in here alone? Hell, he'd bring her carcass to haunt me if she were dead. My pulse ices over at the thought.

I promised to be there for Meira, but I let her down at the one time she needed me the most. All because of the weasel I'm going to murder. He betrayed me, and I should never have left him alone in the prison. Of course, he had allies to break him out... I fucking hate hindsight, but would I change things if I had my time over? Not if it meant not finding Meira.

Rage collides into me, and I roar more like a lion than a wolf at how fucked-up everything turned out.

I lunge forward, shaking the bars. "Let me the hell out!" I bellow.

"Brother, why would I do that?"

I spit on the floor between us. "You are not my real brother, but you are everything like your father."

His expression twists in a flash from a calm demeanor to a raging bull. He bursts toward me, nostrils flaring. His ice-blue eyes narrow, while his white hair sits wildly around his face. I want him fuming so he makes a mistake, comes in for me. Desperation for a savage fight rattles through me, and my sights are set on the wolf I should have eliminated long ago. I should have listened to Lucien and Bardhyl. But that's not a miscalculation I'll make again.

Mad stops just out of reach from me, strangely in control for someone who rarely thought before he acted. His entire body trembles, and he inhales heavily, the struggle to hold back clear. He stands as broad as me, but runs from most fights. So I poke the bear.

"Father betrayed us, hated us, beat us. You loathed him for what he did, and yet you became the monster you feared as a child."

"You're a fucking weak leader," he spits. "Father was right about that, it seems." He cracks his neck and lifts his chin. "Your pack is crying out for a solution to the undead, but instead, you play trading games with a damn Alpha who has a cure for his members. You're a laughing stock, and I'm no longer sitting back and letting you kill everyone here as those abominations break into my compound again."

I clench my teeth, grinding my back molars, but I refuse to let him get to me. He's a liar. The relations I have with other Alphas like Ander in X-Clan is the way of the future. Not stealing or bringing war to our doorstep from deceit.

"You're a fool." I growl. "Ander's serum is not a solution for us. It's tailormade for *their* race of wolves. You risked everything by—"

"And I'd risk it all again to save this pack!" he shouts.

I huff. "You mean to save yourself."

A guttural snarl reverberates from his chest. "Your time is over, brother. I've been your lackey long enough. Now it's time to show you how a real pack is run. And that little slut of yours will spread her legs for me, and her blood will help me bring immunity to the pack... *my* pack!" He slams a fist against his chest, his head high, so fucking proud of himself.

All I can think about is ripping out his throat, my hands curling into balls. If there's one bright light to come out of this asshole's mouth, it's his admittance that Meira is alive. That sliver of hope floods me with the determination to never stop fighting.

"So, you have what you want, what the fuck do you want with me?" I snap, needing to know his motivation and understand how long I have to escape before my time is up. Mad does everything for a reason that benefits him.

I'm under no illusion that Mad will finish me. He knows as well as I do that I will never just stand by and watch him take my pack from me.

He bursts into maniacal laughter and begins to stroll toward the exit door. "How else do you think I'm going to claim your wolf girl?"

Sonofabitch! I'm his bait.

Meira slipped away from him, and now he's hoping she will come back for me so he can trap her.

For the love of all things, I pray to the moon goddess

that Meira runs as far from this place as possible. If I escape, I'll find her even if I have to search the entire world. For once, I hope she runs.

LUCIEN

"*T*hat fucktard, lying, wankface cockroach," Bardhyl murmurs under his breath as he paces back and forth in our small prison. Pale blond hair flutters over his broad shoulders, his vivid green eyes narrowing as he scowls. He's a damn huge bear of a wolf, a Viking who's eager to fight.

My head still hurts from whatever the hell was jammed into me with the syringe, and now we were brought back into the compound to be tossed in the dungeon.

Jolting, I sit upright, my head spinning, and I scan the filthy cell, the barred walls revealing that the other three prisons are empty. We're down here alone. "Where're Dušan and Meira?"

"No idea. But we're going to break out of here and find them." He pauses in front of me as I climb to my feet.

"It's close to impossible to get out of here. We made sure of that." The window isn't in our cell, and we've had these bars and locks secured to resist a wild were-wolf's attack.

"We will with sheer brute force." Bardhyl growls

with each rapid breath he takes, clearly not thinking straight.

I rub the side of my neck, where I feel the lump from the injection. Mad's ambush came so fast… the bastards must have seen us coming and we walked right into their ambush. *Fuck!* I cross the prison, a mere three paces, and stare out into the dark hallway, finding the door into this basement shut. There's no sign of a guard watching us, and keys are never kept down here for obvious safety reasons.

"With brute force! Didn't you hear me?" Bardhyl stomps toward me.

"No need to repeat yourself. I ignored you just fine the first time. You know as well as I do these dungeons are unbreakable."

He snarls, and I glance over to him as he punches the brick wall. The dull thump that comes with it must hurt, but it doesn't stop him.

"Hold on to your anger. Maybe there *is* a way to break out."

Bardhyl snaps his attention my way. "I'm listening."

"The door hinges on the prison cell are the weakest point. When we had these made, we had several that kept easily snapping off. So if we're lucky, maybe one of these has a weak point."

Bardhyl huffs, squaring his shoulders. "Well, this I can do. I'm the master at breaking things." He marches over to the door, and I track alongside him.

Unease simmers in my gut about where exactly Meira is. I keep telling myself she's with Dušan, but something tells me that's too easy and we need to find her urgently. When Mad is involved, the worst-case scenario is most likely.

I curl my hands into fists at the possibility of what he'd do to her and shake my head, my muscles tense. I already lost my first mate... And I never imagined finding someone else to love, to connect with my wolf, but Meira is that and so much more. My heart squeezes as my throat thickens.

She can't be dead. I'll die before I go through losing her.

CHAPTER 3

MEIRA

I straddle two worlds. The human side that comes from my father, and the wolf from my mama. I grew up being told I'd never truly belong anywhere as long as my wolf refused to show. But now that she has, I don't know how to return to my human form, so what am I supposed to do now? Go hang around in the wilderness with actual wild wolves? I half-sob, half-snicker at the notion.

How in the world am I meant to be with Dušan, Lucien, and Bardhyl? I've been a human for so long that it's all I know, and I kinda liked it. Now, I pace back and forth in the cave up in the mountain, my paws moving swiftly over the stone floor. In a strange way, it almost feels like I'm flying at how fast and easy the movement comes.

A hawk screeches in the distance, and I turn my attention out of the cave's entrance where storm clouds roll over the sky, and a rumble bellows somewhere over the land. Miles of treetops swing back and forth in the rising wind. Dušan's compound lies behind this mountain, and my insides churn every time I think about him and my other two captured men. I want to believe Mad won't hurt them, but I don't trust a single thing about the bastard. I want to rip him to shreds.

"Come over here," Jae says in her soft voice, pulling me from my thoughts. I find her kneeling by the small fire. "I'm going to help you change. You saved me. Now it's my turn to repay the favor."

I startle, staring at this young girl, maybe thirteen or fourteen years old, taking the lead to save me. Her round face glows red from the fire and she has lots of freckles over her nose and cheeks. Her short, dark hair sits messily, and everything about her looks adorable. Even the jeans two sizes too big for her and cinched in by a belt, not to mention her T-shirt with a penguin riding a sleigh on it.

I trot over and flop down on my belly, legs bent under me, but it feels uncomfortable, so I shift and awkwardly stretch my front legs out in front of me. Ah, that's slightly better. Heat from the flames embrace me, and a wave of exhaustion comes over me.

"Relax," Jae says to me. "My sister, Narah, taught me how to change back when I first transformed a couple of years ago. It's as easy as exhaling, but you need to be calm."

Speaking and doing are two very different things. I look up at her and groan with a rushed breath.

She reaches over and strokes the top of my head with her small hand. The impression snakes down my back with the most soothing sensation I've ever experienced, and my eyelids are fluttering with the need to close them.

"There are places in this world that are riddled with secrets and danger," she explains. "But one thing for certain is that our wolves will always be there, and that we have control of our animal side. Think of all the things you experienced in your life up till now, and how afterward, you became a slightly different person. Every day changes you."

I study Jae, who now sits with her legs crossed in front of me. Her words are profound and deep for someone so young, and I'm guessing she is parroting what her sister told her. Maybe one day I'll get to meet her sibling, as she sounds wise.

Jae's fingers scratch over my ears delicately, and my eyes close. "You are in control. Call your wolf inside you."

A gentle ripple skims through me, the warmth from the fire soothing me with its sputtering sounds, and I'm half-falling asleep from Jae's soft petting. A single thought of my wolf retreating crosses my mind, and a sudden sweep of fur brushing against my insides begins.

My mind turns over to memories of going apple picking with Mama as a child, my breaths heavy. And then darkness sweeps over me.

"*M*eira, are you hungry?" a soft female voice asks, then someone shakes me harshly by the shoulder.

In a heartbeat, my memories roll over me like a truck, and I flip open my eyes to Jae's face. She's looking down at me, chewing on something, and the smell of grilled meat has me salivating.

"What are you eating?" I say, the words out loud. I'm human. With a gasp, I lift my hands to see they are in fact hands. No fur or claws or anything animal-like. "Oh, hell yes, I'm back to being me." I get up quickly, staring down at my naked body, cut and bruised, but I changed. It didn't seem too hard to do, though it put me to sleep, so hopefully, that's not a common side effect.

"Thank you so much." I glance over to Jae as she bites into the small drumstick, her chin greasy from the meal. The fire spits and crackles from the two rabbit rotisseries sitting over the flame, and I'm starving.

But my thoughts swivel to my three mates captured by Mad. Behind me, rain drizzles over the land, the sunlight cowering behind the heavy clouds staining the sky.

"I have clothes for you. Come eat before rushing out there," Jae says, smacking her lips.

I follow her pointed finger to the wall across from the fire, where a pile of clothes waits for me. "Where did you find them?"

"At the back of the cave. Told you I was here before, and one thing my eldest sister taught me was that everywhere I stay, I leave a small survival pack."

Dragging on the baggy pants, I pull at the corded string so they don't fall off me, then reach for the black T-shirt. "She sounds smart. You never know when you might be back at a cave. Case in point here."

"Oh, it's not just for me, but for any woman in trouble and needing clothes, fire supplies, and a warm blanket."

I'm partly gobsmacked by her admittance. Why has her idea never crossed my mind before? I was so busy surviving, keeping away from everyone, that helping others who are just trying to live never occurred to me once. And now, I make a note in my mind that it's something I intend to start doing.

I stroll over to the fire and plonk myself down on my heels, already reaching over for a piece of rabbit.

"You were busy while I fell asleep, and I would love to meet your sisters one day." I rip free a drumstick and sit back, eating. The meat is a bit tough, but it's hot and fatty, making it everything I need.

She shrugs, gnawing on a bone before going in for another helping. "I never made it to our spot." Her voice grows faint and she stares into the flames, the blaze dancing in her eyes.

"So tell me, what happened after you ran away from me?" I ask, trying to distract her a bit from the obvious pain of not reaching her sisters. Jae told me last time that they'd gotten separated, but they had a meeting point if that ever happened. Smart. I've heard of people spending weeks trying to cross paths with someone.

"I didn't want you to try stopping me, so I took off to meet with my sisters. One person on her own is easier to slide through the woods unnoticed than two, especially from the undead." She holds herself strong and her fighting spirit reminds me so much of me.

Most likely, I would have done the same in her position.

She swallows the mouthful and wipes her mouth with the back of her hand. "I didn't hear the Alphas sneak up on me. I should have been more careful, and now I'm even farther away from the meeting zone."

"Your sisters will wait for you," I urged.

"I know they will," she answered adamantly. "She made me agree that we'd meet there even if it took years."

The hope in her voice tears through me. I used to believe in so many things before I watched the Shadow Monsters kill my mama. After that, I lost my hope in this wretched world we live in that eats and spits you out daily if you let it. The only way I survived was to become selfish, to accept that no one would come rescue me. I spent many nights crying myself to sleep, and it doesn't get easier being alone. But how can I say those things to Jae when she holds on to that thread of possibility like a lifeline?

"How about we make an agreement?" I suggest. "You don't run away anymore, and I will help you track down your sisters with the Ash Wolves."

Her eyes widen with shock. "Are you mad? No Alphas help Omegas, don't you know that? And I don't intend to be captured."

"You won't be. I have three mates, all Ash Wolves, and well, I need to rescue them from the assholes who tried to kidnap you. Then they will help you get back to the waiting spot, I give you my word." There was no doubt in my mind that they would help.

Jae shakes her head. "You worry about what you need to do, but I don't need your help."

"We all need help sometimes. Like when I rescued you from that rogue Alpha in the woods over a week ago, plus today."

She stiffens, her shoulders squaring. "And I saved you and got you to shift back into your human body. We're even."

I laugh and collect the rest of what's left of the half-eaten rabbit. "I just want to help you, Jae. You leave items in a cave in case other females are in trouble because you want to help too. It's okay to accept assistance."

Her brow furrows instead of fighting back.

Only the crackling fire floods the silence as we eat.

"Why don't you come with me?" she finally says. "Narah will welcome you to stay with us. There will be no Alphas to command or try to rut you." She snarls after saying the words.

And I realize then, she doesn't quite understand the concept of meeting a mate. But I understand. I spent so long hating males, seeing them as nothing more than wanting me as their slave. And some of them are that way, but not all of them. The connection with a fated mate is unbreakable and captivating and alluring. I want to scream that I'm away from mine while they remain in danger. At the back of my mind, I keep wondering if I still have leukemia, seeing as how the Shadow Monsters are keeping their distance from me. But I push those thoughts aside. I can't think about that when I have Alphas to save.

The ache in my chest burns for them, but I'm also not an idiot to know Mad would have wolves out there searching for me. The pouring rain outside is my savior, concealing our scents and that of the cooking rabbit.

That's why this is the time for me to check the perimeter of the compound to see how the hell I'm going to break in to help them.

"My place is here," I answer, something I never thought I'd ever say. For all my life, I've run away.

Except that stops now. The time has come for me to claim what is mine and fight for my three wolves.

I discard the rabbit bones into the fire and wipe my hands down my pants, then get up.

"Where are you going?" Jae asks, a quaver threading through her voice.

"To scope out the Ash Wolves' compound. I need to break in."

She trembles, as if the mere thought terrifies her. "That place is filled with Alphas. Are you sure you don't want to come with me and leave this war zone behind?"

"I've never been more certain in my life about anything. But I hope you change your mind and don't go anywhere," I plead, though based on her past behavior, I doubt she'll listen to me. "Whatever you decide, stay safe."

"You too." She returns to eating, while I head out of the cave and into the tragic weather. It may be wet and cold, but it'll conceal me from the monsters out here.

I have no idea how I'm meant to save them, but I guess I'll come up with something once I reach the pack home.

"Good luck," Jae murmurs behind me.

Yeah, I'll need it.

CHAPTER 4

MEIRA

*R*ain drenches everything, slips under my clothes, and I'm soaked to the bone. But I welcome the wild weather to keep away the Alphas searching for me, no matter how much I'm trembling with the cold.

The canopy of leaves overhead mostly protect me as I press up against a wide fir tree where only the occasional heavy drops fall onto my head. From my location, I get a clear view of the Ash Wolves' compound.

Thunder roars and the ground trembles, sending the branches into a tremble, throwing more water onto me. But I don't move, even as an icy drop slides down my spine.

A metal fence, about fifteen feet tall, closes in around the settlement. Left and right, it stretches outward. I've circled the perimeter from within the woods already to scope out my potential entry points. There are three into the place.

First, the main entrance gate with two snipers sitting up on the stone posts. There's another on the opposite end from me with one guard, and a third gate to my left at the rear of the settlement. And I remember the guard on the back door. He stood outside my room when I was first brought into this pack, and he always smiled at me. Plus, I've seen him talking to Dušan a few times, and you can always tell a lot about a person by the way they treat others, especially prisoners. I don't even know the man's name, but there was awe in his gaze when he spoke with his Alpha. Perhaps it had to do with him being older than the other guards, so if I trust any of them, it would be him.

Yeah, it's a risk, but what else can I do? I need a way in. Scaling the fence is close to impossible, and breaking it down will bring all sorts of attention. My plan is to sneak in as undetected as possible.

I chew on my lower lip, my stomach churning as I'm standing out here as an easy target should anyone come in from behind me. I keep looking over my shoulder, but with the heavy rain, I can't detect anyone.

The more I stare at the brick fortress beyond the lofty fence, the more I'm reminded of Dušan and the first time he brought me here. Terrified, I would have done anything to escape capture, and ironically, now I'll do anything to get inside.

Steadfast stone walls, the pointy towers, the crenellations across the top. I can't stop thinking about the time Lucien took me up on the top balcony for breakfast, and we shared our first kiss. Later when I escaped my room, the Viking beast, Bardhyl, tracked and dragged me back inside. My heart clenches at the memories, and an urgency drums through me to get to my men faster. Every second that passes, I drown farther in thoughts that I'll lose them. But I can't allow my worries to pull me under. Not until I do everything I can to rescue them. So I need to cause a distraction at the opposite end of the enclosure. Then, I can finally slip into the compound.

I scan the open land and find no sign of anyone, so with my head low, I push out from behind the tree and hurry through the woods. Running, I remain in the shadows and follow the downward sloping land toward the front gates.

While scouting the entry gates to work out which guard looked easiest to convince, I discovered a recently dead deer carcass down in this area that I intend to use for the interference. Now, my heart beating frantically, my lungs burning, and I'm mentally gathering my energy to triumph.

Cause a disturbance.

Then bolt back up to the rear entrance.

Beg the guard to let me in. It's a long shot, but I'll try anything right now.

Rain pelts down on me, the sky growling, and I rush forward when the ground suddenly slips out from under my feet and I fall on my ass. "Argh," I moan from the sharp pain of landing on a branch. Mud coats my pants and hands. "Crap." I get back up, taking the hill slower this time.

Dead ahead, I come around a cluster of trees where

the terrain flattens, and where I last saw the dead animal. Except now two Shadow Monsters are hunched over the thing, gorging, their slurpy sounds sickening me.

"Okay, maybe this will work even better," I whisper, meaning I won't have to lure them to me. I skid to a halt several feet away, and that's when I catch movement deeper in the woods, more undead coming to the scent of blood. At least a dozen of them lurch amid the trees.

"Oh, shit." They'll make this harder if I don't move now.

Sucking in a deep breath, I throw myself forward, cringing on the inside that I'm actually going to do this. Reaching the rump of the deer, I grab its hind legs. They are cold and damp to the touch. Thank goodness it's not a huge animal.

Then I haul the thing, directly out of the undead's reach. The creatures don't seem to even notice me but lurch after their meal with outstretched hands and gaping mouths dripping with blood.

Groans from the woods draw my attention to the other monsters coming this way.

So I move with speed, shuffling backward, tugging this half-eaten carcass and doing my best not to look at its open ribcage or I'll be sick.

One zombie latches on and bites down on its neck. As I drag the deer, the undead loses its balance and falls, still attached on with teeth and fingers. Their weight resists me now, and I swear under my breath at the fucking thing.

My heart pounds in my chest, and the rain is unrelenting, soaking me. It drips down my face and into my eyes and mouth.

Glancing behind me, I approach the edge of the woods, and behind that is a clearing between me and the fence of at least twenty feet.

I scan the area and find no one there, so I move fast with the deer and creatures.

Emerging from the woods, the sheet of rain pours buckets over me, slamming into me ferociously. I slide the deer over the muddy ground, one zombie still clinging on to its neck, eating, while the other staggers after us.

Fear pummels into me now. Those guards in the compound shoot on site, and I'm in open territory with their enemy.

My arms tremble with exhaustion, but I keep wrenching the damn deer over the bumpy ground and shrubs. I pivot and tow the meal closer to the edge of the settlement. Farther around the corner stands the main entrance, and well, I need to create a big enough diversion that draws attention to this end of the settlement.

After the last break-in Mad caused, I'm guessing most of the pack members will be hypersensitive to uncover a horde of zombies clustered together near their home.

On cue, the dozen monsters emerge from the woods, so now I have little time to waste.

Gritting my teeth, I fight the dead weight and two damn creatures eating the deer. I want to scream but keep my mouth shut. Those in the mob chasing after us are moaning enough to make a racket.

A shiver races down my spine, my body shaking over the thought that I'll get caught.

My back hits the wall and I dump the animal to the ground, my muscles screaming with pain, my legs straining, and I wipe my hands down my soaking pants. Scraping the rain from my face, I peer around the corner. No trees or people. There's a driveway at least fifteen feet away, leading to the main front gates. Peering up, I can't make out anyone, but I know the guards are there.

Growls rise behind me, and I snap around, my pulse racing. The other zombies have arrived and all are pushing over one another to get to the carcass.

Goddammit.

Two Shadow Monsters are in a tug-o-war with part of the deer they tore free. I don't even try to make sense of what part of the body they're fighting over.

Instinct kicks in, and I lunge toward them. Like a crazy person, I snatch the long bone, still covered in meat and fur, and wrestle it away from the zombies.

They are so slow to react at first that they snap toward me with savagery. A shiver races down my spine at the hunger in their eyes, but I remind myself it's the food they want, not me. They would have attacked me by now already if that were the case. The idea that I am still sick flutters over my mind, but I don't have time for that.

I pivot and rush around the others in a wide sweep,

carrying a damn deer leg, and now that I look down at the hoof, bile hits the back of my throat.

The moment I reach the corner of the fence, I hurl the leg as far toward the front gate as possible.

The thing lands with a thump about seven feet away, then rolls a few more, landing in a small puddle that splashes.

Undead shove past me, moaning, pushing me aside. At least half a dozen of them take the bait. I swing back around the corner and avoid being seen.

My heart booms in my chest, and I bolt toward the woods. This is my moment to escape and head up the hill.

But farther up the slope, four large gray wolves approach. I startle, tripping over my feet as my stomach drops through me. They are Ash Wolves, most likely Mad's search party for me. *Fuck. Fuck. Fuck.*

I throw myself to the ground where the undead roam to reach their meal. The bastards walk over me, bony feet against my back and head. I wince at something kicking into my side, then a Shadow Monster trips over me. The shrubs around me whip wildly in the weather, rain battering into my back.

In the distance behind me, gunfire pops. I flinch. The guards are taking out the zombies. How long before they come to investigate this side where I'm hiding from the wolves?

Terror seizes me, and I don't know what to do.

My hand flies forward and parts the greenery for a view. The wolves are running this way already, and I'm trembling. Have they seen me?

I shudder, and adrenaline shoves into me. My mind screams to run. Fucking run!

But I don't move. Not an inch. My brain is on overdrive, sparking and every nerve snapping. I'm no stranger to danger, but this is me cornered with no way out.

Bang. Bang.

The shots come again, louder, closer. I jump in my skin with each shot.

I won't allow myself to be caught.

When a feeding undead suddenly lurches upward from the deer in front of me, I jump into action.

Scrambling to my feet, I dart behind the creature, lowering my head to hide, fisting the torn shirt it wears. I stay close behind the putrid thing that has me gagging from the stench of rotting flesh.

I shove him sideways, shuffling to remain hidden. It moans, stumbling on its feet as it fights the direction I'm forcing it to go away from its meal and into the woods so I can hide from the wolves.

I keep looking over to the wall, expecting to find the guards popping up on the fence any second now. I suck in every rapid breath, terror raising the hair on my arms.

Peering over the shoulder of the undead man in my grasp, I see the wolves charging down the hill.

A whimper slips past my throat. I need to get into the woods. The high pitched howl pierces my ears. It sounds close and comes from somewhere back in the compound.

Panic buttons have been pressed and my distraction

worked to get their attention, but I'm not meant to still be caught in the chaos.

A blinding light flashes over the land, followed by an earth-shattering boom of thunder. I shudder as the sound shakes me to the core. And as if it weren't raining hard enough before, now the heavens split open and fall unrelentingly heavy, blurring my vision. Rain drums incessantly on the trees and grounds, dinging furiously as it hits the metal fence behind me.

I push the damn zombie to get moving as it attempts to turn around, but I won't let go of him. Pushing my shoulder into his back, I drive him toward the woods as I keep concealing myself from the wolves, praying they haven't seen me. Its moans of protest are lost beneath the storm ripping away all noises.

Suddenly, the stupid zombie trips and falls sideways, taking me with it. I cry out and fall.

I'm soaking, and the wolves are almost upon me, leaping down the hill, one of them sliding over and crashing into a tree. I'd love to laugh, but I'm too busy trying not to die. I clamber to my feet and dart right the last couple of steps into the woods just as a wall of Shadow Monsters emerge. There are dozens of them, careening right for the dead deer, some already reeling to where I tossed the leg. They hustle against me, driving me back at first.

Hell! I burst into the mass, fighting their shoving and shoulders knocking into me or them stamping on my feet. But I push my hands against them and carve a path for my escape.

I stumble into the woods from where more emerge, and I want to kiss them for just saving my ass.

All right, that's a bit much. I will never lay my lips on these disgusting things. Freeing myself from the tangle of putrid bodies, elbowing and thrusting past me, I search for the wolves.

Growls flitter somewhere in the distance. I start making my way up the hill from within the woods. The back entry into the settlement is my goal.

A bloodcurdling cry shatters the silence, and I quiver, missing a step.

I keep going up the hill but can't stop looking back to where a wolf is engulfed by the creatures, while the three other wolves lunge at the monsters.

Bang. Bang.

The shots start again, and the war I've unleashed is in full throttle.

I can't think about anything but using this time to get inside the compound. I planned a distraction, and fuck, I got one hell of a commotion.

Running up the hill, my thighs ache, as do my lungs. I grab on to low-hanging trees to pull myself up over the steeper sections. My feet keep slipping out from under me, and my heart beats like it's intending to burst out of my ribcage.

I look back and catch enough of a glimpse of the battle, but if the wolves survived, it's too difficult to tell.

Farther behind me, there are three or four Shadow Monsters following me… hard to tell how many in truth with the shadows and rain. They aren't moving in a mad rush for food at me, either, which makes me think they are confused. The rain washes away scents easily, I guess.

The battle grows in the background as I make my way swiftly to the rear of the compound.

I stop for a moment and steady my racing heart as I suck in shaky breaths.

Thunder cracks overhead, the trees whipping in every direction around me, the wind pushing against me when I finally emerge from the woods into a clearing at the back of the settlement. I'm huffing and puffing. I need a few seconds to just calm down or speaking with the guard will be impossible when I attempt to convince him to let me in.

The mental pictures of my three wolves hurt and on death's door pushes me to keep going. Chills flare over my skin while bile rises in my throat that I might lose any of them. I almost want to laugh at how easily I call them 'my wolves' when there is still so much I want to learn about them.

But it sure as hell isn't going to happen if I'm daydreaming about them, either.

I race alongside the fence, for any kind of protection from the ravenous weather beating into me. Ten feet away, the narrow gate comes into view, and when I look up, the guard from earlier is gone.

Crap. I run my hand over my face in the rain, but it's useless as more water is coating me, yet I can't stop doing it.

Standing around won't help me get this done fast.

I hurry toward the gate, my gaze constantly drifting higher along the fence in case a guard pops up and mistakes me for an undead. Panic makes anyone trigger happy.

The gate is made of solid metal with no windows, and I knock on it, then instantly feel stupid. I doubt anyone can hear it, so I call out, "Hello!"

Again nothing.

Have the guards all gone to the other side? Which is a good thing, right? So I press down on the handle of the door, which of course doesn't open. I frantically glance around for a solution, for anything, when I find an oversized fallen branch as thick as my leg.

Looking back up, I see there are still no guards on the stone posts along the metal fence.

Desperately, I lunge toward the branch and haul it closer. There's a wooden platform over the gate entrance where I saw the soldiers stand guard earlier, so I need to get up there.

With quivering arms, I lift one end of my new ladder and carry it closer, then drop it up against the wall. It comes to about chest height. It needs to be higher, so I leave it there and rush to the other end.

I might end up pulling a muscle, but I don't care right now. I crouch down and lift the thick branch and shove it forward, inching forward with my steps. The tip slides up against the wall until it hits the lip of the fence across the top. Rain pelts down, stray leaves thrown into me, and this timber is unsteady as hell. But I have to make it work.

41

Searching around me, I find several rocks about the size of a huddled fox, and I collect one. Tucking it at the base of the branch to keep it wedged in, I'm partly terrified of my contraption.

But the wood is thick enough and damn heavy, so I put my foot on it, bouncing it. Suddenly, the tip slips sideways from the pressure, making a scratching sound against the metal. Hell, this is going to fail miserably. Stepping back, I take in a deep breath, shake my arms, and just run. No overthinking this.

My first step is solid, my balance strong, and I press forward, my arms jutted out on either side of me in my crazed climb.

The branch suddenly dips out from under me, throwing me sideways and to the ground. I swallow my scream as my stomach lurches and I hit the ground hard with my hip and shoulder. Muddy water splashes me, and I groan from the dull ache pulsing down my back.

Sonofabitch.

Getting back up, I study the branch, which is wedged in where the door and frame marry. At least it's held in place. Up on my feet, I try again and again, and by the fourth time, bruised and battered from falling, I'm burning up with fury that this damn thing won't work.

I rush at it once more, reaching halfway up, farther than I'd achieved previously when the flex in the branch starts to bend from my weight. Adrenaline driven, on my next step, I throw myself forward and madly snatch the top of the fence. Gasping for air, I dangle from there for a few moments.

My entire body shakes, muscles screaming with pain.

I need to get over the damn thing, I have to. I lever one leg up against the branch and push myself up. Then I throw a leg over the top of the lofty fence, straining to pull my body to follow, my heart pounding from exhaustion. I roll onto the wooden platform and lie there for two seconds to just breathe because I can't believe I made it. I want to laugh at the craziness I've just gone through, but that will have to wait.

Getting back up, I find I'm definitely alone. Finally, something is going right for me.

Several howls come from much farther away, and from my vantage point over the tops of the trees, the whole territory comes into view. The land sloping downward to the castle-like structure, the pack members running down to the front gate, the houses where pack members live.

Hurrying, I rush toward the wooden ladder leaning against the platform and scurry down. At the base, I search for anyone, but it's quiet.

So I slip right into the cluster of trees and sprint to the castle, my feet slapping the wet ground with each hurried step.

There's movement to my right, and before I even look around, I dive behind a tree, then look out. A man is marching to the rear gate I just climbed over. Adrenaline rises faster and my brain is firing off panic like a shotgun. That I'll be caught, that I'll cause my Alphas' death, that this was the wrong move.

I wait. *Just calm the shit down. I've got this.*

My skin feels like it's on fire even when I'm being rained on. I shake like a leaf as I glance out from my hiding location to where the figure disappears somewhere near the back fence.

Then reality punches me in the gut. The branch I used to climb over the fence! *Shit!* I left it propped up against the door. *Idiot!*

Terror seems to swell in every cell in my body as dread grips me. So I do the only thing I can… I lunge toward the Alphas' home.

The woods blur past me, and I follow the path Lucien showed me last time he and I were up here. We had sex, mind you, out in public, and it was ridiculously alluring. A moment forever imprinted on my mind. One of the many times that Lucien made me fall for him and so hard. Just thinking about him has my heart clenching. And this is why I'm running and need to save him and the others before it's too late.

Reaching the side entrance to the castle, I press my back to the stone wall, frantically looking in every direction. Just then, someone bursts out of the doorway and looks in the opposite direction from me, missing me completely just standing feet from him. He bursts into a sprint toward the front gates.

I'm plastered to the wall, petrified he'll turn around, but he never does as he vanishes around the building.

Gunshots ring in the air, popping, one after another. Someone's shouting; others are yelling. Must be from the guards.

A dinging bell rings from the direction of the back

fence. I cringe. The guard must have discovered my branch. Well, that didn't take long.

Quickly, I slide into the building and pray with everything I have that I don't bump into anyone. I recall someone mentioning prisons in this building, and from what I've read, cells are always in the basement of castles.

No time to waste, I hurry down a quiet corridor with dark stone walls and the torches on the walls flickering. The wind howls savagely in here, my skin suddenly icy cold. I'm heading to the large set of stairs I remember in this fortress going underground. My head swims with so many doubts that every move I make might be wrong and my undoing.

Voices come from up ahead, and I shudder. Terrified, I lash out toward the first door I find and shove it open. I dart inside, my pulse banging in my ears. It's someone's chamber, judging by the messy bed and table with a jug and cups. I also spot a blade inside a sheath on a belt, so I sprint over and snatch the weapon, just in case.

Back at the entrance, I press my ear against the wooden door and listen as I wrap the belt around my waist, the blade at my hip. It's super large and even in the final belt hole, there's a bit of wiggle room, but it will have to do. For those few moments, I try to calm my raging pulse. I've been going non-stop and I might pass out. I remind myself I can't afford to make any mistakes.

Loud footfalls pass like whoever's out there is

running, and I don't leave the room until I'm certain they are definitely gone.

Stepping into the corridor, I swing my gaze left and right, and with no one there, I move with haste to the stairwell farther ahead. The hairs on my nape shift, and my brain is on overdrive.

I rush downstairs and arrive at a door. The stairs curve around and lead farther down. Is this the basement? Because it smells rank enough that it could be? Then what is on the next floor down. I'm chewing on my lower lip over what to do but find myself drifting to the door and listening for any sounds.

Quietly, I open it and in front of me are a set of prison cells. Both are empty, so I stick my head inside to check out the rest of the room.

"What are you doing here?!" a male's voice snaps behind me.

I flinch around, my nerves shot.

A huge guard with wet hair and clothes clinging to him like he's just run in from outside is thundering down the steps toward me. He has a hooked nose, and I've seen him amid the wolves fighting alongside Mad in the woods. Fuck, why did it have to be him of all people coming down here?

His eyes grow as he really sees me… recognizes me.

Shaking, I stumble backward into the nearest cell and trip over my feet, falling over. I recoil on my ass as he marches right up to me, hands curling into fists, his jawline clenching.

"Meira!" a familiar voice calls me from within the room, and I swing my head to the left and lay eyes on

Lucien and Bardhyl inside the cell at the end of the row. They're gripping the metal bars, appearing just as shocked as I feel. Sweet hell, they were in here!

I hurry to get up when the back of the guard's hand collides with my face. Pain explodes down my cheek, and I'm reeling, my back smacking the floor. I'm crying out with excruciating pain, clasping the side of my face.

"Got you, you little bitch!" he snarls.

CHAPTER 5

DUŠAN

I close my eyes, my back against the ice-cold wall, and I'm drowning in fury. Spiraling, falling so damn fast, I'm losing control.

Meira.

She floats in my mind as I slip in and out of panicked thoughts and fucking blind anger at Mad.

I always gave him everything, made him my second-in-command, permitted him free rein in my pack. But it wasn't enough for the greedy sonofabitch.

I assumed I'd handled his demands and outbursts well but still gave him enough leniency so he didn't feel any less important. The Ash Wolves' pack came from his father, and I claimed it by fighting almost to my death to stake my claim from other Alphas. Mad never helped and always ran from danger.

He's gutless, a terrified asshole who would rather sit back than battle in the way of the wolves. Instead, he manipulates and steals.

A nerve pulses in my neck each time I think of incident after incident where the clues were right in my damn face, but I overlooked it again and again because I considered him family.

I pitied the fool, remembered the shit we both went through as kids, how I covered for him so I got the beatings from my step-father, not him.

Maybe that's the problem. I've protected him for so long, he's become complacent, arrogant, entitled.

No fucking respect for anything I've done for him, or for the pack, and he only sees his own selfish desires.

My foolish oversight will never happen again.

A groan sounds from up ahead, and I slide open my eyes to the guard leaning against the wall outside my cell, ordered to watch over me. Most likely in case Meira finds her way to me, which I want to laugh at. She doesn't even know we have dungeons in the basement, and I'm hoping she's smart enough to keep her distance from this place.

I climb to my feet, stretching my back, gaining his attention.

Nico watches me, and I know him well, so to see him betray me like this sits like barbed wire in my gut.

"I saved you years ago." I groan, then clear my throat.

"That you did," he answers, his voice strong, as though ready for this conversation.

"And yet you so easily break your loyalty and change allegiance."

His mouth thins and he folds his arms over his chest. "It's about survival, Dušan, you know this best. It's why you created our pack home. But times change, and there is no shame in admitting your ways are not going to ensure we remain safe. We live surrounded by fucking zombies." His voice climbs, his arms falling by his side.

"What has Mad promised you? Immunity from the undead? He's wrong. There is no such thing. We all carry the virus in our veins already. We die and we become one of them. We get bitten by a zombie and we're the undead. He's making empty promises. The serum he stole from our partnered packs is made for the X-Clan race of wolves, and it won't work for us." I suck in a sharp breath. "His action could bring that pack to our doorstep to annihilate us. So now you have two enemies outside your home." I'm partially lying, as I promised Ander the serum Mad stole back, and I intend to keep my promise, even if I have to pry it out of Mad's cold, dead hands.

Nostrils flaring, he growls under his breath. "The bitch is immune. Everyone saw her walk right through the mass of zombies unscathed. She isn't X-clan. Mad told us how you intended to keep her for yourself, to protect yourself while letting us live in fear so we followed you."

I'm seething. "A fucking lie."

"He promised everyone who showed him loyalty that they will receive the antidote once he caught her. We all live in fear, especially after they broke into the compound through the fence so easily. If you were smart, you'd stop fighting against your brother and help him find the cure for us all."

"That's where you're wrong," I answer with a growl in my voice. "Meira's sick and dying and that's why the undead leave her alone. Not because she's a cure." I need to get through to him so he sees the truth. My whole pack's future is at stake.

Nico blinks at me, thinking through my words, and about fucking time. "So she's immune, which means something in her blood or sickness may hold the key for all of us. Why can't you see this and do something to help all of us instead of insisting there is no way to help us? It's why so many have turned their loyalty to Mad." His face contorts in disgust.

"That's not how this works. Open your eyes. Our wolves abolish all illnesses, and she is half-human, half-wolf. What works for her will be killed off in our blood system."

He snorts and turns away, refusing to hear the truth.

My hands fist, my nails digging into the palm of my hand until it hurts so much, I can't think. I'm burning up with rage at how Mad planned everything out to undermine me all these weeks, maybe months ago. And these fools... *Fuck!* They're all scared, which was Mad's intention all along. Terrify the pack into submission with his fake promises. Sad thing is he believes Meira is the cure. Transformations eliminate all human illnesses, so when Mad discovers Meira is no longer immune to the zombies herself...

All fuck's going to hit the fan, isn't it?

BARDHYL

*M*eira's cries shatter through me like shards of glass.

"Leave her the fuck alone," I bellow from the cell I'm locked in with Lucien. My knuckles are white from how tightly I strangle the metal bars, throttling them.

Lucien is rattling the door with fury.

My eyes are locked on Meira. Always on Meira.

She cries and kicks and scratches the brute daring to lay a hand on her. I'm trembling, my wolf surging through me, my skin pricking with the change.

In my mind, I'm already ripping his throat out. I always push back the hunger from my wolf, try to tame him before I lose all control.

But not anymore... My heart is pounding, fists by my side.

"Bardhyl, I need your help to get this damn door down."

I whip my gaze in Lucien's direction as he kicks his boot into the bottom hinge of our prison.

The guard snaps his attention our way, snarling and twisting to come over, when Meira jumps onto his back, slamming a fist into his head.

Damn fucking brute swings around and throws her off with ease.

Her scream as she hits the floor burns in me like scalding acid. She's mine... my mate, and I am livid with the hunger to kill the guard for defying our Alpha, for ambushing us, but most of all, I'm going to rip his head off for daring to touch what belongs to me.

"Get the fuck over here!" Lucien shouts, and I march over to the door as he backs away.

I kick my heel with all my strength into the bottom hinge. The door shudders, the metallic groan echoing across the room.

I don't relent, don't feel anything but madness in my veins.

Meira's in the bastard's clutches. He holds her by her throat, lifting her off her feet. Lucien is yelling at them, and I'm barely holding back my wolf, except there's no use letting him free until I'm out of this cell. The more I watch her hurt, the more my head spins, and I'm breaking on the inside. It kills me to hear her cries, to do nothing.

I slam my heel again and again into the hinge, when finally, it gives a loud, metallic crack.

"Finish it!" Lucien commands.

I kick ferociously, my hands balled into fists and a growl in my throat as I put everything behind the thrust.

Metal warps, the bottom half of the door near the hinge buckles and snaps away from the bar.

Lucien lunges forward, shoving a shoulder into the door so it pushes away, offering a slight gap. I'm right there and shove my hands into the side of the door, pushing with all my might. Together, we bend the bar upward just enough for escape.

That's all we fucking need.

Lucien slides out of the prison cell first.

But before he can pull the metal back, the guard appears suddenly from where he was beating up Meira at the other end of the room. He now crash-tackles Lucien to the ground. I didn't even see him rush this way, too caught up in getting free. Lucien kicks him in the gut and scrambles back up while lunging at the bastard.

My gaze swings to Meira, who lies on the ground in a heap, blood on her face, nose, and jawline. On the ground near her lies a blade, and my heart plunges to my feet.

Did the asshole stab her?

Rage engulfs me, and I shove my shoulder into the bent door and squeeze out, bursting free. My wolf erupts out of me as I snatch the back of the guard's neck, dragging him away from Lucien and hurling him into the wall.

I roar, my body pulsing, aching, burning with the change. Clothes rip off me, falling away in shreds. Seconds is all it takes, and I'm on all fours, covered in white fur, leaping at the man. His head twists around to see me charging.

His mouth falls open in a silent scream, and his fear taints the air. He took too long fighting to bother changing. Too late.

My wolf is right there, nudging me while the corners of my vision blur in blinding rage. All I can see is red, and this fuckwit is going to pay.

MEIRA

*A*n agonizing sting flares along the side of my face. I groan, scrunching up the eye where I was hit and push myself to sit upright.

The prison cells surround me, metal bars, a terrible stench. But my attention swings to the explosion of growls and blood and cries from the opposite end of the room.

It takes me several seconds to clear my vision and work out what in the world is going on.

White fur, and the guard on the ground standing no chance, while Lucien stands in his path to ensure the asshole doesn't go anywhere.

The growls, the shouts bounce off the walls, and when I push to my feet, the room tilts.

Then Bardhyl in his animal form charges. The guard screams, and I turn away, not wanting to see this attack. He deserves to pay, but right now from the way he hit me, nausea washes through me. It takes everything in me to not throw up. I'm aching all over from being the prick's punching bag.

I hold on to the metal bars, taking deep breaths, while the savagery of growls and ripping and bellowing floods my ears.

"Hey, gorgeous, I got you." Lucien is by my side, his arms looping around me, and I sweep around to face him. We're pressed together, and I cling on to his shirt, needing closeness, needing him.

"I missed you," I murmur, then glance over to the bloody assault, which will be over in seconds now. I'd seen the way Bardhyl fought back in the woods, remembered what I'd been told about his wild wolf. So I doubt this one guard stands any chance against him.

Lucien's hand slides under my chin and turns my head toward him. "Focus on me, beautiful." He leans in and steals a light kiss. It's short and closed-mouthed, but the fire he ignites inside me awakens a storm of emotions. Desire. Sorrow. Anger. And a desperation to never lose what is mine ever again.

"I wasn't sure if I'd see you again," he whispers against my lips. "It would have killed me."

His words pierce right through my heart. He mirrors my feelings exactly, and as ridiculous as it sounds, tears prick my eyes. There's an asshole having the shit beat out of him, and I'm drowning in fear of losing my mates. I've never once imagined that finding my soulmate came with a savage torment if I lost them.

All I can think about is Lucien's first soulmate dying, and I can't even begin to understand how he survived such a loss.

"You really think I'd let Mad get the better of me?" I answer as I press myself to Lucien's chest, his heart pounding in my ear. I don't want him to see the tears or how easily I fall apart because of them. He holds me tightly and kisses the top of my head.

Mama always told me life is hard. Don't expect anything to be easy. You've got no one to count on but yourself. And those words kept me alive for so long. I am convinced they are the only reason I survived living in the woods. They helped numb the darkness in the hardest of times when I swore I was going mad.

That's how fucked-up I was. Looking back, it's so

clear. But at the time, I held it together by holding on to my hardened life. Maybe I've softened since first coming into Dušan's compound, or I found a new reason to fight for my life. More specifically three reasons.

I've searched for a purpose to life, and with the overwhelming sensation slamming into me at how much my soulmates mean to me, I feel weird. Though I know the truth. I finally fit in somewhere… with someone.

"Bardhyl, end this," Lucien suddenly commands, then he lowers his hand to my cheek and his thumb wipes away my tears.

He doesn't say anything, simply holds me. I glance up and look into those spectacular steel gray eyes, the smile on his lips, and my words tumble past my lips. "I think I love you."

The moment they leave, my cheeks heat. What is wrong with me? Is this the place to confess to such feelings? In a prison?

"Baby girl." He breathes heavily, his smile contagious and in every way captivating. "You are everything to me. My life. My future. My sun. I love you too."

His kiss comes swift and covers me in goosebumps. More than anything, I want to be away from danger for a change. For so long, I've been running from everything and everyone.

And now for the first time, that is no longer me. A guttural growl has us pulling apart, and we both glance across the room.

The guard whimpers, curling in on himself, bleeding and battered. It surprises me that he still lives. Bardhyl stands near him in wolf form. He looks at us, a gleeful expression sweeping behind his eyes just as he lifts his back leg over the man and pees on him.

"For fuck's sake, Bardhyl!" Lucien turns away from him, shaking his head.

I laugh, but it hurts my jawline from where I was punched. In fact, I want to cry out with excitement. I finally found Lucien and Bardhyl.

"Where did they take Dušan?" I ask.

"We don't know. He wasn't with us when we ended up here." Lucien's arm around my waist squeezes like he's afraid I might go too far from him.

Bardhyl trots over and nudges his head into my side. I reach out, looping an arm over the back of his neck, drawing him to me. He's burning hot against me, his fur splattered with blood.

Lucien pulls away first, breaking our embrace, and as much as I want to protest, I know we're in danger the longer we remain here. "We need to go now," he says.

Time with them is always too short, and my gut churns with concern. "We need to find Dušan first."

"Down in the dungeon below us. Bet that prick Mad tossed him in there." Lucien takes my hand and leads me to the door, Bardhyl at my back, and I take one last glance at the guard at the end of the room. He's slumped against the wall, not making a sound, but his huge eyes are staring at us, his empty gaze haunting and terrified.

Bardhyl left him alive on purpose because he had to have known these Ash Wolves made a massive mistake in betraying Dušan, yet he believed this man could repent.

Fear makes people desperate, and that's when shit goes sideways. But everyone fucks up sometimes. I misjudged all Alphas for so long, while Bardhyl lives with the agony of those he killed back in his home town in Denmark.

I glance back at my Viking mate still in wolf form, following close on my heels, and while everyone might see him as a terrifying warrior, I see someone else.

Someone who might be trying to atone for his past mistakes.

We all step out of the prison, my heartbeat quickly rising. Just as we swing toward the descending curving steps, a loud thud comes from down below.

Footfalls slap the stone floor, and panic races down my spine.

Lucien's hold around my hand tightens, and he's flying up the stairs, me in tow, and Bardhyl alongside us. He growls low to himself.

As we run away before detection, Dušan floods my mind, and I can't stop the images of him lying down there being tortured from playing in my mind. And I hate myself for leaving him behind.

CHAPTER 6

LUCIEN

*W*e force ourselves to run faster, me pulling Meira by the hand to keep up, while Bardhyl takes the lead. He sniffs the air to prevent us from running into anyone, taking us left and right down corridors. He knows this place inside out.

Voices and shouting booms from outside the building, coupled with the distant popping sound of guns going off. I don't know what's going on, but it sounds chaotic. Better for us to slip out of here undetected. Though leaving behind Dušan is a punch to the gut, and there's only one place I can think of to hide to get my thoughts together on what to do next, which is where Bardhyl is headed. We discussed our escape plan to get out and go find Meira. Seems the little fox discovered us first.

When I glance over, there's an innocence behind her pale bronze eyes, coupled with fierceness. She doesn't whimper despite the guard having attacked her but steels herself against me as if ready to confront whatever danger emerges.

I fucking adore everything about her, and my heart clenches as her words back in the prison float in my head.

I love you.

Three words I never expected to ever hear again, and it plays heavily on my mind. I accepted my loss long ago, and that my future would be filled with women in my bed, not my heart. Until Meira. Except this isn't the place to fall apart and get all mushy. I need to get my shit together.

We sprint down an empty corridor, my heart in my throat at the thought of being found, so I keep looking behind us.

Bardhyl careens left around a corner. He's going for the side exit from the building and into the settlement grounds. Perfect.

"Quickly," I whisper to Meira, who's huffing but still keeping up with me.

My thoughts ping-pong in every direction. I will fight to the death to protect my soulmate. To defend our home. To safeguard those we consider family, currently living in fear within the pack. And then there's Mad, the fucking prick. He is a certified psycho, and I told Dušan this long ago. But you can't reason when it comes to family. I know this, but it doesn't change my mind.

It sucks we had to devolve to this chaotic disaster for Dušan to finally open his eyes to who his stepbrother is: one twisted sonofabitch.

Everything about him is screwed, always has been.

From the times I caught him assaulting two newly arrived Omegas in our woods, feigning he was helping them. To his constant goddamn spying on everyone. No one does that unless they are up to shit.

Meira's hand slips in mine, but I hold on to her tighter as we dart down the darkened hallway. There are doors on either side of us. These are the staff quarters and our kitchen. Beyond lies a door leading outside, always locked from the inside.

Bardhyl skids to a halt at our exit. Letting go of Meira, I shuffle past Bardhyl's big ass and find no key. I try the handle. Locked.

"Stand back." I kick the damn lock. A clang sounds.

"Wait." Meira interrupts, and we both turn to her. "I entered the settlement from the rear fence, and they already know I've probably broken in, so there might be guards out there. I caused a diversion at the front gate, but I don't know how long it will hold. Is there anywhere else we can go without going outside?" She glances back down the corridor. "Maybe we should return and find Dušan."

"Hold on," I start, trying to process everything she told me. "How did you escape Mad's men in the woods?"

Even Bardhyl makes a rumbling sound in his chest.

She's still breathing heavily. "Everything happened so fast, but I had my first transformation after they attacked and you two were knocked out."

"Holy fuck!" I drag her into my arms. "You had your first shift… Hell, this is massive." I look her over, and she's not harmed. "You survived." My heart beats so hard. Gone is the worry of how we were going to find a way to fix her. This is the best news, especially considering everything else is falling apart.

Bardhyl is right there, rubbing himself against Meira's legs, letting her know he's there for her.

She gives a small laugh as she pets Bardhyl behind the ears. "When they injected me, it must have triggered something in me and I changed." A frown creases her perfect forehead. "It freaking hurts to transform."

I chuckle and embrace her before lowering my face to her and kiss that sweet mouth. Short and sweet, and now I desperately long for time with her alone.

"So you ran from them?"

"Yes, and then let's just say, the horde of zombies who showed up suddenly saved my ass."

"You were damn lucky those things didn't get you too." She must have been fast in her wolf form.

She blinks at me, her mouth parting, like she's going to say something, but she nods. Something swims behind her gaze, an unease, but we don't have time for this now. She'll tell me later what happened in the woods after I was knocked out.

Bardhyl groans and headbutts my leg, then looks at the exit. Yes, we need to get the hell out of here.

I turn to the door and steel my shoulder, then ram it into the wooden surface. It groans and splinters in response, rushing open in a wide swing.

A burst of rain and wind slams into me, blustering wildly, snatching at my clothes and hair, howling.

The storm booms overhead, darkening the world, as though night has arrived early to claim the land.

A small clearing of grass stands between us and the array of homes surrounding the large cobblestone courtyard where most of the pack lives.

Bardhyl growls and shoves past me, leaping into the field, sprinting toward the rear of the homes that back onto the woods. Exactly where we need to go.

Meira's hand glides into mine. "Let's go," she says, determination fierce on her gorgeous face. Blood and dirt stain her cheeks and chin, her dark hair a mess, but to me, she is still beyond perfect.

We both rush outside into the wild weather battering into us, rains drenching us in seconds, icy cold against my skin. There's no one around, the commotion from earlier coming from the front of the compound. As much as I want to explore and find out what the heck Meira did, I can't risk being seen.

Gravel crunches under our feet as we hurry past the first few small houses and follow the narrow trail behind the homes to our right. Meira keeps up, her gaze sweeping over the woods to our left.

The alarm bell from the rear of the settlement is going off, and my skin crawls. They will definitely be scouring the area, and they aren't stupid, so they'll know it's Meira. My mind strays to leaving Dušan behind, except I can't risk Meira's life.

Get her to safety, then I'll return and find my Alpha.

Running, Bardhyl takes a sudden swing right into a small backyard with a tiny vegetable garden, and he charges up to the back door, where he turns. He waits for us, his ears pressed to his head with impatience.

"Is this Kinley's place?" Meira asks. "Why are we here? We can't endanger her. We can't be here."

"Trust me, gorgeous, Kinley's got the best way out of here and only we know about it."

She looks worried, but I don't have time to explain this out here.

I step past Bardhyl and open the door. Kinley's house is rarely locked.

We rush inside, where there's heat in the house, coupled with a fire stove burning in the kitchen we just stepped into. I lock the door behind us.

"Who's there?" Kinley's soft voice calls out from the main room, and I go in first, scanning the dimly lit living room to ensure she's alone, which she is. Curtains cover the windows, the small fireplace spitting embers against the metal grill in the fireplace. Kinley sits in her chair by a small table piled high with books, her teapot, and cup. She wears her hair short for convenience. She's paralyzed from the legs down. Like Meira, she's also half-human, half-wolf. A rogue wolf attacked her during her first change, and it was her fated mate's wolf energy that saved her from dying when her own wolf broke out of her. The rogue wolf severed her nerves and she lost the feeling in her legs. It's a fucking tragic story, but she's alive and we're grateful we still have her.

"It's me, Lucien. I've got Bardhyl and Meira with me," I say in a lowered voice, moving forward to collect several logs from the basket and toss them onto the dwindling flames.

"Why are you all here?" Her voice cracks and worry taints her words. She blinks over at Bardhyl and Meira as they enter the room, and a smile splits her mouth. "Everyone's looking for you, girl."

Smiling, Meira makes her way across the room and kneels next to her, taking her hand. "Someone had to save these Alphas."

Kinley laughs, and she pats Meira's hand.

Bardhyl is pacing back and forth near the door, keeping guard. Being here is risky... Anywhere in the settlement is with Mad in charge.

"I experienced my first change," Meira tells Kinley, who gasps with startled excitement, then scans my gorgeous babe head to toe.

"And everything's all right?"

"Yes. I think. I'm not too sure yet, but I'm not dead, so that's a bonus."

I trace the curve of Meira's body, searching for anything to show she's not fully recovered after her first transformation. The way she talks is like she's not convinced yet she's healed. A chill slides down my back at the thought that she hasn't told us everything yet.

Bardhyl gives a short growl, grabbing my attention while the two women talk. I head over to him just as electricity skips down my arm. His body begins contorting, stretching, growing. The familiar sound of bones cracking and skin popping fills the room. Before I step back, he's standing in his human form, naked as a doorknob. There's way too much cock on show for my liking.

"Put it the hell away," I snap as I turn my back to him, smirking because I love getting him all riled up.

"Bardhyl," Kinley says. "In my bedroom, I have spare clothes in the cupboard. Always have spares."

He doesn't say anything but marches across the room and vanishes into the hallway. I don't miss Meira staring at the big guy, at his nakedness on display, or the way her eyes glint at seeing him exposed.

I have no doubt she'd stare at me with the same desire if I stripped right now. Though with the way Kinley is looking my way with amusement it's as though she can read my thoughts, I walk away and close the distance to the window. Pulling back the curtain an inch, I scan the grounds outside.

The rain is coming down in sheets, puddles covering the courtyard, and figures are darting about. But how much longer before they start searching houses? The gates out of the fortress grounds would be heavily manned, so using those to exit are out of the question.

I turn to Kinley, who's still chatting with Meira, but she lifts her gaze on my approach. "You know why we're here," I say.

She nods.

"Why is that?" Meira lifts to her feet as Bardhyl returns, and I look over as he strolls into the room, carrying a pair of black sneakers, too small for him.

The dark pants he wears are plastered to his thick legs, the fabric appearing thin, and it leaves nothing to the imagination. His black, long-sleeved top has a V-neckline and pulls taut across his chest. He pulls at the material, and if there's one thing I know about Bardhyl, it's that he loathes constricting clothes and prefers to be in his wolf form. Sure, those were two facts, but it's like he chose those pants on purpose to display his wares.

I turn back around to Kinley, noting Meira doing a double-take of Bardhyl. I roll my eyes. "Okay, focus." I grab everyone's attention, all three staring strangely at me. Hello, who's wearing tights clinging to his cock? It isn't me!

"So, are we hiding out here until we go rescue Dušan?" Meira's voice is full of hope, then she smiles wildly as Bardhyl hands her the sneakers. She's been running around barefoot, and the big guy is soft when it comes to Meira.

"Thank you." She wraps herself around him, hugging him, then peers up at him. He leans down and kisses her quickly. My heart beats faster and it has zero to do with jealousy, but everything to do with admiration at how much Meira has tamed the beast in him.

I hate to be the bearer of bad news, but... "We're getting out of the settlement now. Homes will be searched soon, and we'll be no help if we're imprisoned again."

The lovebirds pull apart and Meira's expression falls. "Wait, we can't leave without Dušan. Can't we stay here and go back for him later?" She puts her shoes on, tying up the laces.

"I wish we could, but we can't risk you getting caught. We'll be back for him, I promise," I explain.

Begrudgingly, she nods, her mouth tight.

"I have a bag under the sink filled with blankets and water," Kinley says to Bardhyl. "Go fill it with food from the pantry. Meira, help him. There's also a fire starter kit and dry kindling and wood to take."

"What's going on?" Meira asks.

"We have another way out," I say. "Go help Bardhyl before we end up with only salt." He coats it on everything he eats.

I face Kinley as the other two hurry into the kitchen. "You are a blessing."

"What I am is prepared. Just like you and Bardhyl have been in case a day like today happened." She smiles, but there's concern behind her eyes. She knows as well as I do that danger comes in many forms and our Alpha only really trusted a handful of Ash Wolves. He may have given his stepbrother lenience, but he didn't trust him. Which is why Mad has no clue of our backup escape plan right here under his nose.

"Go quickly before it's too late," Kinley says.

I lean in and hug her. I've always seen Kinley as my older sister who looked out for me, who told me stories and helped me get through the devastating sorrow after losing my soulmate. "Be careful," I whisper.

A sudden burst of voices comes from somewhere outside. I break free from Kinley and dart across the room to peel back the curtain a bit. In the courtyard, at least a dozen pack members stand guard as Mad marches toward them. The sight of him makes me curl my hands into fists, fury bleeding through my veins. I shudder with anger and urgency to rush out there and make the asshole pay for what he's done.

I can't hear his words, but his arms are waving about, all while it's pouring rain out there. I'm under no illusion that he won't be sending out a search party through the settlement to look everywhere. It's what I would do.

I whip around and say in a quiet voice, "We leave now!"

Darting into the middle of the living room, I roll back the rug spreading over the floorboards and reveal a trap door I'm way too familiar with. I reach down and drag the metal latch free, then wrench up the door.

The gaping mouth of darkness greets me, bringing with it a cold chill. There's a ladder that goes down into old tunnels that crisscross under this land from ancient times. Dušan had Bardhyl and me work to secure the passage from here and right out into a secret spot in the caves in the woods. Years is what it took, sweat and fucking aching muscles to unblock cave-ins, and now it's worth all the damn time we spent on it.

"Whoa!" Meira states as she emerges from the kitchen, Bardhyl behind her, a large bag swung over his shoulder. "Is this our way out?" She sounds almost scared.

"Yes, and we need to go now! Hurry up." Voices from outside escalate as though they're moving closer.

"The torch," Kinley reminds me, rolling her wheeled chair forward, ready to drag the rug back over the trap door once we're gone.

I take a thick, wooden stick hidden near her fireplace and plunge one end covered in cloth and oil into the fire. It takes instantly, an orange blaze flickering and coming to life.

Bardhyl has already jumped into the tunnel, and

Meira is on her way down the ladder, and she looks at me with uncertainty, but there are no complaints.

"I'm right behind you, gorgeous," I assure her.

Though, in truth, I wish I could fly her out of here so she didn't have to run and hide, but I can't, so I'll do the next best thing. Protect her from the fucking demented wolf on our doorstep.

CHAPTER 7

MEIRA

"Hey, you okay, angel legs?" Bardhyl asks, slowing his relentless marching through the tunnel and turning his head toward Lucien and me. Flames flicker from the torch he grasps, tossing shadows across the tunnel walls.

In reality, it's more of a sauna as I'm sweating like a beast. The rains aboveground seem to have made this place a sweltering and stuffy cocoon. Each breath gasps as I draw it in. Luckily, a light breeze brushes past every now and then, and I crave more before I pass out.

I wipe the perspiration from my brow and push away the hair stuck to the sides of my face. "How much longer?" Compact earth covers the walls of the tunnels, wooden arched beams keeping the place from caving in. "Feels like we've been walking for half a day. I really don't like being closed in here." Pain coils in my chest at not seeing a way out. We've passed several passages spiking in different directions, but the men insist this is the right path. But what if it's not and we get lost underground, going in circles?

My pulse races and I'm frantically looking behind and forward to where only darkness awaits.

Shadows dance under Bardhyl's eyes, the pitch-black snatching away everything else in its grasp. "Not long now. I'd offer to carry you on my shoulders, but…" He glances up to the low ceiling.

"I want to get out of here." My voice wavers and more sweat drips down the side of my face.

Lucien reaches into the bag he's carrying over his shoulder. He pulls out a bottle with water. Yanking the cork top, he offers it to me. "This should help."

I swallow past my dry throat and greedily accept the bottle with two hands. Pressing the opening to my mouth, I tilt it back and gulp down several mouthfuls. Cool water runs down my throat, chasing away the heat and dryness clinging to my insides.

"We spent many weeks working down here, fixing these old tunnels," Lucien assures me. "We are very close to reaching the end. Just a bit longer, beautiful. All right?"

I nod and wipe my mouth as I hand back the bottle. He takes a drink then passes it to Bardhyl. Soon enough, we are on the move again.

"What were these tunnels used for before?" I ask, needing a distraction from the sensation of the walls closing in around me. I've never felt so claustrophobic before. Then again, I've never been in such tight confines with no way out. I think that's the problem… a lack of escape and feeling trapped.

"This is Râșnov Fortress built by Knights to protect local villages against invasion from other countries," Lucien explains. "Afterward, the Hungarians and Saxons expanded the location, so it could have been any of them. But most likely, it was used as a way to defend their land, using these passages to surprise invaders."

"Remember those two skeletons we found down here?" Bardhyl asks.

Lucien starts laughing, leaning against the wall alongside me. "I swear they died while having sex. It was vanilla sex, but still freaky to see them in the position. Now *that* is a good way to go."

"Really?" I butt in, trying to hold back my laughter at what they remember from this tunnel.

Bardhyl smirks. "There are only two ways I want to go. Either in battle, or buried deep in…" He pauses, looks at me shaking my head, and shuts his mouth. But the rest of the conversation dissolves and the flame on his torch flicks wildly to the point of going out.

"Well, hopefully, that never happens to us," I respond, rubbing the goosebumps out of my arms. "And for the sake of all things, don't let the light go out." A small whimper escapes past my lips.

"It'll be fine. We won't let anything happen to you," Bardhyl says. "Even if the flame goes out, I can get us out."

"That doesn't reassure me." I wrap my arms around myself, hating how this confined space is affecting me so much. "Does it feel like the tunnel is getting smaller?"

Lucien pipes in. "Two of us can stand side by side, babe. It's not narrowing. But I agree, it's not a big deal if the flames go. Means we no longer have to stare at the sausage in Bardhyl's pants."

"What?" Bardhyl and I say in unison, turning to Lucien.

He sighs and blows a long breath out. "I wasn't going to say anything, but fuck, bruh, why did you select those pants? Your plums and cucumber are sticking out like a damn sore thumb. I mean, you almost made poor Kinley faint back in her house when you came out with your bed snake on show."

Bardhyl glances down, lowering the torch, and I can't stop myself but follow his gaze. The fabric clings to his cock, which sits at an angle, and hell, he is a huge boy even when not turned on. I must agree that when I first saw him in those pants, I almost choked on my breath because the material concealed nothing, curving over his ridge and bump. The saying about guys having three legs is not wasted on Bardhyl, and my skin heats at the image.

"Why are we talking about this now?" I ask, unsure of Lucien's point, except that it comes from a place of jealousy, and I don't want Bardhyl to feel bad if those pants were all that fit him.

"It looks incredible, right?" Bardhyl answers, and it's not the response I expect.

"Told you, he wore them on purpose to fling his pecker around. There was a reason Kinley sent you quickly to get dressed. Then you came out like this." Lucien flings his hand at him.

Bardhyl laughs and is already walking away. We are

hurrying up behind him, and I'm just shaking my head that this topic is even being discussed.

"There was another pair. If I knew you'd be this jealous, I'd have brought them out for you."

Lucien scoffs and reaches down to grope himself. "What I'm packing leaves Meira gasping, but I don't wear fancy pants to draw attention to my ammunition."

"Hmm, don't bring me into this," I murmur as we walk faster.

"Babe, you are completely in the middle of this sandwich," Lucien answers.

While Bardhyl still laughs, he glances over his shoulder. "Later, you can try on my pants and then we can let Meira judge who looks best in them."

"Um, no," I respond.

"Deal!" Lucien answers.

I roll my eyes. "Seriously, I'm not sure why guys are so obsessed with the size of their penises. You don't see females going around flashing their... their flowers for comparison."

"There'd be nothing wrong if they did," Bardhyl responds. "I wish you would."

"Yes, finally we both agree," Lucien adds.

I glare at Lucien, who winks at me, and while the discussion is absurd, my knees wobble slightly at how easily he affects me.

The path curves to the left and only once we clear it does a small light come into view from up ahead. I'm suddenly bouncing on my toes. "A way out!"

A whistling wind curls around us, and relief washes

over me. "We've reached the end. That's the best sight in the world."

I'm moving faster, the men right there alongside me.

"Feeling better?" Lucien murmurs.

I turn toward his smiling face, and it takes me a few moments to really understand what he's talking about. Then it collides into me like an avalanche. "You orchestrated that whole conversation about Bardhyl's pants to distract me, didn't you?"

He blows me a kiss while Bardhyl faces us, and those delicious eyes narrow seductively.

"You bastards," I tease. "Here I thought you both had major jealousy issues. Though I will admit, those pants are super tight." This time, it's me who laughs about the fact that they so easily fooled me. "Thanks." I move to hug them both, and for a few moments, we hold each other. How in the world did I get so lucky to score these smartasses as my mates?

Finally, we take a step out of a gaping hole and into an oversized cave, with its opening at least twenty feet away. I hurry forward, never wanting to be in another tunnel ever again.

The sight of the woods stretching out before us, the fresh smell of pines and rain fills the air… I missed it. I can't see exactly where we are, but we are definitely outside the compound.

"It wasn't that terrifying," Lucien murmurs as he pushes the strap of the backpack higher up his shoulder.

Bardhyl walks toward us, his nostrils flaring as he takes in a deep inhale, his chest rising. "Do we remain here until the right moment to sneak back for Dušan?" he asks.

"No. I mean, yes to finding Dušan, but we can't stay here," I answer before Lucien gets a chance. "There's a cave up on a hill near the settlement and my friend Jae is waiting for me, I hope. It faces away from the compound. With the rain, we shouldn't be detected. I just don't know how to get there from here." I'm speed-talking, wanting to get away from here, as I hate the open tunnel. Mad and his men could be barreling after us right now.

"What side of the settlement is your cave?" Bardhyl asks.

"The same side where we were attacked by Mad."

Lucien pulls out a blade from his boot and winks. "So we've got a bit of walking to do. Let's join your friend while we wait then."

Bardhyl straightens his posture before offering me his hand. "You run with me and lead the way once I get us to that side."

"Okay. I'm ready."

His hand grips mine and we hurry into the pounding rain. Its coldness leaves my skin covered in goosebumps, and I duck my head as we dart into the forest.

I'm freezing and my heart beats overtime that we might bump into Mad's men. Or Shadow Monsters. It's not me I worry about, but my two wolves, and I just pray we make it safely.

Rain assaults the forest around us, thunder growling in the sky, and we don't stop. I'm pretty sure if I do, I'll fall asleep in seconds. Though I'm also starving. My thoughts keep going to the cheeses and dried meat and bread we took from Kinley. I can't even remember the last time I ate. Starvation drives me to run faster.

I don't know how long we've been running for, but when we pause, I'm out of breath and lean against Bardhyl, who holds me, gasping for air himself.

"Hell, please tell me we're near the hill." Lucien drops the bag to the ground, hands on his knees, sucking in rushed breaths.

For a long moment, no one says anything, but we all breathe heavily. Drenched, we look like drowned rats, and I might have laughed if I weren't so exhausted.

I glance around us and know exactly where we are now… in the woods at the rear of the settlement where I scaled the fence. And farther to my right, the mountain rises like a giant. "Up there." I point, and Lucien groans. "We're close."

"Fuck. When you said *hill*, I assumed a small hill, not a freaking monstrous mountain to scale." He huffs and picks up his bag.

Bardhyl stiffens, his eyes locked on something behind me, and suddenly, he shoves me to stand behind him.

I stumble to catch my balance, terror strangling my lungs. Have we been discovered? I step out from behind him, my muscles bunched along the length of my back.

Farther ahead near a cluster of trees stand three Shadow Monsters. They don't charge us in a mad rush to attack. Instead, they watch us like the ones I saw on my run toward the back of the compound. I assumed they were lost from the herd, and technically, they wouldn't have been drawn to me. But why aren't they coming for Lucien and Bardhyl?

"What's wrong with them?" the men ask in unison.

"I don't know, but the more I look at them, the more I recognize them. Not only did these three follow me in the woods before I came to rescue your asses, but they were part of the horde that attacked right after I ran away from Mad and his men gave chase."

All three of us just stare at them for a few moments, but they're too far for me to make out clearly if they're the same Shadow Monsters or different ones. They look so similar.

"We move and keep an eye on them." Lucien has already drawn his blade, and I take the lead toward the mountain.

Every few steps, I look back to the undead following. They aren't running and keeping a fair distance.

"Something's up. Since when don't those fuckers attack?"

Lucien has a point and I don't know the answer, though could it be related somehow to me still being immune? I don't see how.

"I should probably mention," I start and then my voice fades as worry creeps over my thoughts at what I'm about to reveal to them. Do I really want to tell them about my immunity and have them jump to the conclusion that I'm still sick? I've never felt stronger than when I transformed, but I also want to stop hiding secrets.

"What is it?" Lucien asks as he starts our ascent,

moving quickly, the rain slowing to a trickle. Sticking to the paths with less foliage and more trees to grab on to helps us travel faster.

"Somehow, I'm still invisible to the undead. I don't know how, but—"

"You're still sick?" Bardhyl pauses and steps in my path. "You said you transformed."

Lucien takes my hand in his. "How can this happen?"

I shrug, and I want to hide from them, instantly regretting I said anything. I hate the pity in their voices, the strain in their eyes. That was the old me... the reject no one wanted, and I thought once I changed, I'd become someone new. Someone who fit.

"Not sure how or why. I don't know if I'm still sick or maybe the injection Mad jabbed into me made me temporarily immune."

I glance over my shoulder to confirm the zombies have stopped at the base of the mountain just staring at us. So, what is the deal with them then?

Little makes sense. "Please, can we keep going and not stand around here," I say.

"Tell us everything," Lucien insists, so I do just that, keeping my voice low. I summarize what happened from the moment they were knocked out by Mad's men to when I found them in prison. I explain it all, including my distraction and the zombies.

"Fuck that!" Lucien growls. "You can't be sick. Your wolf side heals everything."

I'm not quite sure whom he's trying to convince then. Himself or me.

"We need to have her blood tested again," Bardhyl states.

"That's not happening while Mad's taken over," Lucien corrects him in a distressed voice, then he lifts my hand to his mouth, where he kisses my knuckles. "Even more reason to destroy him and claim back our home."

I melt on the inside to hear his devotion, to watch it slide over Bardhyl's face. They both keep looking over their shoulders, and I nudge them to continue climbing. The quicker we are in hiding, the more we can relax and talk about everything.

"I've never felt better," I tell them as they keep stealing glances my way. "The sickness I experienced before is no longer there. Maybe the zombies not sensing me now that I've had my first transformation is a temporary thing."

"I'm thinking the same," Bardhyl says.

The rest of the way, we travel in silence, and only the rain hitting trees echoes around us. Each time I check the path behind us, the undead follow, and I'm terrified they'll suddenly snap into their frenzied forms and attack my men. Or are they scouts for other zombies? Ridiculous. They're undead and don't have any brain capacity to work as a team in such a manner.

I swing back as they approach, frustration building in my chest, as I don't want those things scaring Jae.

"Get lost," I call out as softly as possible, flicking my hand at them to leave. "Go away!"

They freeze and just stare at me with empty, dead

eyes. Who were these three in their previous lives? Humans? Wolf members?

My men stand on either side of me as the Shadow Monsters slowly turn around and start trekking back down the mountain.

I'm gobsmacked, completely and utterly convinced that didn't just happen.

"Are you kidding? Did they just listen to your command like you're their queen?" Lucien gasps.

"I-I t-think so! No, this can't be right. How?"

"You've become the Zombie Queen," Bardhyl says almost in awe, like he's proud for me to carry such a title.

I cut him a sharp glare. "Don't even joke about that. Seriously, that is not a thing, right?"

"We need to keep moving," Lucien says, taking my hand to join him, but my gaze remains locked on the three Shadow Monsters lurching away from us at my command.

This must be a mistake, a coincidence because they must have smelled blood somewhere close.

My stomach rolls in on itself, and I can't even convince myself I commanded the Shadow Monsters.

And Bardhyl's words float over my thoughts, refusing to leave me.

Zombie Queen.

That's ridiculous. There's no such thing.

CHAPTER 8

MEIRA

*W*e stumble into the cave at the top of the hill, the trees behind us swishing, and coupled with the drumming rain, I can barely hear myself think. So I step deeper inside, scanning the enclosure for Jae.

Lucien and Bardhyl stand alongside me, dripping, their bodies almost blocking out all the light from outside. I move to allow a little illumination to spill into the cave.

Rain drips down my body, leaving small puddles around my feet, and unease settles in my gut.

"Jae!" I call out, even if the cave is small enough that she can't be hiding anywhere. All I see is the burned-out fire, a small pile of blankets and clothes in the back, and an old glass bottle. She left... again, and I want to scream at her for not waiting for us. Why would she go out in the rain?

"She's long gone." Bardhyl states the obvious as he

studies the fire. But it's not him I'm angry at… Maybe *anger* is the wrong word here. I'm disappointed with Jae.

That's what floods my veins. I want to protect and help her. I know how hard it is to live alone in the woods. And she doesn't even have the immunity against the Shadow Monsters like I do.

I look over my shoulder to the heightening storm, the spray of water coming in and coating my face.

"You're not going out there to search for your friend," Lucien says, like he can read my mind. Though he's right, and I tense at the realization. All I can think about is rushing out there to find her.

Foolish. She could be miles away, and I have no clue which direction she headed. I can hazard a guess, but what about Dušan? I won't abandon him, distracted by something else.

He is what matters right now, his survival, or I may lose him forever.

I sigh and turn away from the entrance, moving deeper into the cave. I ignore my churning gut and decide that I will search for Jae once we rescue Dušan.

"Fire, shelter, and food," Lucien says, dumping his bag on the stone floor at his feet. "We have it all, so we need to prepare and find something to block out some of the cold wind coming in during the night." He and Bardhyl get to working on the fire first.

I march to the rear of the cave and paw through the clothes. We're soaked to the bone and something dry and warm would be perfect. I also grab all the blankets I find, then begin laying them behind the kindled fire.

Bardhyl finds broken tree branches in the cave that just keeps on giving and throws them onto the blaze.

I finish laying the third, large blanket over the other two for as much insulation as possible from the freezing stone floor. There should be another blanket in Lucien's bag, and I have every intention of snuggling up to the men to steal their warmth tonight.

"What's our plan for rescuing Dušan?" I ask, though I keep speaking, not giving them a chance to respond. "Do we break in at night and go search for him in the dungeon?"

"Something like that," Lucien answers, while Bardhyl focuses on stacking more wood on the fire.

I blink, staring at both men, knowing them well enough to understand when they are placating me. They never accept things so cavalierly. "I hope you're not thinking of ditching me and going back on your own?"

They both raise their gazes toward me, revealing their true intentions.

Bastards.

"We are not splitting up. I almost lost you once—not again. I'm tired of being alone and losing everyone I care for. I won't let you do that to me." I don't even know where this came from, but something stings in my chest at how fast I get worked up.

Bardhyl closes the distance between us in two long strides, lays his hand on my cheek, and lifts my head to meet his gaze—beautiful green eyes that appear paler tonight. "We will fight to escape hell itself if it means coming back to you, but we are petrified of something happening to you. Can you understand why we make the decisions we do?"

He leans in closer and whispers, "Losing you will destroy me. And being away from you is the hardest thing. But we won't put you in danger." His lips brush against mine, stealing my chance to respond.

I ought to push him away, but instead, I melt against him, cupping his face, and kiss him back. Since Mad attacked us, it's been a relentless rush to escape, to find my men, to survive. Now, I let myself slow down and pitch closer, our bodies pressed together, our clothes soggy. I don't care about anything but being with Bardhyl and Lucien. I've missed them terribly.

My other man clears his throat near the fire and we pull apart, then glance at Lucien's unimpressed expression. "While I'd love to join you two, we should find a way to block out some of the wind from the entrance. The cold spilling in here is hellish. Then Meira won't be so cold when we strip her down." He raises his eyebrows in my direction and gives me a small nod to indicate it's happening. His gaze sweeps over me and pauses on my lips before rising back up to my eyes.

The mischief in his gaze is ravenous, and how can I feel anything but pure rapture when a gorgeous man says such things? I lick my lips, swallowing the lump in my throat.

Bardhyl looks at me, nodding. "Be back soon, beautiful."

Then he whips around and heads right out of the cave with Lucien, both turning left where there had been a cluster of trees, with large branch potential for covering the entrance.

A coldness sweeps inside, sending the fire into a wild flicker, while my skin shivers. I'm soaking wet and I need to get changed before I die from the cold.

Rushing over to the pile of clothes Jae had left in the cave, I grab a small pair of black leggings that have a hole across the knee, and a baggy sweatshirt, both too small to fit the guys. Quickly, I peel my shirt off, the fabric stuck to my skin, so I wrench it off me. The wind coming from behind me sweeps over my bare back, and I tremble. Damn, it's icy to the touch and my teeth are chattering. Just as fast, I pull down my pants, dropping them in a wet mess with my top.

With shaky hands, I grab a fluffy jacket that looks way too small to even fit me and frantically wipe the water from my body. Rapidly, I collect the leggings from the pile and step into them. Dragging them up my legs is a nightmare. They're tight and the fabric glues to my skin from not drying myself enough.

Fighting the damn thing, I get it halfway up my thighs, when the snap of wood has me twisting my head around.

In the doorway, Bardhyl and Lucien are caught frozen, the wind whipping against them, blowing their hair over their faces. They're holding large branches covered in leaves, seeming to have forgotten they're getting wet as they stare at me.

"Hurry up," I tell them as I wrestle to heave the pants up and over my ass.

Hastily, I pull the tee over my head and down my

arms, then I tug it down over my stomach and turn around.

"You didn't need to rush for us," Lucien adds as he and Bardhyl layer the cave opening with half a dozen branches in a crisscross fashion from inside the cave. They've also managed to bring in several large rocks for use at the base of their structure. Branches are sticking against the narrow sides of the enclosure, bent and shoved into place.

There are still some gaps here and there in the layers of branches, but instantly, I feel the change in the fading cold. With the fire crackling, this cave will be cozy soon enough.

"And we left a small opening here," Bardhyl states, pointing to the base of the structure near the edge of the exit. "For toilet breaks."

Speaking of which, I step forward for just that. "This looks great. Thanks. I have some dry clothes for you in the back to change into." I peer outside through the holes in the covering to where night falls over the landscape and the rain has eased to trickling.

"I'll be right back. Toilet break." I rush outside and don't steer too far, but it's freezing out here, and the rain catches me just as I push back inside through the gap.

"It's going to be a chilly night," I say as I straighten, but my voice flatlines.

My eyes land on both men standing on either side of the fire, butt naked, glancing my way with smirks.

"Careful. Before you burn something precious," I

tease as I wander closer to chase away the cold clinging to me.

Neither of them move from the blaze, and I join them, stretching my hands out to warm them up. "So, what's the plan?" I ask, fighting the urge to lower my gaze over both of them. "Food."

"Getting stripped firstly," Lucien answers swiftly, grinning at me, and I feel Bardhyl's gaze on me, both like wolves in waiting for the perfect moment to strike their prey.

I laugh, mostly for show. "So you saw a bit of ass and that's got you both hot and bothered already?"

"Do you need any other reason?" Bardhyl asks, and he's being serious.

I roll my eyes at them, even if on the inside, I'm extremely impressed and slightly turned on by their eagerness. "Let's eat. I'm starving."

They don't even hesitate and jump into getting dressed, both of them in loose shorts, and shirts a size too small. "Fine, food first, then stripping," Lucien reiterates.

Bardhyl is bringing out food from the bag. The white tee he wears forms across all those hard planes and muscles. Damn, he is toned. Lucien strolls over to me as he tugs on a long-sleeved tee the color of a sunset. The fabric is tight and also hugs every contour. He stands over me and pushes loose dark strands of hair off my face, while I can only think of how gorgeous he looks. Clearly, I'm unable to form thoughts that don't concern me picturing them naked again, muscles flexing, and me all over them.

"Sounds like a plan," Bardhyl begins. "Food first. Take a seat and we'll join you."

I eye him as he blows me a kiss and goes to assist Bardhyl. I'm beyond exhausted, and I might fall asleep while eating.

Soon enough, I find myself sitting cross-legged on the blanket, the fire warming me up, and my two men joining me. We're having a mini picnic of crackers, cheese, and dried meat, served with fruit chutney. The small salad of tomatoes and cucumbers I roughly chopped at Kinley's is on offer, along with a large slice of fruit cake. This is the biggest feast I've ever had while on the run… which has been most of my life.

"Enjoy," Lucien says as he reaches for a piece of the meat. "It's no roast pig, but it will do. And it's more than what Dušan will have to eat tonight."

I lower my head and send my thoughts to Dušan, praying that he's safe and we'll save him hopefully tomorrow. Glancing at Bardhyl and Lucien, all three of us sitting in a semi-circle around the food, I notice they also have their heads low, praying for their Alpha.

When we start eating, no one says a word, and my reason has to do with the sheer hunger I'm drowning under. I help myself to everything, except for the cake. I rarely get to taste such a delicacy, so I'm saving it for dessert.

"After I kill that fucking asshole, Mad," Bardhyl starts with a mouthful, then he swallows it, "I am cooking up my famous Viking stew for you. Three kinds of meat, potatoes and carrots, plus spices that will warm your insides. You will love my cooking."

"You're making me hungry while I'm eating. Is it a family recipe?" I create a stack of cheese, meat, and cucumber slices in my hand.

"A dish my father made for us growing up. I loved his saying that it made even the Berserkers stronger in battle. So of course, I'd insist on having three bowlfuls."

Lucien pushes a large slice of tomato into his mouth. "When I grew up, my dad would always tell me to love without strings attached. He helped around the house, always went out on hunts, so he didn't quite say those words, but rather showed it in his actions. In the way he aided others in need, how he worshipped the ground my mother walked on."

"He sounds like a romantic," I muse, unable to pause my thoughts drifting to the father who bailed out on Mama and me, who was too afraid to stay behind and look after us.

I can't protect either of you, he'd shout. *Meira is weak because of me. She'll always be an outcast.* He's human and couldn't live with himself, so it was easier to be gutless and run away than stay with us to make it work. I clench my teeth. Even after all these years, I struggle to forgive him, and part of me blames him for Mama's death. If he'd stayed and helped, maybe we would have been staying somewhere else and the Shadow Monsters would never have killed her.

My eyes prick, and I hate how quickly he still affects me, but it's not him I've cried for. It's losing Mama. I lower my head, pretending to stare at the spread of food as I blink away the tears. *Don't live with the past*, my mother said to me. *Always look forward.*

"That he was." Lucien nods, breaking my concentration, and it takes me moments to remember what he is referring to.

I breathe heavily and push aside the thoughts of my past as I can't do anything about what's happened, but I *can* control my steps forward. I found three men I will never abandon no matter what.

We eat with only the company of the crackling fire. It's only when I look up at each of the men that I recognize the expressions they wear as their thoughts drift miles away. Lost in their past. After all, it's all we all have left in this broken world that takes and takes from us. Luckily I have them in my life now, which wasn't always the case. Those are memories no one can erase, so what we have left, we cherish.

Exhaustion must have taken its toll, because after finishing the cake and licking every sweet crumb off my fingers, everyone settles into their own routines. Bardhyl packs up the leftover food into the bag, while Lucien stands and wanders over to check the barrier over the cave entrance.

I collect the crackers in a small plastic bag and fold it closed before handing it to Bardhyl. Our hands graze, and I soften at how warm he feels.

"You all right?" he asks, but I can't stop looking over at Lucien, about ten feet away, his back to us. It's clear he needs time alone with his thoughts.

"Is he okay?" I whisper behind the snapping sounds of the blaze.

Bardhyl nods. "Losing his parents so long ago to a

rival pack still affects him. Just give him a bit of time. He always bounces back."

"I lost my dad when I was really young, and then my mama, so I know the feeling." Leaning over the blanket, I use my hand to dust away the crumbs from our meal. "But I don't want him to hurt over what we can't change." The words spill from my lips, and I feel hypocritical, seeing as how I can't even get over the loss of my mama.

Zipping up the bag and pushing it aside, Bardhyl comes and sits next to me, his arms draped over his bent knees. "You care for him a lot, don't you?"

I nudge him with my shoulder, but he doesn't budge because he's a rock. "If you haven't noticed, I care about all three of you... a heck of a lot more than I ever thought I would. I mean, I accepted long ago that I wasn't intended to find my fated mate. But look how that's turned out."

The look he cuts me, those sexy eyes narrowing, makes me smile and forget everything else. This is one of his magic tricks I notice, and one of the many reasons I've fallen so deep for him.

He takes my hand and kisses each fingertip. "Once in a lifetime, everyone should meet someone special, maybe even three of them at once. Someone who ignites their world, who changes everything."

His words are the most beautiful things I've ever heard, earnest and passionate. Since meeting him, it took me a while to understand Bardhyl was so much more than a powerful Viking warrior with a berserker wolf. Beneath the layers is a man who suffers, who carries darkness from his past. But most of all, he is an Alpha who wants to be loved. I see it in the attention he gives me, the tenderness in how he holds me, the words he shares. Everything from when his hypnotic gaze meets mine to when he fucks me like a man driven mad by emotions he can't control.

"Do you think Lucien still misses his first mate?" I whisper, almost regretting at once that I asked such an intimate question.

His hand slides across my back and curls around my waist, drawing me against him, chasing away any space between us.

"Soulmates exist," Bardhyl assures me. "There is no such thing as an accidental meeting of souls. It was all meant to be." He glances over to Lucien, who stands at the mouth of the cave, staring into the downpour outside through the gaps, the sound of rain hitting the mountain hypnotic. "Just like you've given your heart to the three of us, Lucien will always hold on to a piece for Cataline. It doesn't mean he loves you any less."

"I know," I say, and part of me wonders if the ache I feel in my chest has more to do with feeling his sorrow of losing his first partner, rather than jealousy. "You know, I never used to believe in soulmates—well, until I met you three. Heck, after watching the undead kill my mother when I was fourteen, I stopped believing in anything but survival, including my own happiness."

He leans in close and kisses the side of my head. "Which is why I will hug you tightly every chance I get so all your pieces can fit back together. Until you remember how incredible you are and find that happiness you lost so long ago."

I tilt my head up and look him in the eyes. He has green eyes like the forest, and I fall deep into them, offering myself to this Ash Wolf. "You three are the part of me I always needed and never knew until you found me."

"No matter what happens, I want you to know that to me, what we will face, whatever the outcome, it is worth it. Being with you is everything, loving you, claiming you. Everything is worth it."

My heart flutters at his devotion, his words imprint on my mind so I never forget them. He shifts toward me, and I twist around too as his hand glides through my hair. I adore the way he looks at me, how when I'm in his arms I feel incredible, free, and safe. Add to that my body buzzing with an electrifying arousal. In any of their company, a single touch ignites my desires for them, entices me to their sides.

His eyes are deep and penetrating as he looks at me. His heartfelt musings have gone, a mischievous sexy expression now replacing it. We are stuck in the cave while the storm wreaks havoc outside, and all I can think about is how much I thought I'd lose my three wolves, how I want to crawl into their arms and remain there.

"I missed you," I murmur.

A delicious smile crawls over Mr. Gorgeous Warrior's lips, and my toes curl in response.

We come together, a slight pressure on the back of my head where he holds me just as he wants me, and he says, "Remember what happened last time we were in a cave together?"

My heart thunders behind my ribcage, and heat pools instantly between my legs because I will never forget. Clasping on to my confidence, I hold his gaze. "I learned my lesson already," I tease. "I'm never doing deals with you again."

He laughs, the sound like honey... sweet and addictive. And I don't wait another second. I close in and press my lips to his.

Seconds is all it takes for his fingers to curl over the elastic of my leggings, and I push a hand against his chest. "Um... what are you doing?" I have no plans on playing easy after his games the last time we spent together in a cave.

"Oh, you thought we were joking earlier?" Lucien's breath washes over my neck. I flinch at his sudden appearance and turn to face him as he gives me a sinfully sexy smile. He's back to his flirtatious self.

He leans in, kissing my lips over my shoulder. Like the storm raging outside, our mouths clash, even our teeth clinging together. And he's tugging down on my pants while Bardhyl wrenches up my top.

And I let myself fall into their arms and into this sexy fairy tale I've missed so much.

CHAPTER 9

LUCIEN

*H*arder. Faster. Insatiable.

That's how my little beauty kisses me, twisting her body toward me as we remain seated by the fire, holding my face in case I plan to get away. I'm close to bursting with desire at her passion, at how much affection comes from her when she's with me. We get lost in each other's company as I push down on the tight pants she wears, needing more.

They need to go.

Bardhyl is at her back, leaving kisses along her neck.

Meira is everything I want, every soft curve, every delicious taste, every tempting morsel that I'm craving. She's glorious and perfect.

She reaches between us, her hand gently clasping around my erection through my shorts, palming my cock. I'm so fucking hard, and I hiss at her teasing touch.

Bardhyl drags her top up and over her head, breaking apart our kiss. I use that moment to rip those pants off as she lifts her butt off the floor. Her body shudders in the speed and force at which I strip her. My gaze sweeps over her jiggling breasts and straight down to the small mound of dark hair between her legs.

My cock twitches as I catch a glimpse of her lips glistening from arousal before she clenches her legs, hiding from me what's mine.

As Bardhyl slides his arms around her waist, embracing her from behind, his large hands glide up and cup her perky breasts.

I use that moment to stand and lower my shorts. I step out of them, kicking them aside as I pull my T-shirt off, also tossing it behind me. Meira has the back of her head nestled against Bardhyl's shoulder, moaning as he pinches her nipples between his fingers, tugging them.

Dropping onto my knees in front of my queen, I watch this gorgeous woman who is our soulmate, whom we almost lost. I'll do anything to keep her safe and by our sides because losing one fated mate in a lifetime is more than I can survive. So I made the decision when Meira ran from us that I'll give her everything I have. To remind myself this was my second chance. I put my sanity on the line, my future, my heart… and I don't regret a thing.

I reach over and clasp her bent knees, running the tips of my fingers up to her hips, rousing her from her elation with Bardhyl. Sweeping my touch back down to her knees, I try to pry them apart, but the little minx resists me. She looks at me with a dirty little smile, and I lick my lips as Bardhyl laughs.

"You're going to play hard to get?" I say, flicking Bardhyl a knowing look as my hands grab her hips.

In one quick movement, he shuffles back on his knees, his hands tucked under her armpits, holding her up as I swiftly lift her ass up and off the blanket.

The shock has her shifting to escape us, her breath hitching, and in her mistake, her locked knees fall apart. "Hey, two against one is no fair."

"Who said anything about fairness?" Bardhyl murmurs, mirth in his voice, and he's enjoying the show just as much as I am.

My pulse pumps harder, faster through my veins as her sweet, wet pussy reveals itself to me, her pink folds needing attention. Hands sliding under her asscheeks, I nudge my shoulder forward to spread her legs wider, which dangle over my shoulders now, and position myself right between her thighs, eye level with what's mine.

She bucks for escape while she's in the air, both of us kneeling, holding her. Despite her actions, she laughs. "Put me down."

One swipe of my tongue over her sex, and her protest turns into a surrendering quiver. I inhale her perfumed scent that goes straight to my cock, my balls tightening, and I seal my mouth around her juicy offering and suck. She tastes sweet and so aroused, that I can't stop from eating her like I'm devouring a peach.

Memories flood my brain of all the times I've claimed her, how they were too few and infrequent. What we shared is not enough and I have every intention of rectifying that. But the more I lick and drown in her pussy, the more all those thoughts fly out of my mind.

Bardhyl groans with his own growing arousal, mingling with Meira's cries of pleasure. He gently lowers her shoulders and head to the blankets, while I grip her hips, latched on to her, holding her pussy nice and high. Her ass rests against my chest, so I take her weight.

He makes quick work of stripping, and his cock springs out of his shorts.

Meira reaches out for him. She sucks on her lower lip, then murmurs, "Come to me."

I continue to lick and nibble on her inner lips. My tongue strokes her all the way down to her entrance, where I plunge into her.

She writhes beneath me, her legs quivering with the approaching climax. I feel it in her taste, in the swelling of her lips. Everything about her consumes me, while my need to release thunders through me.

Her body shudders as I slowly pull on her clit, and the image of her squirming and moaning undoes me. I invade every inch of her with my tongue, flicking with speed.

Her pelvis rocks against me with her mounting need.

She reaches over and palms Bardhyl's thick shaft, pumping him back and forth. He roars, while I'm floating in my own fantasy. I can't get enough of being buried face deep in her radiant throbbing core. This is everything I dream of. That saying about guys being an ass or tit lover… I'm a pussy man through and through.

The three of us bond in carnal desires, needing this pure connection after almost losing her. Unable to stop watching her, all I want is to hold her in my arms, never let go. She's so beautiful, so innocent, so captivating.

Meira looks up at me, her expression overflowing with desire and confidence. She is no longer the scared girl whom Dušan brought to us from the woods, the girl who escaped Mad's capture, the girl who kept running from us.

She is a goddess.

Her body quivers harder, her moans louder.

"Meira! Not yet. Don't you think about cumming," I command as I lick her sweet candy juice from my lips and chin. With her weight on me and holding her with one hand, I run two fingers across her spread offering. She's velvety to the touch and so wet.

She turns over to look at me as she slips her lips over Bardhyl's cock, taking him deep into that gorgeous mouth. Her fiery eyes drown on the edge of her orgasm. I see it in her eyes, how close she is.

Bardhyl pushes in and out of her mouth, and I sweep my touch down her slickness and press them into her opening. Her eyes widen as her inner walls clench around me, squeezing, and she moans from what's coming.

"Not yet, Meira," I remind her and I pull free just as Bardhyl slips out of her mouth.

MEIRA

*T*he way Lucien says my name melts me, my whole body tightening. Those big, strong hands grasp my ass, his face buried between my thighs. My attention is glued on these two men's bodies... powerful as steel, biceps bulging. There is something primal that makes the feminine side of me go crazy with lust over these men.

I try to respond, but only a faint moan slips over my throat as Lucien lowers my hips back to the blankets, and I want to scream. The ache deep inside me pulsing, and I'm out of my mind with holding on as they pause.

"That's totally not fair," I protest through gritted teeth, drawing my legs together to bring forward that exhilarating promise of pleasure.

"Not happening." Lucien nudges my legs back open, holding them wide.

"I think she needs a bit more encouragement." Bardhyl growls, a deep sound growing in his chest, one that reminds me of hunger.

"I'm ready to burst like a volcano."

They exchange glances and smirk in a way that slightly scares me as to what they could be up to.

Lucien lowers his body over mine, and I arch my back in anticipation, then rock my pelvis upward to meet him.

"Please," I whisper.

His mouth claims mine, kissing with an aching desire, and I return the favor, needing him so badly. The tip of his cock glides over my entrance. I must have him in me.

He lets out a delicious groan, and a flush of heat washes over me, a desperate yearning. Balancing on the fringe of a climax, he teases and teases, never fully giving me what I want.

"Lucien," I beg into his gorgeous lips, tired of waiting.

He laughs, then pulls back.

I sit up, but before I can protest, Bardhyl reaches down and collects my hand. "Come to me," he assures me.

He's standing, his cock stiff and glistening from my mouth, and I can still taste his salty deliciousness.

Once I stand to face him, he makes little effort of leaning in and grasping the back of my thighs. In seconds, I'm up in his arms, my legs wrapping around his waist. I shift my pelvis back and forth, rubbing myself over the tip of his hardness.

I grip his round, iron shoulders as he closes in, our foreheads touching. "You've been away from me too long, sweet cheeks."

Unceremoniously, he slides into me, his grasp on my hips pulling me down. That earlier ache intensifies as he goes deeper, stretching me. I cry out at first from his sheer size, and the pain turns into exhilaration.

"Take all of me," he murmurs, the corded muscles in his neck twitching. He's fighting the urge to just fuck me like a wild animal.

Buried in there, he kisses me, then draws out halfway, and slams back into me. The rhythm escalates, intensifying.

My arousal billows within me to the point of explosion... I'm chasing the climax, desperate for release.

Lucien's strong hands clasp my waist from behind, and his chin props on my shoulder. "Are you ready for both of us, beautiful?"

I'm not exactly in a state to think straight, as I'm floating on clouds, and right now I want more. So much more.

"Yes," I purr, remembering the last time I was taken from the rear and how incredible it felt once I got over the initial shock.

Bardhyl pauses his thrusting and steals my mouth with his as his hands part my ass cheeks.

Lucien wastes no time. His fingers glide over the wetness, over my rear, and I'm already so turned on, so wet, I'm ready to go. Positioning the tip of his dick at my entrance, he takes his time and presses into me.

I stiffen, but I'm in good hands. His mouth is on my shoulder, leaving a trail of pecks as he slowly nudges into me, widening me.

Right now, I'm filled to the max with two huge cocks, and while the thought might have had terrified me months ago, now it's everything I lust after.

The three of us gradually fall into a rhythm of both men gliding in and out, alternatively, igniting an overwhelming friction. There's fire between us, burning us up.

I'm sandwiched between my two men, holding me in place as they fuck me.

My body shudders, the sensation sending me into the clouds. I cry out with each thrust, my breaths racing.

They gasp for air and groan their own pleasures, the three of us lost in the pleasure that our bodies tangled together to create.

I ride the two cocks, bouncing on them, my whole body contracting as my orgasm slams into me.

I scream, my body convulsing, and everything goes white for a few moments. In that same moment, Bardhyl stiffens and growls, shoved deep inside me, and I feel the end of his cock knotting, growing within me, filling me, locking in place.

Two pumps later, and Lucien's fingers digs into my waist, bursting with his own pleasure. I don't know how he fits, but his knot also swells. It's strange, but the pressure of them growing inside me triggers a deeper level of satisfaction, like somehow my body makes it clear I belong to them. They've staked their claim and I'm theirs.

The three of us moan, and I'm floating as they fill me with their seed. I feel it pulsing out, its warmth flooding me.

For years, I've struggled to find my place and home. I told myself things were perfect, but they weren't.

It's clearer now than ever that life back then was never simple, but a disaster waiting to happen.

"Wow," I exhale deeply. Swallowing hard, I chase my breath.

"You deserve everything," Lucien says, while Bardhyl sucks in a small inhale as though he's still going, pumping his seed inside me.

Seeing his handsome face lost in lust reinforces all my desires and how fast I've fallen for them.

It isn't long before the haze behind his eyes clears and he smiles wide. "Fuck! I need more of that."

I lean forward and rest my head on Bardhyl's chest, feeling more at home now than I ever have. It's not about the location, but the people I'm with that makes me feel that way.

Bardhyl and Lucien lower themselves to the ground, me still pinned between them, still joined.

Before I know it, we're lying on the blanket on our sides, near the flames. I doubt I'll get cold tonight. Bardhyl offers me his bicep to lay my head on, while Lucien presses his chest against my back and runs his fingers gently through my hair.

A slow smile creeps over Bardhyl's mouth.

"What's funny?" I ask, exhaustion quickly replacing the earlier adrenaline. Snuggled between my men, there is nowhere else I'd rather be.

"I'm seeing a pattern with us and caves." He laughs, the sound like warmth wrapping around my heart.

"Sure, but not all caves will mean sex."

Lucien slides hair off the side of my face. "I'm with Bardhyl on this one. All caves we stay in must come with sex."

Bardhyl chuckles and he nods his approval to Lucien.

I roll my eyes even if I can't stop smiling, but as I

rest, worry creeps into my thoughts. How I may be enjoying a moment of perfection now, but we're not even close to being out of the woods.

Especially when Mad will be expecting us to come for Dušan.

CHAPTER 10

DUŠAN

*T*he punch to the gut sends me to the floor, blood coating my mouth. I suck in each raspy breath, clutching my middle, curling in on myself. *Goddamn idiots.* When this is all over, they'll be on the chopping block along with this fucker, Mad.

I'm furious that men who once were loyal to me have betrayed me. Now, they don't even look me in the face, ashamed of what they've become, but it didn't stop them from changing allegiances. They believe this liar glaring at me will be their salvation. Well, they can all go down with Mad.

I cough, spitting blood on the stone floor, looking out at the two guards.

But it's Mad's twisted smirk I zero in on. He's standing outside my prison cell having the time of his life seeing me at my lowest.

Fucking sonofabitch, I want to rip his spine out. Our pack was a family, a home… Now, it's as broken as the rest of the world.

I wipe my bloody mouth with the back of my hand, sitting upright and slumping against the back wall of my cell, bruised and strained from the beatings. But Mad needs me alive and I can play this long term. My healing will thread me back together soon enough. Even if the frigid chill from the constant rain all night and day licks over my bones, and my sides burn from the kicks I received.

"Tell me," I start, my voice croaky, and I spit more blood onto the floor. "Is this everything you'd hoped it'd be? You getting a big fat erection over claiming the pack and being the big chief? But we both know you're still a coward." *Fighting* for dominance with honor is the way, not the trickery bullshit he's pulled.

I am way past caring about not antagonizing Mad.

He snarls, the hatred palpable on his face, and I can't help but smile.

"You're living on borrowed time, brother. Make the most of it, because your wolf girl will be mine by the end of today. Then..." He shoves away from the wall and stands tall, running his hand through his white hair. "I will no longer have a need for you. No one will." He strides toward the exit, but I'm not finished with him.

Mad's a fool and lets his anger rule him.

"Word has it that the smaller rogue packs up north are uniting and have their eyes on this land." I hate giving him any insight, except my intention is to make him realize the situation is much more than about him taking leadership or an antidote for the zombies. "You will have the X-Clan pack coming for revenge for stealing their serum, along with the northern barbarian pack. How many of the pack do you think will remain loyal by your side when your promise of freedom proves to be a hoax?"

He jerks his head to look at me over his shoulder with a wry expression.

I've touched a raw nerve and he knows it… Maybe he never thought this through, but that path he's taking will be a wretched one.

"Is that your attempt to plead for your life? Ain't working."

I half-chuckle. "You think this has anything to do with me? Unlike you, I care for this pack's members. They are my family, but to you, they are your servants." I shrug, cutting a glance to the two guards listening in. They lower their heads and don't meet my gaze. "Just pointing out a massive flaw in your plan."

"This has nothing to do with you any longer, brother." He growls. "You are my pawn until I get the girl. That's all you are, and I don't take advice from pawns." A snarl hangs off his last word, and I smirk at the thought that I've pissed him off.

Good. Maybe my point will get through to try to save the pack from slaughter from the oncoming dangers. Except with my brother, nothing is predictable.

He charges out of the prison with the guards. I sigh and draw my bent knees to my chest, hugging my legs, wincing as the ache flares through me like someone is holding a flame to my insides.

I have every faith in the world that Bardhyl and Lucien will escape their capture. Seeing as they are not with me, I can only assume Mad has them in the other prison cells, which aren't built as strong as this one.

Mad doesn't really care about them… it's me he wants to torture. Whether it's sooner rather than later is another story. Yet Mad's words swirl on my mind about him having Meira by the end of the day.

What does he have planned?

An urgent need grips me to break out and find her first. The desperation squeezes my lungs, hurting more than the strikes to my ribs.

I glance up at the door to the dungeon, the only way out of here. I'm too deep underground for a window escape, and I ease up to my feet. Every inch of me screams with pain. The guards left me alone down here with the other two empty cells and a rancid smell of wet earth, with the trickle of water coming through the walls from the wet ground outside. It's been thundering endlessly since yesterday, and I grasp on to hope that this is not where it will end for me. I'll fight to get out. Still, that thread of doubt lingers.

The main door to the dungeon room swings open, and I lift my gaze to the guards dragging someone unconscious by their arms. The man has pale blond hair, is built like a bull, and is wearing black jeans and a fitted leather jacket. They toss him into the farthest cell from me. My first thoughts leap to Bardhyl, except this man has short hair, and it has been a long time since I have seen anyone wear a leather jacket. Mostly because they're hard to come by.

Slamming the cell door, the guards march out, and I

turn my attention to the newcomer. He lies on his side, curled, unmoving.

"Hey," I call out, but he gives no response. He's been knocked out.

Taking a deep inhale, I sniff the guy's scent to place him.

Strong wolf musk, perspiration, and beneath that lies his unique smell, akin to a saltiness in the sea. Who exactly is this stranger and what is he doing on our land?

What is going on out there?

I stumble toward my cell door and turn to study the main door of the room, listening for any faint voices from the guards.

Silence.

Mad is long gone, and his plan worries me.

A shiver tracks down my spine and it has nothing to do with my demise, but Meira's safety if Mad captures her. I return to my neighbor and will work on waking him to find out what's going on.

BARDHYL

"Get the hell up. We need to leave now!" Lucien's voice rips right through my sleep and tears me awake.

I snap upright, my heart thundering, and I half

expect attackers in our cave. Scrambling to my feet, Meira's eyes flip open and she groans with confusion.

"What is going on?" I bark at Lucien who's gasping for air like he's been running.

"Mad's men are coming up this hill. Saw them when I went out for a piss. We transform into our wolves and run from here."

"Run where?" Meira climbs to her feet, clutching the blanket she's wrapped around herself, her eyes darting to the cave entrance and back.

"Somewhere safe," Lucien says, the energy in the air thickening with the electricity of his teetering change.

I'm shaking my head, panic coiling in my gut. "If they're out here searching for us, then this is our chance to retrieve Dušan."

"Yes." Meira is nodding her head, stepping forward. "No more running because you two are not safe out there with the undead. So we do this now. But how far are the wolves from us?"

"At the base of the hill," Lucien answers.

I adore my angel's resolve, and I wrap an arm around her shoulder and drag her against me.

She glances up, her smile tight and eyes filled with trepidation, still she pushes herself up on her tippy toes and steals a quick kiss. The softness of her lips cushion against mine, but she draws away just as I turn to take her fully into my arms.

"We don't have time for this," Lucien reminds us, his foot tapping the stone floor.

"I know," Meira says, her voice shaky, and she throws her arms around him, kissing him on the lips just like she had with me. "We go after Dušan," she reiterates.

Begrudgingly, Lucien nods. "Fine, I'm outnumbered in votes, but we leave now."

"Let's do it." My skin already pricks as I call my wolf forward and unleash him. He shoves past my barriers and spills out. It's always a race for him, needing freedom, to chase, to take control. But not yet, boy.

Serrated pain carves through me as bones crack, skin splits, and I growl from the deepening ache. Just as quickly as my transformation had hit, it vanishes. I drop to the floor on all fours. Colors morph into muted hues, the world is sharper, crisper, the scent of the pines outside fresh and ripe.

A deep rumbling snarl reverberates through my chest, and I shake myself, my thick pelt fluttering. I never feel as free and ready as when I'm in my wolf body.

I twist my head toward the other two remaining in human form, chatting quietly, Lucien holding Meira around the waist.

I trot closer, feeling like I've missed something.

"Close your eyes," Lucien says. "And only think of your wolf easing forward. Call her to you."

A shiver clings to my heart. This is only her second shift, and not once had it occurred to me that she'd struggle to change. Guilt strikes me in the gut, but it's done now, so I leap toward the cave opening to check on the intruders.

Sunlight beams brightly today, and it's way past morning, so how long had we slept in for?

Silently, I sneak into the shadows of the woods, sliding from one tree to the next down along the sloping terrain.

I sniff the air, catching the wet fur and wolf scents on the upwind. I pause near a rock ledge on the side of the hill with a deadly sharp decline. At the base, three wolves search the area. The rain should have covered my scent, but Lucien is right. We can't risk it.

Gradually, I ease backward, stepping out of sight before I turn and make my way back to the cave. I rush past lofty trees and jump over shrubs. My heart beats faster that we had let our guard down by sleeping in so long. Low branches swipe over me, droplets from the storm splash across my face.

A sudden howl shatters the peace. The echo of paws pounding the ground fills the air, growing stronger the more I listen.

They've picked up on my scent.

Fuck!

I throw myself forward faster, the cave coming into view and still no sign of Lucien and Meira.

A growl thunders past my throat, a warning to Lucien, and I pray he helped Meira transform.

We've just run out of time.

CHAPTER 11

MEIRA

My wolf rips through me so fast and sudden, that panic grips me. I shuffle about, wincing, needing to somehow stop the pain burning over my body. It didn't work. I'm still human, and part of me is freaking out that she'll fully take control of me this time.

"Relax. Don't be afraid of it," Lucien's voice floats around me, while my heartbeat thunders in my ears. I'm trying to concentrate on his voice and don't seem to be doing a great job.

Sharpness digs through every inch of my body. My body heats up, almost as if I'm on fire and about to explode. It's not different from the first time… transformations are damn painful, and my wolf is coming out harder than the first time.

"Meira, stop fighting it."

I take in a sharp breath and thrash wildly, my clawed feet scratching the stone ground. I twitch all over and suddenly collapse on all fours, shuddering. My vision blurs back and forth from present to dark spots. Just as it had on my first transformation.

Seconds later, and I'm inhaling deeply, my pulse on fire, no longer in my human form. Now, I stand on four paws as my wolf, and I lift my head, sniffing the acrid smell of the burned-out fire, the muddy earth outside, the delicious scent that is all Lucien. There's something freeing about being this way, except just as I have that thought, my wolf rises through me like a shadow. She's always there, always pushing and pushing me aside.

I twist my head toward Lucien, and his approving smile is all I need to calm down.

He runs a hand down my back, the touch like the most incredible massage in the world, and I soften against him.

A sudden growl from outside the cave has us both snapping our attention to the opening, my pulse spiking at the threat of danger.

"They're coming," Lucien announces, and a spark of energy abruptly flares over me. His body shifts from man to beast in seconds, so effortlessly while mine felt achingly painful and slow. He meets my gaze, and I stare into familiar pale steel-gray eyes that don't change in color from when he's in his human form. Thick brown fur covers him, his long ears swivelling, taking in all sounds.

The air thickens, and a chill grips my spine. Gone is the peace with my wolf. Something different overcomes me—the heightened awareness of every sound, every movement, of survival.

Lucien pivots and darts out of the cave.

I scramble after him, desperate to keep up, my wolf pressing forward, steering me toward the enemy. Panic burns me, and with every inch of willpower I steer myself back around and chase after Lucien. Tensing, I concentrate on every step, every move, and part of me is convinced my wolf feels stronger.

Coldness wraps around me.

Around me, the earlier smells are now tenfold, smothering me. From the muddy soil the rain has stirred, the pine trees, the smell of fire smoke in the distance I assume is coming from the Ash Wolves' compound.

I sprint right after Lucien, who swings left from the cave and we're bolting down the slope between the trees.

I see Bardhyl running with us, his white pelt like a blur amid the shadows, leaping over shrubs, his frantic movements belonging to someone fearful. He's an Alpha where little scares him, so his reaction terrifies me.

Our pursuers are close.

He swings toward us, glancing at me for a split second, a powerful energy swirling behind his gaze. The three of us in wolf forms leap down the hill, cutting our escape with extraordinary speed. It startles me how fast I move, not too different to flying, I like to think as my paws barely touch the ground as I lunge downward.

We pick up our pace and sprint over a rushing creek when I spot the same Shadow Monsters lingering not too far from where I'd sent them to leave me alone. And I clearly see there are four of them. Like before, they don't make a motion to chase after us. The more I look at them, the more I can't help but feel like I remember the one with the massive scar on the side of its bald head. Then the memory comes to me like a storm. It tried to attack Jae after I untied her from a tree. It's the same damn Shadow Monster I fought and bit. Why is it acting this way now?

An ear-shattering howl from somewhere behind us shatters the silence in the woods, and I twist my head around.

Two figures charge after us. They have our scent and their call would alert others. How long before the place crawls with Mad's followers?

Lucien doesn't pause, and I rush to keep up with him. Bardhyl has fallen behind me, keeping me always in view. I can't ignore how protective they are and how much I love that about them.

Ears alert, I listen for anyone sneaking up on us, for sounds, but the farther we race, the more my lungs tighten. But I don't mind constantly moving. It keeps my wolf occupied.

I don't know how long we've been running. Lucien never slows, and only when movement at the edge of my vision grabs my attention do I look around at the surrounding woods.

Shadow Monsters push through the forest, streaming forward from our right. Lucien lurches away abruptly at having noticed them too.

Crap! Terror floats on the back of my mind that we've ended up in a swarm of them. Maybe this isn't the best path to run.

When I look behind me, Bardhyl is practically on my heels, our trackers closing in, except there are now close to a dozen in their wolf forms charging this way.

My chest clenches at the sight.

I tip my chin toward the horde of undead noticing our commotion, and I pray we are quick enough to escape them while the Ash Wolves at our rear are taken out.

Abruptly, the mass of undead on our right pour toward us with such speed that it takes me aback at first, my heart galloping. They're coming for my two men.

Lucien swings a sharp left and right to where the forest is less dense, where he has more of a chance to escape. Bardhyl does the same, nudging me with his head to follow.

I swing my attention to the Shadow Monsters, to the Ash Wolves, to my two men darting away, and it's all happening too quickly.

Slivers of seconds to make a decision.

Bardhyl looks back at me as I pivot in the opposite direction to him and lunge at the undead that move fast. I want these creatures to focus on our enemies instead.

I slam into a dead man, bringing us both to the ground. He reeks of death and putrid things. Brittle bones snap beneath my weight on his chest cavity, but it makes no difference to these creatures. He's already rolling to get up, groaning. I scramble forward and tear down the next monster, and another. Sure, they keep returning, but I'm slowing them long enough for my wolves to escape.

In a chaotic dance of leaping and tearing them off their feet and shredding clothes, I stop as many as I can. Already, half a dozen swing toward the wolves careening toward my men.

When I stare out that way, Bardhyl and Lucien stand by a twisted grand old tree, farther away, barely a shadow, but I know it's them.

Frantically I study how nimble the Ash Pack moves toward my men while curving away from the encroaching zombies. The members don't see me, not while I'm surrounded by the undead.

Problem is that the moment I step out to join my lovers, I will reveal myself. Instead, I recoil deeper into the river of undead emerging from the woods.

Desperately, I stare at my men, imploring them to get the hell out of here, hoping they understand. I will find them. Our only saving grace is starting to see some of the zombies chasing after the Ash Wolves.

When I swing my attention back to Bardhyl and Lucien, they're gone.

My heart twists and hurts, but it's for the best. With the Ash Wolves out, better for me to remain near the undead for now... at least until I can make a clean break.

Jittery nerves rush through my veins and I jostle about following the flow of zombies heading after the Ash Wolves. They shove past me, moaning, flooding the air with their reek. I may hate them, but they have saved my ass a few times. Beggars can't be choosers.

When I can no longer see the Ash Wolves in the woods up ahead, I start to pull away from the undead and decide to keep going in the direction Lucien had been taking us initially, away from where the Ash Wolves and zombies headed. I pray that once they shake off the Ash Wolves, they'll resume their course in this direction too.

Woods blurred, closing in around me, this part of the forest is tightly packed with trees, and sunlight barely pierces the canopy overhead.

Shivers of panic blaze over me. The farther I travel and keep looking over my shoulder, my stomach hurts. Maybe I should have tracked after my men being chased by the Ash Wolves but kept my distance? Did I make a mistake?

Pausing for a moment to catch my breath and slow my drumming heart, I wrack my mind for what to do next.

There's no one following me that I can see when a twig snaps behind me.

I whip around, teeth bared, my rage unleashing. My thoughts fly to the Ash Wolves, except my gaze lands on Jae and the three huge men by her side. They are dressed in clothes too clean, too perfect to be from anywhere in this place. Pants, boots, long black coats, and wild hair. Brutality gleams in their eyes. The sight of them scares me and reminds me in many ways of three bears rearing up on hind legs before they attack.

With their sheer sizes, these large men standing at least six-foot-five or higher look like beasts to me. They aren't from around here, so where the hell did they come from?

"Meira," Jae says at first, stepping closer, her hand stretching out to me. "Don't be afraid."

The man with honeyed hair, cropped short, snatches her arm to hold her by their side.

Yeah, right, don't be afraid, she says.

Jae frowns and glares up at her captor, then shakes her hand free. "She's not a danger, but an Ash Wolf. She saved me from the zombies and from the rogue wolves. She is with me."

I tilt my head to stare at how confident Jae sounds, and I'm proud of her in that moment, but these three men she keeps company are nothing but danger. Does she know what she's doing?

The man who took Jae by the arm steps forward, which tells me he is the leader of these Alphas. I can smell it on all of them in fact, feel the Alpha heat that radiates from them like fire. Just as Omegas like me give off a certain scent, so do these men.

But I'm no fool... Alphas search for two things when they hunt in the woods.

Food.

And women to claim. To trade. To rut.

I sure as hell didn't come this far to end up back in square one.

I recoil from them, Jae's mouth dropping slightly as she sees me retreat. I am not a match for three men. I know my limits, but none have made a fast grab for me either.

"Meira, please," she pleads. "They aren't rogue. They arrived here from the north, and they'll help me find my sisters."

North... my mind swirls with the rogues who live

there, how there are only small pockets of wild Alphas working together. Fear climbs through me.

"Your friend tells the truth," the leader assures me, his voice deep and husky.

Three pairs of pale eyes study me, their expressions not concealing their intentions if given the chance. To me, there is nothing alluring about them and only fear collects in my chest for me and Jae. "Change and we can talk, Ash Wolf."

I want to laugh as I will not take his word, but Jae's I will. And for all I know, this could be her code to help her... yet again.

"Please," she insists. "Change so we can talk properly. They just want to know about the Ash Wolves."

The fur on my back bristles. What do they need to know? Their weak points so they can attack while chaos reigns over the pack? Though this also gives me the chance to mislead them and uncover their true intentions. We are already dealing with a demon, and we don't need the devil sneaking up on the compound to take over.

The leader unbuttons his coat, which falls to his hips and shoulders the fabric down his arms, before handing it to Jae. She dutifully takes it and holds it out like a curtain to cover me from these three men who leer at me. Her eyes plead with me, and she truly believes they will not harm me.

My skin crawls because I don't need to be dealing with this right now. But I can't walk away if new predators stalk these woods either.

As Lucien had taught me, I exhale slowly and call

back my wolf, her attention on the newcomers. With a growl in my chest, a protesting sound at these enemies, she slides into me, the pain slithering over me, making me tighten. I won't show these men any weakness.

In moments, I'm standing naked. Quickly I take the coat from Jae and turn my back on the audience to thread my arms into the too-long sleeves. The strong musky male and perspiration scent from the fabric floods me, doing nothing but raising my hackles. Though I appreciate them giving me something to wear, where many males wouldn't. I button up the coat that looks more like a dress on me when it falls to my knees. But it covers everything I need.

I swing around just as the leader grabs my arm, squeezing, and growls. "Let's walk. We need your help, Ash Wolf."

CHAPTER 12

LUCIEN

I skid to a stop near a gurgling creek, my lungs furiously pumping for air, and whip back around. Bardhyl leaps right over the water before he pauses.

Behind us, there are no signs of the Ash Wolves. No sounds, either. The same can be said for the undead. We've lost them.

All I can think about is Meira and how she saved us by turning the zombies toward the wolves coming for us. Normally, I'd stay and fight, especially as I vowed to never lose her again, but I ran. And I hated myself for that, yet to remain meant our certain death among that swarm. Running is not a weakness, even if guilt now twists my insides into a knot so tight, I feel sick.

A sudden spark of electricity blazes down my arms, my hairs lifting. I turn to find Bardhyl pulling himself to his feet, in his human form, the last layers of fur vanishing into his skin.

He cracks his neck, his wry expression bursting with fury.

"Fuck!" is all he says.

Exactly my sentiment. I take his lead and summon my wolf back, my transformation clawing through me. I welcome the pain, the agony, anything's better than the feeling of my heart rupturing.

"We need to find her." I growl, pulling myself up. "She either chased after us or continued in the direction I was taking us up north to the mountains that neared the Savage Sector. It's where Dušan told us to go and hide if things ever got really bad." Wolves rarely visit the area and I figured it might be a good spot to lie low to shake off the Ash Wolves.

"I don't know if she'd go in that direction. She doesn't know that's a hiding spot. We retrace our steps carefully and try to find her here," Bardhyl says, sounding more like he's reassuring himself.

"Fine, but if we find no sign of her, then we can split up between the north and the direction heading back to the compound. Whether she's caught or of her own volition, she will go there eventually, right?"

Bardhyl's response comes in the form of a growl. I sniff the air and don't sense her. "We just need to find her scent."

For the most part, she might be anywhere in the woods, but I'm trying to think like Meira. She saved us from the cell in the settlement, which means she won't steer far and come to track us down.

I glance the way we came, part of me desperate to see her silhouette appear out of the shadows, to know she's safe, but she never comes. I know it deep in my heart that she didn't follow us.

"The woods are teeming with undead and Ash Wolves who've turned against us," I say.

"If fortune is upon us, we will find her in the woods."

"I hope you're right, my friend." Trepidation worms through me at the thought that it won't be that easy.

MEIRA

"*L*et me go!" I wrench my hand from the brute, except his grip might as well be an unbreakable stone.

"You will help us," is all he keeps demanding, walking us quickly back the way I just ran, dragging me alongside him. This Alpha with the palest green eyes makes no effort to slow down.

If luck shone on me, we'd cross paths with the undead, giving me the ideal chance to escape. Worse, we'd bump into the Ash Wolves searching for me. Well, maybe these northern brutes might finish them off for me. Again, offering me plenty of time to run away with Jae.

I glance back over my shoulder to where she speed-walks between the two other Alphas, though neither of them are holding on to her.

"Nikos," she calls out. "Please. You're hurting Meira."

The man hauling me pauses, turning slowly toward

us, his grasp on my wrist constricting. "There is no time to waste." His attention falls to me, his features tightening.

Up close, there are flecks of gold in his eyes, and a fresh scar across an eyebrow still blushing pink. He has thick, long, chestnut hair on the top and back of his head, which is shaved at the sides. It's easy to see him as a wild man, but I remind myself he hasn't hurt me yet, which means he can be reasoned with.

"Just tell me what you want?" I ask, holding his attention. "You want my help, then talk."

The sound of the other two men breathing heavily tells me these Alphas aren't used to females talking to them in such a way.

Nikos, as Jae called him, smiles. "The Ash Wolves have something of mine and you will help us retrieve it." There's no patience in his voice.

"What is it?" I ask immediately.

"That's none of your business, Omega. You will aid us or I will feed you to my two men." His head juts up before I can respond. "Jae, if you want us to take you back to Narah, you will shut the fuck up."

Unease curls in my chest, and I twist to look at Jae, at how white her face has turned. Her shoulders curl forward, like she's trying to make herself smaller, to vanish, but her gaze never leaves mine. Behind her eyes, there's a battle between forsaking me to reach her family, or give that up to assist me.

"You give your word you will not hurt my friend? Narah, hired you to find and keep me safe, but I ask you to do the same with Meira," she finally says.

These men have been contracted by Jae's sister? Hired to find her? Who exactly is her sister to have goods to trade or power to hire such powerful Alphas?

Nikos thumps a fist to his chest fiercely. "My word is yours. We will not harm the woman if she helps us."

Jae nods, and Nikos turns to pull me back into his fast walk, but I yank against him. "Wait. So you want me to get you inside the settlement? Is that all?" My skin crawls at the way he stares at me, but I can't hate Jae for not begging them to release me. We all do anything we can for survival, for our family. I've spent enough time with Jae to know she's true of heart in her intentions, wanting nothing more than to get home and feel safe. We all deserve that, so any anger I feel is for these men who, like the rest, take what they want for greedy reasons.

"Yes," Jae whispers in response instead as she looks away.

Nikos drags me back into our rushed pace. My head swims back and forth to make sense of everything. What did the Ash Wolves take from these Alphas?

In truth, I don't know enough about the wolf packs around Shadowlands Sector, even whom Dušan has dealings with. For all I know, these are disgruntled Alphas coming for retribution against him while they are in the vicinity, and they want me to open the front door for them.

Still, even that theory doesn't sit right with me. Eradicating the top leader of any pack is not an easy feat. Is it a job for just three men? Maybe. Well, I sure as hell will not be handing over my mate to these monsters.

We move faster now, the ground rushing under my feet. Nikos keeps holding my arm, carrying some of my weight so I keep up with his long strides.

Much to my disappointment, there are no Shadow Monsters on our path.

"If you tell me what you're looking for, it will be easier," I break the silence. "I'll know where to sneak you in from. I mean, I assume you want to be snuck in, or why else drag me there like a madman?"

He doesn't make a sound or even glance my way, but we rush over terrain covered in dead leaves and twigs. Our approach is easily heard by anyone nearby, though it doesn't seem to faze him.

Behind me, Jae and the other two men remain close. Any attempt to escape won't get me far. I can tell this by the size of these men alone. Three against one, basically.

"Meira." He snarls, somehow making my name sound dirty. He leans in closely. "Listen carefully. These men have been starved of a good rut for weeks since our departure." He grabs me by the chin, hurting me. "Keep pushing me, and I'll gladly watch them take their turn with you. After that, you will still help me collect what's mine. The decision is yours."

I freeze as my panic flares. But I don't flinch or dare show him how furious he makes me. In my mind, I want to make him suffer, to hurt, to cry with pain. Jerks like him get off on seeing the terrified impact they have on others.

"Please, Meira, just do as they say," Jae pleads, and I

hear the quiver in her voice. Despite these Alphas coming to collect her, they still scare her. That much is obvious.

But I hold Nikos' stare. He's trying to get under my skin. "Fine, we'll do this your way," I finally say.

He lets me go and snatches my arm. "We always do."

We're off again.

I exhale hard. I'm seething on the inside, shaking, but I shouldn't expect anything different. My whole life I steered away from males for this reason. Most Alphas rarely relent and never see Omegas as anything but their slaves.

His threat haunts me with every step. I lift my head and we move swiftly through the woods, while the whole time, I keep wishing the undead would find us. Then, when they eat these assholes, I'll not feel a morsel of guilt.

My legs ache from the pace we maintain and how we've been moving nonstop for what feels like forever.

The firs and the hills in the distance are starting to look familiar. We're nearing the compound, and nerves bunch up under my skin, as I have no idea what to expect. I'm stuck between a mountain and a hard place with two adversaries after me.

Please let Bardhyl and Lucien at least be somewhere safe.

We stop abruptly and even before I can make sense of what's going on, I smell Ash Wolves on the cold breeze, but not my men. Shadows rise ahead of us alongside the trees. A dozen of them approach in animal form, snarling.

A shiver worms down my spine. "We need to leave," I whisper to Nikos. "Before it's too late."

"I never run!" he bellows, his gaze jerking toward the encroaching danger.

He leans in and whispers, "Answer everything I ask you truthfully and I promise to release you." He steps forward, hauling me alongside him by my arm.

I have no clue what he's talking about. Fear grips me, and I slide in close to him, wanting the ground to open up and swallow me. If Mad gets me, he'll never let me go. He'll torture me, and eventually kill me when he finds I am not the answer to his demands for immunity. I'm no fool and know exactly what he wants, how terribly this will play out for me and my wolves.

"I want to speak to your Alpha!" Nikos shouts, loud enough for everyone to hear.

There's no response at first, and I curse my grasp on his arm. Does this crazy northern wolf know what he's getting himself into? That he is literally exposing me to a den of starved wolves?

His fingers around my wrist never loosen. His hold is cruel, and I don't know whom to be more afraid of. I make no move to fight, only watch as a man steps out of the woods up ahead.

Wolves scour the land around us and with each passing second, the chance to escape fades on the wicked wind tugging at my coat.

The man has short hair. He's someone I remember seeing in the compound a few times. He would definitely recognize me, and I slide farther into Nikos' shadow.

"You called for me," the stranger responds, his chin high, his shoulders broad. Except I'm confused, as this man is not Mad, so whoever he is, he's faking. Or is Mad somewhere around us in wolf form, watching?

Nikos leans toward me and whispers, "Does he speak the truth?"

"He's not the leader," I answer softly.

"Who is he?"

I shake my head. "I think a guard."

Nikos bristles, clears his throat, and turns back to the imposter.

"Your men took someone who belongs to us. I am willing to overlook it as an accident, but I am here to get him back. Bring him to me now, or your blood will spill."

I glance up at Nikos, half-impressed by his cockiness, considering there are only three of them against a dozen Ash Wolves. Either he's the best fighter in the world, or he's bluffing. But whom exactly did Mad kidnap from this man anyway?

The imposter spits on the ground between us, his face twisting into fury. "You trespass on my land and dare threaten me?"

He flicks a hand at his wolves, and before I take a breath, we're being attacked. I jerk backward, but Nikos holds on to me like a freaking lunatic.

"We need to run." I gasp.

Half the wolves charge at us, their teeth exposed, their ears flat against their heads.

Nikos skims his hand up my arm, and to the back of my neck, pulling me closer to his side. "Hold still."

A swish of wind suddenly rushes past me, a blur moving so fast, I flinch and bump into Nikos. My initial mistake is thinking an Ash Wolf attacked from the side, except it's the two northern wolves at my back leaping forward into battle.

White as the snow, these creatures in animal form are bigger than any wolves I've ever seen, even larger than Bardhyl, and he is massive. These northerners could easily stand as tall as me at eye level.

Shivers crawl up my arms, but I can't look away from how swiftly these two monsters pounce on the other wolves. One bite and bones crack. Whimpers and terrified Ash Wolves dart to escape. Whimpers flood the air, it's a bloodbath, the tangle of fur and fangs and dust.

Who the hell are these Alphas?

I glance back to Jae, who is close to us now, her head low, hugging herself, not watching the assault. I want to tell her she will be safe, but there's no way I can make such a promise for either of us.

"These damn fools. Don't they know we'll kill them all?" Nikos murmurs to himself.

It all happens so fast, and before us lie dead bodies, bloodied and broken, transformed back into human form. I scan them all for Mad's face or anyone I recognize. Nothing on both accounts from my vantage point.

The imposter falls to his knees before Nikos, the monstrous wolves on either side of him, filling the air with their growls. Red stains their white fur, mouths dripping with blood. The sight alone leaves me trembling. An absolute massacre surrounds me, and it hardly took any effort.

In the distance, more Ash Wolves appear, which isn't missed by Nikos' wandering gaze. He might have fighting machines under him, but even he would have to realize he will fall against a full pack.

"I will ask one last time," Nikos states. "I don't want war between us, but I will destroy every last one of you. Bring me who you stole now!" he bellows. "And to show you I am a fair man, I will give you back one of yours."

He whispers in my ear, "Change of plans." His large hand shoves me in the back, and I'm stumbling forward before I can stop myself.

My heart pounds in my chest frantically, and suddenly, I'm backpedaling. That idiot just threw me into the lion's mouth.

I glance back to him, to Jae. "Please no. Don't let him do this."

"Deal!" a dark voice responds as strong fingers clasp around my wrist.

I snap around and come face to face with the imposter standing inches from me, sneering. "Got you," he mouths.

I pause and try to still my shudders, then look back to Nikos one more time. "Please. They'll kill me."

Jae's tugging on his arm, fear twisting her expression. "Don't let them take her. She needs to come with us."

"We made a deal," the ass holding on to me snarls. "She's ours, and I will have my men fetch your man."

No, no, no! Rage fills my veins. I haven't come this far to be caught. I swing around, my fist flying, and I clip the asshole Ash Wolf right in the face.

His grip loosens as he groans, clutching his bloody nose.

I rip free and whip out of there.

He suddenly grabs me by the hair and wrenches me backward. I stumble, my feet buckling out from under me, and I hit the ground on my ass. I cry out, holding on to my hair to stop the excruciating pain.

Jae is screaming and running to me, but Nikos snatches her by the arm. "No, this is not our fight."

"Bastard!" I bellow at Nikos. I've been right all along about these Alphas never seeing females as anything but commodities. And this prick has just sold me out.

CHAPTER 13

DUŠAN

"*G*et the fuck up!" The growl rips me abruptly from my sleep.

I jerk upright in seconds, my heart jolting into a race, only to find there's no one in my cell barking orders at me.

Movement from my right draws my attention to the farthest cell, where the other prisoner lays. Alen, a guard I recognize with a scar down the side of his neck, stands above the prisoner, kicking him in the leg. Two more guards wait outside the cell.

I tried talking to the prisoner earlier when we were alone in here, but he was knocked out, which I can only assume came in the form of the same injection Mad jammed into me. Though I didn't need to speak to him to identify his Alpha scent. With it came the acknowledgement that I don't recognize him. A rogue? Maybe. Or even someone from a nearby pack surrounding Shadowlands Sector. There are many I haven't had the chance to meet yet, but then again, I'm selective when it comes to whom I'll consider working with.

"Did you hear me?" Alen bellows.

The stranger groans awake, the side of his face red from where he was sleeping on the stone floor.

Leaning over him, Alen snatches him by the hair and yanks him upward. I hear the low rumbling threat rolling through the stranger's chest.

"Leave him the fuck alone," I command.

Alen's head twists in my direction, his lips warping into a wry grin. "Don't fret. Your time is coming."

"And *you* have forgotten your place. Something I will be certain to remind you of when I claim back my pack."

He barks a laugh, though I hear the unease threading through the sound. Yeah, he *better* be scared. Sitting here alone has given me a lot of time to think about how I will run my pack from now on. At first, I accepted that these traitors were frightened and that meant they were doing anything to save their own hides. And while that is still true, there's a vast difference between those who bow down to Mad to show allegiance out of fear and those who happily carry out his dirty work. The latter is whom I will never forgive for their betrayal.

I refocus on the newcomer, who's on his feet, and a lot taller and broader than I first realized. Dark hair sits cropped short around the edges and back, while longer along the front.

Alen reaches for him, but this man is fast and snatches his arm, twisting it around his back in seconds. He shoves the guard face-first into the metal bars.

I can't stop laughing. "Make it hurt," I sneer.

The other guards rush in just as the Alpha slams his foot into the back of the open door, which goes swinging into their faces.

I'm howling with laughter at the incompetence of these men Mad entrusts. I know each of these Ash Wolves and there is a reason they never gained a high position in my team of warriors.

When it comes to this stranger, he is something else and might make a good addition to my team.

He cuts me a look, a slight nod of acknowledgement that we aren't enemies here.

The other guards finally make their way back into the prison as the Alpha pulls back, hands in the air. They lay into him, punching him until his knees hit the ground and he curls in on himself.

"Fuck him up." Alen wrenches away from the bars, his nose bleeding. He wipes the mess with the back of his hand, dragging a line of blood across his cheek.

I curl my hands into fists. "He's had enough!" I yell.

The other two stand over the prisoner as Alen shoves past and delivers a fist right to that prisoner's face, sending him flat on his back.

"Take him. Looks like today's apparently his lucky day after all."

I stiffen, unsure what's going on, suddenly taken aback as they grab the prisoner's legs and drag him out of the dungeon.

I pace up and down my prison cell for movement to stretch my legs. Annoyance burns through me at the thought that I'm still stuck in here and have no damn clue what's going on outside.

I don't remember how long I wear a path into the floor when the main door opens with a creak.

My head jerks up and settles on Meira stumbling into the dungeon, Alen shoving a hand into her back.

Devastation sinks through me to see they caught her. Bile swirls in my gut.

"Meira," I call out, rushing to the corner of my cell, closest to her. Mad implied she'd escaped from him, but the bastard must have found her. To see her is like someone let the sun into the room. Her head turns in my direction, her eyes huge with the realization of finding me.

"Dušan." Her soft voice cracks with emotion, her arm reaching out for me when she's ripped away and forced into the last enclosure. The door shuts, and the guards leave us alone in the room.

I clench my jaw and focus on Meira stumbling to catch her balance.

My little wolf pauses and swings to the side of her cell facing me. She grips the metal bars, her knuckles white, her dark hair messy around her shoulders, dirt streaking her cheek like war paint. It suits her.

"Dušan," she repeats. "We tried to come back to get you, but it's madness out there."

"Are you hurt?" I ask, scanning the long, black coat she wears. It's two sizes too big for her. Her bare feet are filthy, and she reminds me so much of the wild girl I picked up in the woods when we first met. The only difference is that there is no hatred in her eyes when she stares at me, only painful longing. "You changed into your wolf."

She nods enthusiastically, her smile forced at a time I would have thought she would be cheering.

"Something's bothering you?" I ask, waiting for her to answer.

She pushes loose strands of hair from her face. "Despite transforming into my wolf, it seems I'm still invisible to the undead. I don't understand what that means. Am I still sick?" Her tone softens, like it hurts her to admit that out loud.

"Are you vomiting blood like before?" My voice thickens at the notion. She was supposed to heal once she shifted, but if she still suffers from leukemia, does that mean the disease will take her from us? This isn't what I want to hear when everything else is fucked-up.

She shakes her head. "I feel strong and like nothing can touch me."

I huff and lick my dry lips, attempting to make sense of why she's still immune. Was I wrong this whole time and maybe Mad is correct—she holds the key to our salvation? I seethe at the thought that he might be correct about anything. Just because immunity is in her blood doesn't mean it's a solution for the rest of us.

"I will do everything in my power to get you out of here so we can work out why you're still resistant." The swell of overwhelming admiration in my chest threatens to suffocate me at the thought of how much she's grown on me, how much a part of me she has become, how I can't bear to lose her. She looks at me, giving me that gorgeous, lopsided grin, and I want to bellow with frustration and rage.

There's an empty cell between us, and more than anything, I wish I could hold her, kiss her, and tell her we will get out of this somehow. She breaks our gaze and lowers herself onto the cold floor, tucking her legs in beside her. It doesn't take her long to get as comfortable as she can, while every fiber in my body is close to the breaking point at being so far from her.

She wipes at her glistening eyes. "I'm so angry. We ran from the Ash Wolves, and I got split up from Bardhyl and Lucien. Then I bumped into the girl I told you I met in the woods last time, Jae, except she was in the company of three northern Alphas. I've never seen anyone transform into such monstrous wolves before. Dušan, they were like Bardhyl, but bigger and scarier."

My mind whirls with what she tells me, with the stranger who occupied her enclosure not long ago. Up north, there are many rogue wolves and packs, more akin to barbarians in their behavior. But that Alpha I saw today appeared calculating and not a rogue. Could he be from up in the Savage Sector?

"That northern asshole traded me for someone else Mad had kidnapped. And the worst part is that Jae is with them. Whoever they are, apparently, her sister hired these goons to come find her."

That tells me Mad's men intercepted the outsider pack and must have taken one of their own. That's who the Alpha in here was before.

I grind my jaw at hearing how my fated mate has

been used as a trading pawn. Fury bleeds through me that anyone dared lay a hand on her in the first place.

"Guards are all over the woods," she says. "I just hope Bardhyl and Lucien are safe."

With the Ash Wolves tracking the surrounding forest, my Second and Third will lie low until they get the chance to come in here through the tunnels. Unless the location has been compromised.

"What else is going on out there?" I ask. "Is Mad part of the search too?"

She leans in closer, pressing her face between two metal bars, and it kills me that there is an empty prison between us and I can't hold her or brush away the terror painted on her face. "The man who negotiated with the northern wolf declared himself the Alpha of this sector. But he's just a guard. And if Mad had been there at the time, he'd have rushed out the moment he saw me."

I nod. "You're right, which means he doesn't yet know you're in here or he'd be here in a flash."

My chest tightens, but I refuse to voice my concerns to Meira. Mad's plans are straightforward. Now that he has Meira captured, there's no more need for me. My end is near. Sweat rolls down my spine, and I ought to be fearful, but what I worry about more is what the lunatic will do to my beautiful mate if I'm not here to stop him.

Lucien and Bardhyl are my last hope.

"We'll get out of this," she assures me, most likely picking up on the deepening of my concern.

I've fought my whole life for a better place for our

pack. And the one person I protected all his life will now be my undoing.

I glance over to the door, my racing heartbeat sounding like a countdown until my stepbrother marches in here for Meira. I swallow the bile at the back of my throat. Anger echoes in the confines of my head, and I try to push away the mounting dread. I comb a hand through my hair, needing to shake the nerves away.

"Dušan, are you all right?" Meira interrupts my thoughts, and her singsong voice draws my attention to her. Her beautiful eyes study my every move, every reaction.

My mouth curls into a smile, but on the inside, I break, my emotions spilling free. To never look on her face again, to never feel her warmth, to never hear her laugh destroys me. And in its place, fury builds over me, swallowing me. I ball my hands at the thought that Mad will do everything to take her away from me.

"I refuse to believe we won't make it out," Meira says, and it takes me a few moments to roll the word *believe* over in my mind for it to finally settle into my thoughts. For so long, I'd been that person that convinced the pack members we were safe in this compound. To have faith in me and believe their future is secure from the zombies. But little did I know, the true enemy was in my ranks this whole time.

I shift my gaze to Meira's beautiful face, which I've memorized, every line, every curve, every color. She's a painting in my mind I will never forget. "You're right, gorgeous. We will get out of this."

I take a seat and listen to her as she tells me about her rescuing Lucien and Bardhyl, her diversion with the undead, and even some strange zombies that seem to follow her. Which is unusual in and of itself, but I can only imagine it has something to do with her still being immune to the undead.

Her voice calms the beast inside me bursting to go ballistic at being locked up.

Everything about her is addictive. She smells so good, like the fresh meadow on a spring morning. I crave to feel her body pressed against me, her soft breasts, her long legs wrapped around me, the fire between her thighs. I miss her terribly. We may share the same room, but she's too far away.

I want out of his fucking prison now!

When I meet her gaze, an ache reflects inside them. She senses my agony and suffers herself from the hellhole we've all fallen into since Mad started playing his games.

This will end with blood. His and mine. I won't go down without taking him with me.

CHAPTER 14

MEIRA

A click from the door into the dungeon wrenches my attention away from Dušan. With it, I stiffen, grasping on to the metal bars, straining to see who's entering.

Mad storms inside, his gaze sweeping from Dušan to me, then he lets out a loud exhale. His smirk infuriates me. "My men told me they caught you, but I didn't believe them. I had to come and see you for myself." The tight curl of his mouth covers me in goosebumps—and not the good kind.

I shuffle backward in my cell, terrified of what this crazy man has in store for me. The look in his eyes belongs to someone who cares about only one thing: himself. And I am merely a stepping stone to him, a way to get an upper hand in this twisted world.

"You're a fucking monster," I cry out. "Let us go!"

He ignores me and steers over to stand outside Dušan's prison, three guards following closely.

As one of them opens his prison door, a flare of

panic spikes through me like razor blades. I suck in each racing breath and drag myself to my feet.

I stare at them, my eyes pricking, because I'm not stupid and know exactly what's happening here.

Mad has me, so what need does he have of Dušan? Leaving the Alpha alive is a danger that will have Mad looking over his shoulder for the rest of his life.

Two guards approach my soulmate and take an arm each. Dušan doesn't fight them… four against one, he won't win. So he willingly stands up, holding his chin high, his lips tight.

I choke on a desperate breath, drawing their attention. But I only have time for Dušan. I look into his eyes, trying to remember how to speak while terror climbs through me, building slowly like a tempest. It comes faster and faster, my chin trembling. All I see in return is a man swallowed up by a destiny forced upon him. The struggle on his face to be brave for me shatters me.

Now I see why he doesn't put up a fight. So the last thing I see of him isn't a panicked man, but the fated mate I fell in love with.

Someone strong.

Confident.

Stubborn.

But beneath the layers is a man who's dying to keep it together.

A tear slides down my cheek. "You can't do this." I gasp each word, glaring at Mad.

"And why is that?" Mad asks, like he has every intention of giving me a chance to convince him to save my soulmate. But he's placating me, humiliating me.

I wipe the shedding tears with the heel of my hands and square my shoulders. "Because you are a piece of shit, and you'll never be anything else compared to Dušan. You use bribery and fear. You're weak, and I will murder you the second I get a chance."

Rage bubbles through me. My wolf sits in my chest, pushing and pushing for release. But not yet. When the time is right, I will slaughter him.

Mad rolls his eyes at me, half-chortling. "Big words from someone who will soon be nothing but a rat in an experiment."

I shudder at the thought, at the inferno burning through my veins at this asshole who doesn't deserve to live.

"It'll be all right," Dušan reassures me. He always puts me first. Except today, that's the last thing I want.

Death has walked into his cell to collect him, and all he cares about is my wellbeing. "Mad," he says. "If you still retain a thread of brotherly love for me, then you will promise me to not hurt Meira. Give me that as my last wish."

My knees buckle under me, my chest cleaving in half. This can't be happening.

Mad responds to Dušan with a threatening growl. "Did you show me mercy when you tossed me into the dungeon, when you stripped my title in front of others? You deserve death, and I'm going to make sure you suffer while I watch. And as you take your last dying breath, it will be my face you see smiling."

Dušan's expression darkens, his shoulders curving forward, and his wolf growls through his chest.

"You fucking asshole!" I cry out.

Mad simply laughs, and he makes me so mad, I want to scream. Fury battles inside me, an explosion of heartache and frustration at the thought of being stuck in here.

They shove Dušan toward the door, and I rush to the front of my prison, sticking my arm out. "Please, don't do this! I'll do anything you want, Mad. I beg you."

It's Dušan who still looks at me, holding my gaze while my tears run rampant down my face.

He smiles, and I'm crying, unable to stop. "Our souls will always be united. I promise this won't be the last time you see me. I love you, Meira."

He's forced out of the prison, with the guards and Mad following him. Before the main door is barely closed, Dušan turns ferociously onto two of the guards. Brutally, he slams into them, bringing them down to the ground.

The door claps shut.

I freeze.

I can't breathe.

I'm falling apart.

Growls and thuds erupt, the banging and shuffling escalating. *Kill them, Dušan.*

I wait breathlessly for him to return. To find out that he finished them off. To take me away from here.

It takes moments for the blast of noises to flatline. Silence.

Anticipation coils around me, suffocating me.

The longer I wait, the more I deflate, and my insides incinerate with anguish.

Never had I dreamed that I'd fall in love, let alone with three men. But to have one ripped from me is like tearing my heart physically out of my chest.

I collapse to my knees, crying loudly in my hands, hissing my anger through clenched teeth.

Seconds pass.

Minutes.

He doesn't come.

Dušan never returns.

He's gone.

My world breaks into pieces that will never be put together again.

In my mind, all I see are his wolf-blue eyes, the softness of his lips cushioning against mine, the soft whispers in my ear of what he promised me. Everything we shared had been taken from me and I can't bear to fathom a future without him.

A sob breaks through me.

Those memories sit inside me like horrible, jagged shards of glass.

Tearing me.

Shattering me.

Killing me.

Selfishly, all I can think is that I wish I'd never fallen in love with anyone.

BARDHYL

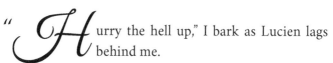

"Hurry the hell up," I bark as Lucien lags behind me.

"Hold your fucking horses."

Frustration crashes through me that we haven't found Meira anywhere in the woods.

When we started to go north, we finally caught her scent. But it brought us right to the back entrance to the settlement. And that meant one thing.

She's been captured. There's little other reason she'd be using that entry when the woods are crawling with Ash Wolves.

I wipe the trickling blood from my busted lip with the back of my hand. Lucien and I took out a small group of Ash Wolves we found searching the woods, and in all honesty, we couldn't resist. The idiots were men we knew. Lowest of the scum in our pack, easily manipulated into being loyal to that traitor, so that small service to clean out our tribe was the least we could do.

Now we burst through the tunnels in human form. We wedged several boulders at the cave's entrance leading to these tunnels, just in case anyone finds it.

I glance back. Lucien finally catches up, bouncing in the dark. He's a shadow I easily discern with my wolf eyes… Partial transformation has its benefits.

"Had to make sure it was securely in place," he murmurs.

Both of us frantically bound forward in the narrow

tunnel, darkness chasing after us, and all I can think of is Meira.

"We rescue Dušan first, then the three of us bombard Mad. I'm tearing his head off." I growl.

"Fine, I'm laying a claim on ripping out his spine. But on one condition." Lucien doesn't wait for me to respond. "He's alive so he can feel pain. I want him to fucking hurt so much, it burns inside me with urgency."

"That assmuncher is going down," I bark. "Then I'm dancing on his grave. Well, actually, you can do it with your cowboy boots, seeing as how he hated them."

His brow bunches up, eyes widening. "What the fuck? He hated my boots?"

"Bruh, he laughed about you to others. When I heard him doing it, I hit him so hard, I knocked one of his back teeth out. Never heard a word after that about your boots."

"You're a good friend, you know that? If there's anyone I'd share my soulmate with, it's you and Dušan."

"Don't get all soppy on me."

Lucien laughs and pats my shoulder as he shoves himself past me, nudging me into the wall on purpose. "Hurry the hell up," he mocks, but he keeps laughing softly.

I burst after him. We both know these tunnels like the back of our hands, every turn and every dip.

Once we reach the end of our passage, we enter the small makeshift area with a ladder leading up to Kinley's place.

Wasting no time, I race up the steps and pause just below the closed trap door.

Placing my ear as close as possible to the wooden panel, I listen. Nothing. Not even vibrations to imply Kinley has visitors and they're walking around.

When I'm confident we're clear, I bang my knuckles twice on the horizontal door.

I glance back down to Lucien and he just stares at me, shrugging. Kinley rarely goes out, and I doubt she would with the chaos in the settlement.

Unease hardens in my gut at the idea that something happened to her. I can easily break through, except I want to make sure before I destroy this entrance.

Swinging back to the wooden panel, I take hold of the metal latch, ready to rattle it in case Kinley has fallen asleep.

The creak of wood echoes down here, and I release the latch, rushing back down, just in case it's someone else up there. Another creak.

Lucien and I slide into the shadows around us when a female voice calls out, "It's unlocked."

Kinley. Relief washes over me.

I dart up the ladder and push open the panel.

In moments, Lucien and I are in her room, the trap door shut and covered by the rug. I search the whole house to make sure we're alone.

Lucien is by Kinley's side, giving her an update on what's been going on. He's always been great at making connections with others, much more than me, so I leave it up to him.

"Have you heard anything?" he asks her.

She shakes her head. "Everyone is scared and most

families are staying hidden in their homes. No one wants Mad in charge." Her words quaver.

Lucien holds her hand and reassures her. "He's going down," Lucien assures her, and when she glances over to me, I nod. Suddenly, I feel awkward just standing there.

"We need to go," Lucien explains. "Keep the doors locked until we return, all right?"

"Of course. But put some clothes on or you'll stand out in the crowd."

She's right. Here we are naked. Most in the settlement hold their human forms and rarely walk around in the nude. Well, except old Rog, the oldest member in the tribe, who sometimes forgets where he is.

"I'll get us some clothes," I offer, well aware of where Kinley keeps her stash.

The backroom is small and filled with shelves of folded clothes, a variety she collects for anyone in need. Problem is that most are smaller sizes.

Footsteps close in behind me, and I twist around to find Lucien right behind me.

"You think I was going to trust you to get me something to wear?" He grins, and I sneer back at him.

"You're worried I would get you tights? Don't worry. No one expects you to look as good in them as I did."

He grabs folded blue pants and tosses them at me. I snatch the jeans that appear close to my size.

"What the hell? She had proper clothes in the drawer?" I ask.

Lucien chuckles to himself. "Only *you* wouldn't check in there, right, tights boy?"

I don't care what he calls me. I get dressed, tuck myself in there comfortably, and zip up.

When I lift my head, another piece of clothing hits me in the face. "Goddammit."

He hasn't stopped laughing to himself as he pulls on a slate gray knitted top, already dressed in a pair of black jeans.

I drag on the long-sleeved deep-green hoodie.

Somewhere in the supplies, Lucien has found us boots. "Try these."

Taking them, I waste no time and put on the ankle-high black boots with thick soles. "They're good."

"Let's go do this."

Out in the main room, Kinley greets us with a smile. Despite the fear behind her eyes, she doesn't voice her concerns. Like the rest of us, she knows that the only way to eliminate a tyrant is to stand up to him. And while that is fraught with danger, it's the only way to stop him.

One must fight for what one believes in, my father would always say.

"Stay safe," Kinley says.

In a hurry, we sneak out of her home. The courtyard in front of her house reveals several guards strolling about. No one from neighboring homes has emerged.

I flick a hand at Lucien to follow me as I dart along-side Kinley's home and down the side to her vegetable garden. Back here, a passage runs the length of all the homes, and across from us stands the settlement woods.

A quick check, and finding no signs of anyone, we both sprint left.

The fortress rises before us, steadfast stone walls, towers… No longer the place I called home, but a danger.

Voices come abruptly from the woods to my right. I pause, frantically looking for where to hide.

Lucien snatches the sleeve of my top and hauls me back behind several wooden barrels in someone's backyard. Behind us are fig trees and a small hut-like house made of gray stone. As long as no one looks out the window, we should be fine.

Crouched low, Lucien huddles close. "Did you even look before you ran out so quickly?" he whispers harshly under his breath.

I cut him a glare. "Of course I did."

Tempers are high, but I shake it off. It's not him I'm frustrated with, but what Mad has taken from us all.

Peering through the gap between two barrels, I watch two Beta males talk in hushed voices and head down the path this way.

I tense. I exchange glances with Lucien, who's pointing at them from the back of our hiding spot. He's seen them. If there's one benefit of so many pack members living in the compound, it's that all our scents are so heavily mingled in the air that I pray to the moon and back that they won't pick up our wolves.

While we have no idea whose side they're on, we can't take the risk.

Huddling near Lucien, I watch them with intensity, but in my head, I have it all played out. The moment I sense a whisper of being detected, I will take them both down.

Moments later, they stroll past us, and behind the frantic beating of my heart, all I can make out of their whispers are four words. "He's doing it now."

My mind catapults to Mad, and all I can picture is him hurting Meira. He's got her and is going to cut her up, take her blood, take everything.

Electricity jolts through me at the thought, and a desperate urgency flares over me. I'm on my feet, charging after those bastards to make them talk.

Strong hands snatch the back of my hoodie and wrench me backward.

I stumble, my heel catching on a broken stone in the garden. My stomach lurches as I fall onto my ass hard near the row of spinach. I growl under my breath when Lucien gets in my face.

"The fuck, man?"

I shove him off me. "They know something about Meira."

"You don't know that. We can't reveal ourselves."

Heat pulses in my temples as I twist my head to find the two Betas are long gone.

"Shit." I'm on my feet. "We go now!"

Lucien's lip curls upward. "Keep it the hell together. We stick to the plan. Get Dušan, and then we'll be stronger to take on Mad."

Fury knots in my chest, but I swallow back the anger. "Let's do this then."

Checking the perimeter and finding it clear, we run straight for the fortress and to the side door, where I broke the lock last time we were here.

We burst into the hallway. Shadows cling to the walls.

There's not a soul in sight and the deeper we travel through the compound, the more my stomach knots. It's never this quiet here. Ever!

Lucien sprints down the stairs silently, and I lunge after him, ever vigilant. We go all the way down to the base dungeon, convinced that if Mad put our Alpha anywhere, it's down there.

We curve around the stone steps, suddenly face to face with a guard.

I stiffen.

Lucien stops.

The man is as startled as us at first, frozen on the spot, his eyes practically bulging out of his sockets. I've seen him several times before. Jarrod. A Beta with more muscle than brains.

I clench my fists, but Lucien lunges at him, stealing my fight from me. "You think you can laugh at my cowboy boots?" He growls as they both hit the floor hard.

I roll my eyes and charge right into the dungeon. We have no time to waste.

My sights scan the area for guards, and the cells for Dušan, but I come up short on both fronts.

Instead, my gaze settles on a small bundle at the back of a cell, her heartbreaking cries filling the room.

I stumble forward, my throat thickening. "Meira!"

CHAPTER 15

MEIRA

*M*y head jolts up at the sound of my name, at the familiar voice, with hope threading through my chest.

Bardhyl stands outside my cell, gripping the bars. At first, I can't believe my eyes, but I'm scrambling to my feet and rushing over to him. I crash into the bar door, my arms threading through the gaps to reach him.

He came for me!

Tears never stop falling, while my heart bangs loudly into my ribcage.

"Angel legs," he coos.

"Dušan! They have Dušan!" I blurt out, just as Lucien bursts into the room, his gaze sweeping wide until it lands on us.

"I've got keys," he declares.

Bardhyl and I step back, and in moments, Lucien has the door to my cell swinging open.

I throw myself at my men, all three of us in a tight hug. I can't stop trembling. I want to remain here and never leave their sides, but we are nowhere near safe. Our fight has only just started.

"Dušan," I breathe as I untangle from them. "Mad took him and he's going to kill him. We have to find him."

Lucien's mouth drops open while the corded muscles in Bardhyl's neck twitch.

"Where would he go?" I ask, desperation raking through my chest.

No one responds at first and that tells me they don't hold the answer. I'll scour the whole settlement to find him.

"He'd do it with an audience," Lucien finally answers, and there's trepidation behind his voice. I hate hearing him scared because that skyrockets my own anxiety.

"It'll be either in the courtyard or out in the field."

"We follow the crowds," I squeak, panic sinking in. Terror strangles me.

Bardhyl nods, then takes the lead and wrenches open the main door, while Lucien grabs my hand and we rush out of the dungeon.

"I'm sorry," Lucien says, his face pale as fear swirls behind his gaze. "I promised to look after you, and I lost you again."

"That doesn't matter," I say. "I would do anything to protect you—like you would me. And right now, we need to get to Dušan."

An ache flares in my chest each time I remember the way Mad hauled him out of the prison. My insides shatter at the look on his face.

Dušan's last words linger with me, refusing to leave me. Already, I know that if we don't get to him in time, that memory will destroy me.

Rip me to shreds.

I can't live a life without all three of them with me.

And I can't even begin to imagine how I am meant to go on again. I glance over to Lucien, remembering how he lost his first fated mate. He is braver than I can ever be. Tears well in my eyes each time I think of losing Dušan.

But in my head, it's clear that whatever happens, I will kill Mad.

I will burn down everything. My only salvation is Bardhyl and Lucien, but I'm not a fool. This will destroy them too.

Nothing will ever be the same again.

I feel it in my bones.

Distraught, I gasp for air and race up the stairs with my men.

We sprint out into an empty hallway. There is no pause. We swing right and frantically run to the side door we last used. The answer lies outdoors. I check the corridor behind us as Bardhyl sticks his head outside. With a wave of his hand at us, we hurry into a yard devoid of people.

In that same moment, an ear-piercing siren rings through the air, stealing the earlier silence.

I shudder in my skin, spinning on my heels, half-expecting an army of Ash Wolves to charge down on us.

"Fuck, fuck!" Lucien's hand in mine shakes.

Bardhyl charges to the right and vanishes around the

edge of the stronghold building.

"What the hell is going on?" I cry out.

"That siren goes off only when the undead have breached the settlement."

My head spins. "Zombies have barged in here?"

Lucien draws me closer; the color from his face is mostly gone. "I suspect there's something else going on."

Moments later, Bardhyl careens around the far corner of the building farther away and bolts toward us like the devil himself chases him.

Fear twists his expression, and I feel sick to my stomach. Bile rushes to the back of my throat as anxiety strangles me.

I suck in each shaky breath as the ringing continues.

"I think Mad's sacrificing Dušan to the zombies just outside the compound." He gasps. "The siren must be to call the undead to him."

A shiver grips my spine, and my knees buckle under me.

"I can stop it." Before either of them respond, I rip my hand free from Lucien's grasp and sprint to the edge of the fortress.

"Meira!" he calls after me. "Don't go there!"

But nothing will stop me. My hands curl into fists, feet shoving against the ground, running like nothing else in the world matters.

And it doesn't.

I curve around the corner of the fortress, my heart in my throat, but I skid to a stop as fear ices me all over.

Before me, hundreds of Ash pack members scramble toward the wall of the compound. Many are climbing the ladders, others hurrying to find a way to get up there and see what's going on. Cheers come from a lofty pedestal where I spot Mad laughing. He's drinking a glass of wine or something while enjoying staring out beyond the fence. He has guards surrounding him. They are everywhere. There is no way we can even try to attack him. We're outnumbered, and my priority is finding Dušan first. I can only assume he's what everyone is looking at over the wall.

More Ash Wolf members appear and join the others.

But I can't see Dušan from down here.

Bardhyl and Lucien are at my side in moments, heaving for breath. "Don't run off like that," Lucien reprimands me.

"I-I c-can't see him. Maybe it's not him." Tears roll down my face because even as I say the words, I know the truth.

This is exactly how Mad would dish out punishment. Make Dušan's death a spectacle.

My stomach drops right through me and a scream surges through me at the injustice, at how fucking wrong this is.

"We need to get to him." I scan the area when a group of pack members dart right alongside us. Five of them, but they don't even pay us any attention when they're running to witness the show.

Lucien shoves me between him and Bardhyl as more people move in a hurry. "We can't be spotted."

"There's no way out that way," Bardhyl whispers. "We go through the tunnels."

"No. It'll take too long. The back entry," I say,

pointing to the way I first entered the settlement. "If there are guards, we'll deal with them and get over the fence. We have to get to Dušan quickly."

They both nod in unison.

Checking the grounds, we make a break for it and sprint across the lawn toward the explosion of trees higher up on the rising landscape.

I keep glancing over to the spectators. No one pays attention to us, but the guards are definitely staying close to Mad. Some cheer, but many cry out from what I assume is fear at seeing their Alpha being offered up as a sacrifice.

My heart bleeds for all of us. For the devastation Mad is about to unleash once he gets rid of Dušan. He'll treat everyone like a slave and punish anyone for not obeying him.

Please, let Dušan be alive by the time we arrive there. Don't let there be too many guards at the rear door. I push myself to go faster to reach my Alpha.

Swift and silent
Swift and silent.
Swift and silent.

Dušan

he rope burns into my wrists and around my chest, my shoulders screaming as my arms remain pulled taut around the pole at my back. I thrash and wrestle against my restraints, attempting to find some movement in the pole. But Mad made sure his guards dug it deep into the ground, and any chance of me knocking it over or wrenching it out is impossible.

Fury lashes over me and I jerk my attention over to the asshole. He stands on a platform behind the wall within the safety of the compound, while I'm left outside. An offering to the starved zombies.

And the siren wails around us like a roaring demon. There is no zombie breach in the pack grounds, but a calling for them to come outside the settlement and find me.

This is his final gift to me after everything we've gone through together. Growing up with his abusive father, when I took most of the beatings so he wouldn't have to. I guarded him in the pack, gave him a high ranking position. But nothing was good enough. I should have seen this coming, should have fucking seen it.

Dozens and dozens of faces are climbing up the fence to gawk at me, and I meet every one of their gazes. Dread twists in my chest, but I want them to watch me fight to the end against a tyrant.

Fear fills most of their eyes. All part of Mad's plan… Show them what happens when someone crosses him, and no one will stand up against him. I ache for these Ash Wolves who are left behind under the control of a monster.

But the depth of my pain surges for Meira.

For the agonizing heartache he will bring her. I fight against my restraints to escape and seek my retribution against my stepbrother. The whispers in my mind repeat, *Break free and kill him. Every fucking flying, deceitful, arrogant inch of him.*

I want blood.

Revenge.

Death for Mad.

He barks a laugh, standing up there, making sure no one misses the joy this brings him.

The crowd gathers behind the fence, climbing up to watch me, and they murmur their own whispers.

I seethe on the inside, my wolf crashing into me for escape, but changing will still leave me tied up, my back plastered to the pole just the same. Tugging against the pole, I won't stop. Not even as the hollow ache in my chest spreads through me, swallowing me with the threat that maybe it's too late for me.

Time drags too slow, and I suck in a hot breath beneath the scorching heat. Dread crawls through me as I keep picturing my death. Breathing heavily, I struggle to focus on nothing else but breaking the restraints holding me in place.

"How does it feel, to be on the receiving end, brother? If only you had trusted me instead of turning against your own family." Mad's words are like a whip, lashing over me.

"Fuck off! You are not my brother." My response seems to echo. I have no time for his gloating. I'm barely keeping it together and not losing my shit. *I'll get out of this. I will.*

And still the siren rings.

Then instead of his mocking voice, which I expect,

comes a deep moaning sound that sends shivers down my spine.

Someone screams, and I twist my head toward the woods at my back.

Mad declares, "They're here."

The asshole grins deviously, while my gut twists on itself.

Trying my best not to tremble, I fail miserably. Silhouettes lurch out of the shadows, lanky things with torn clothes and gaunt faces. Missing eyes and limbs. Nothing stops the cursed.

Fighting harder, I yank on the ropes, the burn on my wrists digging deep, ripping at skin. Panic slices through me because this isn't where I'm meant to die. Not like this. Not like fucking this.

More keep shambling out of the forest and the sight shudders me to the core. It's a kick to the gut that despite everything I did, this is where I ended up.

"Beg me," Mad demands.

I'd rather die than grovel to him. Nothing I say will make him change his mind. I've seen the darkness in his eyes, the hatred, the retaliation he thinks I deserve.

I straighten my spine, staring back around to the encroaching monsters. Moving ever closer. Darkening shadows blot the forest. These aren't just a few zombies... but a whole herd.

A tremor jerks through me. Tugging for freedom, I never give up while trepidation claws at my insides. Gone is my calm demeanor as the sound of shuffling feet draws nearer.

A sudden lick of electricity hums along my skin, like

it always does when a wolf shifts. Who is it? There's nothing behind me but zombies staggering closer. The crowd on the fence isn't changing but rather crying in panicked gasps. No one dares demand my release and I can't blame them. Not when that's all the push Mad needs to shove them over the fence and at the mercy of the undead.

Frantically, I tug on the rope, a tornado whipping in my chest with adrenaline and the terror coming for me.

A deafening growl slices through the air and it comes from deep in the woods, away from the settlement.

My heart soars. I pray it's Bardhyl and Lucien. I crane my neck to look back. My men better be damn quick because the horde in the distance grows denser. And I hear the terror in people's voices from the wall, their panicked words. *They'll be too close... There're too many... like last time.*

Such a cluster of the undead can have bigger consequences than the pack losing me, if they crash into the compound with so many spectators just out of reach. For the innocents trapped in there, I worry, but for Mad, it's everything he deserves.

Someone screams, and I flinch at the reaction as the ground beneath me shudders like a small quake.

I wrench my head around as a huge white blur charges toward me.

So fast, so large, I can't make it out at first.

"Bardhyl," I murmur to myself, but the scent is all wrong. It's no one I recognize, yet it belongs to an Alpha. My thoughts fly to the man sharing the dungeon with me. Except Meira insisted they negotiated her for him… so why are these trespassers still here?

The sudden swish of air across my back leaves me hardening my spine. I twist my head to the encroaching zombies.

Nothing is stopping the river from coming this way, and I desperately pull for escape.

Four Ash Wolf guards drop from the fence on either side of me. Seconds is all it takes for them to transform into their wolves. Clothes are torn, skin popping as it splits and bones elongate. Trotting closer, they linger around me in a protective circle… This has nothing to do with them keeping me safe from the zombies, but everything to do with stopping the newcomer wolf from freeing me.

Mad is so paranoid I'll escape, he risks his own men to ensure I am torn apart by the undead, even if he loses a few of his own followers. Except for all I know, whoever these wolves are, they might want me dead as much as they do Mad.

Sadistic asshole.

Tension thickens the air.

I lift my gaze to Mad glaring at me, his lips thinning. I never lower my gaze from his, and for as long as I breathe, I will challenge him.

A howl pierces the air somewhere behind me, and I stiffen against the pole. Seconds later, the pounding of paws hitting the ground booms, coming right up behind me.

My heart pummels against my ribcage. I swivel my head as the four Ash Wolves dart toward the white blurs that burst out of the nearby woods with extraordinary agility. They clash tremendously and all chaos breaks loose.

The crowd is screaming and cheering, while Mad's bellowing commands fall on deaf ears.

And if there was ever a time for me to break free, this is it.

Wriggling my hands in the rope proves harder than I hoped. Fighting the tightness, I struggle to curl my hands enough to fit through the knotted binds.

Frustration suffocates me, and I growl under my breath, rage flaring through me. But I won't stop.

Anger and retaliation float to the surface. I draw on those to fight the ties. I glance up to the spectators watching me from the fence, and it must be clear what I'm doing, but no one says a word. They cheer me on with their gazes, their desperation painted on their faces like war paint.

I suck in each rapid breath, sweat dripping down the side of my face. Every few seconds, I check on the undead. They are mostly out of the shadows now, but more seem to be swaying deeper into the woods coming this way, no doubt drawn by the booming sounds.

My arms tremble, every part of me aching.

Whimpers and cries pierce the air behind me to a resolute ending that one side has lost.

Suddenly, a burst of gasps and *oohs* rise out of the crowd. I strain to look around, but barely a second later, there's a flush of cool air against my back.

The cords instantly slacken and fall away from my wrists and ankles. I stumble free from the pole, rubbing the red marks from where my skin is rubbed raw. I shake the rest of the ropes from my ankles and pivot to find four massive white wolves roaming impatiently at the clearing farther up the hill, staring at me. Blood stains their faces, lips peeling back over razor-sharp teeth stained in blood. Ash Wolves lie torn apart near the woods, their bodies already shifting back to their human forms.

The first few zombies are already throwing themselves at the corpses, gorging on their bodies.

The crowds are screaming for me to run away, and I don't need to be told twice.

Mad is shouting orders at his guards, who are pulling away from him, stricken with fear. My idiot stepbrother shoves one man down off the fence, then another.

"Get the fuck down there and finish them!"

Except his followers are backing away.

I whip around, my heart banging in my chest, when several feet away, the first undead lurches my way.

A phantom hand squeezes my lungs to the point where I can't breathe.

There's no time to wait or think, but I run up in the same direction my saviors dart to save myself.

They aren't stupid and they run.

Behind me, there is shouting, including Mad calling for the guns. And that right there is what is wrong with him. He never thinks anything through. He attracted zombies close to the compound but didn't arrange to have the snipers ready just in case.

Yet I know the bastard. He would have rushed to tie

me up right after discovering he had Meira. No thought process, just hurry and move on. This is why everything he's ever touched went to shit, why so many times I've had to cover for him.

A mistake I will never make again.

Thundering as fast as possible before the bullets start flying, I glance back to the masses of zombies piling over the two men Mad pushed off the fence.

The screams ring through the air while the sirens flatline.

But escape is all I care for now... along with darting back into the compound to rescue Meira.

Up ahead near the edge of the compound, the white wolves pause. They all snap in unison to something out of my view and growl, then lunge to attack whatever it is.

More zombies or Ash Wolves waiting in ambush? My skin crawls. I'm surrounded by enemies already.

Running, I finally careen around the far corner of the fence and slow down, having no intention of barging into something blindly.

Except tremors wrack my body at the sight before me.

Four white wolves in attack pose, low, fur bristled, are facing Bardhyl and Lucien in wolf form.

But between them stands Meira, her arms out wide, as if her mere presence is stopping these two power-houses from colliding and ripping each other apart.

A deep guttural growl tears from my throat and I charge, ready to battle to the end to protect my family.

CHAPTER 16

MEIRA

"*S*top! Neither of you are the enemy." My voice streams over the guttural growls, slicing through the thick air filled with Alpha testosterone and dominance.

I remain trapped between two opposing parties, arms stretched toward each to stand in their way of colliding into a bloody battle. Four monstrous white wolves from the northern regions snarl from my right and two men who own my heart on my left. Lucien and Bardhyl. Yet my pulse rages desperately in my veins. The moment we jumped over the fence, we encountered these damn northerners instead of darting around the corner to rescue Dušan. And time is running away from us.

Tick.

Tick.

Tick.

A growl spills from my throat. "Enough of this. We don't have time to waste."

Gunshots and screams sound in the distance. I flinch with each pop, my nerves like shattered glass.

Frantically, I scan the lofty fence farther in the distance to my left. When we'd climbed earlier we found no guards… but how long before they return?

And where the hell is Jae?

I want to scream and shake sense into all these males. Tremors wrack my body, every inch of me clenching.

The threatening growls from each party send out alarm bells in my head, a warning that I'll just get crushed once they attack one another. Except there're two against four, and I've seen the way these northerners fight in the woods. It's terrifying, and I can't bear to have my two wolves taken out. One on one, I have no doubt they'd be equal opponents, but this match is just unfair.

Agony hits me square in the chest when I think of the massacre this can lead to. Desperation clings to me.

"Jae!" I shout. "If you're nearby, get your freaking butt out here now!" I figure if I have someone else at my back, it might help diffuse this situation quicker. I turn to the northern wolves. "Please, Nikos, stand down. These are my pack members and they won't harm you."

Bardhyl's and Lucien's threatening snarls fuel the tension, not helping my cause. But turning my back to the northerners is asking for peril. I may have spent most of my life hidden in the woods, but even I know to never look away from danger.

The scents of sweat and aggression taste sour on the back of my throat.

A sudden figure emerges from around the corner of the lofty fence.

I jerk my head in that direction, and my mind races, initially picturing a Shadow Monster, but it isn't long before my eyes make sense of who's joining us, sprinting across the open ground.

"Dušan," I bellow, all the anguish and dread melting. *He's alive!* The earlier darkness crowding around me softens. Exhilaration floods me as I realize that somehow he escaped Mad's clutches before we got to him. Whatever is responsible for the miracle, I thank with every fiber of my being.

I grab on to him once he reaches my side. "How did you get free?" I keep looking over his shoulder, half-expecting Ash Wolves and the undead to come running after him.

"These wolves freed me," he announces, his chin pointing to the northerners.

He steps in front of me and faces the biggest of the intruders, the one with the gray streak under his throat.

The wolf steps forward, his pack remaining ever vigilant in their attack poses, their heads low, fur bristled, ears flat against their heads. He's large and is easily Dušan's height. But my Alpha doesn't back down. He stands tall, faces the enemy bravely.

My skin crawls. I clench my fists, and dread grips my heart when the first pricks of energy dance down my skin. With it comes the white wolves' transformation.

Moments later, four men stand before Dušan. Muscular, tall, and unbelievably handsome. Nikos and his two men, then the Alpha that Nikos must have exchanged with me when we crossed paths during the trade.

Bardhyl and Lucien step up next to us, and I'm terrified we're sitting targets here. "We should get out of here," I whisper to Dušan.

Gunfire pops in the distance, and I jump in my skin.

"She's right," Dušan states, breaking the silence. "You barely knew me, but you saved me. But before we can discuss why, we need to move deeper into the woods—and quickly."

No one protests against the suggestion, and we move with haste until we reach a denser part of the forest where I can no longer see the compound, where the shots being fired are faint now.

Dušan doesn't miss a beat and continues his conversation. "You saved me, so I will do anything in my power to permit you safe passage through my sector for now."

The man who steps forward has the gray streak and it isn't Nikos, which surprises me, as I assumed he was the Alpha of this pack.

Their leader is a ferocious-looking man. Short dark hair around the edges and the back, while long across the top. He has small metal rings tied into his hair, adding to the whole wild appearance. I am tiny in comparison to him, and while I search his face for cruelty, all I find is tolerance.

Captivated, I stand close to my men, watching the newcomers, and while I come to terms with realizing the northern wolves might have been the miracle who saved Dušan, I have another thought.

All the naked men.

All the carved muscles.

Heat creeps up the back of my neck, and I shake it off. Keeping my head high, I remind myself this is a tense moment, not a gawk fest. Still, what is it with most Alphas being so well-endowed? Is that something in their genes to aid with the process of knotting?

My gaze slides over to Nikos, who eyes me like he's been watching me as I check out everyone's packages. I grit my teeth and refuse to show him I care. If they're hanging out, hell, I will *inspect the merchandise*, as I once heard a woman say long ago. I never understood it at the time, but boy, have I understood it more recently. The size of the ammunition an Alpha carries ensures a higher chance of procreation, since he can penetrate a female deeper. It's why women want a partner with a long handle.

"I am Ragnar, Alpha of the Savage Sector," the northern Alpha announces, his chin high, chest sticking out. He speaks with a guttural, authoritative voice. His dark green eyes are filled with sincerity. Earnestness that tells me to believe him. As strange as that sounds, I can't help but sense he wears his heart on his sleeve.

He continues. "My men messed up by trading your Omega's life for mine in prison." He glances down at me, his eyes roaming down my body, making me feel as though I'm naked. I refuse to lower my gaze from his.

He clears his throat and keeps going. "I follow a strict code of honor, where no innocents will ever be killed for me or under my ruling. So the woman had her life swapped for me wrongly"—he glares at Nikos—"and as a result, I owed you. But now my debt has been paid to you by saving you from your fate."

Everyone's fallen quiet, and I'm not surprised. It's rare to meet another Alpha with such honorable integrity.

"I am thankful for your honesty and aid when I needed it most," Dušan answers. "If our sector were in better circumstances, I would welcome you into my home for rest and a meal."

Ragnar's gaze sweeps over us. "I have no doubt. You have a lot to clean up and wolves to slay" His voice darkens. "What promise I will make is that I will return to your land with my warriors. If you are not in charge upon my arrival, and this mess hasn't been swept away, I will wipe out all the males on this land, claim the females, and take ownership."

I swallow hard, a shiver crawling up my spine. Though in a roundabout way, he's showing Dušan respect. I wonder how different his view would be if he had his whole army with him right now. Would he take advantage of the situation and claim Shadowlands Sector as his own without giving Dušan a chance to win the pack back?

The thought has me tensing my muscles. I don't know these wolves and while they're granting Dušan respect now, that doesn't mean they're always trustworthy.

Neither Lucien nor Bardhyl comment or disapprove. While the thickness in the air remains, I suspect this is normal behavior among pack leaders.

"If I do not reclaim my sector by the next blue moon, I will not stand in your way," Dušan answers. "But when we do meet again, I propose we make arrangements for our packs to work together."

His response startles me. But I also understand its true meaning. If he's not Alpha of this sector, it'll be because he is dead. A shiver snakes up the back of my legs at the thought because he will fight to the very end before letting Mad steal his pack. Even if we are outnumbered.

Ragnar gives a slight nod, his upper lip curling slightly, then he turns to Nikos. "Get the girl, and we leave."

The earlier darkness grows closer, and Ragnar's gaze lashes over us with his promise.

I don't dare say a word as Nikos marches into the nearby woods. I glance in the direction of the compound, unable to see it, but I still worry about Mad's men finding us. I'm jittery and ready to get a move on.

Bardhyl steps toward the Alpha and starts talking to him in another language... which I can only assume is Danish. When the man responds, Bardhyl breaks into laughter.

I exchange a look with Lucien, who shrugs.

"Meira!" a female voice suddenly cries out. I turn to see Jae running toward me. She crashes into me with a strong embrace, taking me by surprise. "I'm so sorry," she says, taking my hands in hers. "I tried to stop them from exchanging you, but they didn't listen to me. I was worried sick for you." She throws her arms around me once more, hugging me so tightly, I can barely breathe.

"I'm all right." I break free and grasp her hands in mine. "Are these Alphas trustworthy? You're sure they'll take you to your sisters?"

She's nodding before I finish talking and sticks her hand into the pocket of her pants. When she pulls it out, she unfurls her fingers and reveals a gold bird-shaped brooch with a large emerald right in the middle. It's beautiful, and I don't remember the last time I saw jewelry.

"It belongs to my sister, Narah. When they found me, they gave me the brooch as proof." She leans in closer and whispers, "I have to believe my sister hired them." Her lower lip trembles as she offers me a lopsided grin. This means everything to her. Since first meeting her in the woods, she's had one mission: find her sisters. I pray to the moon that she will find her family and these wolves are indeed honorable.

"I really hope so."

"We're leaving," Ragnar announces.

I hug Jae one more time. "I hope we can see each other again."

"Me too." Her voice cracks, and she clears her throat as she pulls back. "Take care, Meira, and I'll miss you saving my ass all the time."

I laugh as she turns and walks toward the four powerful northerners waiting for her.

They quickly vanish into the shadows. *I'll miss you too, Jae.*

Strong hands clasp my waist and suddenly, I'm lifted off the ground as a hot breath washes over my neck. "Hey, beautiful. I missed the hell out of you."

My heart bursts with joy at having Dušan back with us. When my feet touch the ground once more, I twist in his embrace and loop my arms around his neck.

We kiss, our bodies pressed so close and tight, it feels impossible to ever separate again.

"I love you all so much," I murmur. "Let's never be apart again, please."

"Beautiful, you are mine, and I love you." His words touch me in ways I never could have imagined.

Lucien and Bardhyl join us, both on either side of me, embracing me, ensuring they press themselves against me, especially their cocks, like dogs humping a leg. I want to laugh because they're so much more similar than they'd both ever admit.

"I love you, angel legs," Bardhyl murmurs.

"You are my everything, and I love the hell out of you," Lucien adds.

Everything feels surreal and incredible at the same time. I'm falling harder and harder for my men, loving deeper than I ever thought possible. They care for me so much, and I never thought I'd be so lucky. But in no way has this union been easy. The shit we've gone through is crazy.

"We need to get going." Dušan finally pulls back, as do the other two. I remain in the circle of my three men.

"Where to?" I ask. "We can't leave Kinley and all the others in there under Mad's leadership."

"I want to destroy Mad." Bardhyl growls.

"Then we go into the tunnels," Lucien adds.

"My thoughts exactly," Dušan admits. "We just need to lie low to catch our breaths and work out our plan to take back the settlement and Ash Wolves."

I absolutely agree with him, yet a small part of me can't help but feel scared. We barely escaped, barely survived, barely came back together. But as exhausted as I am, I've been frightened my whole life. Hiding. Running.

This time, I'm embracing the fear, the darkness ahead of us, and will walk as far away from the safety of light as I can to make things right. The final battle isn't just about saving a pack... I am fighting to hold on to the one thing I've been missing since losing my mama.

Love.

CHAPTER 17

LUCIEN

"We use the old tunnel room," I suggest, to which Bardhyl scrunches his nose. "That dump. I hate it there."

I roll my eyes at him as we rush over the slope of the mountain to the blocked-up cave leading into the tunnels. Dušan and Meira rush ahead of us, hand in hand, whispering to each other. She's missed him so much, worried for him. All I want is to wrap up Meira in silk and keep her safe from the world. It's ridiculous and even she'll fight me if I pulled such a stunt. But my wolf burns at the notion of us not keeping her protected.

I cut Bardhyl a stare as he hurries alongside me, constantly looking over his shoulder for signs of pursuit. Then he meets my gaze. "We just stay low in the cave," he says.

"It's too open, and we can't exactly have a fire, with smoke coming out of the cave."

"I agree with Lucien," Dušan throws over his shoulder. "We stay in the room."

Bardhyl grumbles under his breath, glaring at me.

"What can I say? When I'm right, I'm right," I gloat.

"I accept no responsibility if we all catch fleas," he responds.

Meira looks back at us, her eyes wide. "Fleas?"

I shake my head at how dramatic the guy can be. "There are no fleas." I scowl at Bardhyl. "Why are you making up shit?"

He eyes me. "So the family of raccoons who moved in while we used the room during our tunnel building doesn't count?"

I want to laugh out loud at him, but I keep my voice low and whisper, "Big bad wolf is afraid of raccoons."

"Fuck you, Lucien. I woke up with one chewing on my ear."

Dušan pauses at the entrance where two boulders cover the entrance into the tunnel. This place is our saving grace. No one knows about it aside from us four and Kinley. Dušan was right to have kept this little project from his brother and it's serving us well.

Without a word, the three of us head to the barrier, while Meira steps aside, studying us. Hands pressed up against the side of one stone, the three of us make quick work to slide it over the stone ground until a gap appears into the tunnel. It's big enough if we slide in sideways.

Bardhyl goes in first, shuffling, and gets jammed halfway, catching around his chest. That time, I can't help but laugh, but I drive my hands into his sides, shoving him through. "Your fat ass won't fit." I groan.

He pops out on the other side and stumbles. "Hell, that was a tight squeeze."

Meira is giggling to herself as she easily steps inside. Dušan is next, then I follow.

We emerge in complete darkness, but the small room we made during our reconstruction of this tunnel isn't too far and it's easy to find. I take the lead. "Follow me."

The darkness is a welcome friend. I spent weeks… *months* here during construction. A task Dušan gave me when I newly arrived in his pack, and while I didn't realize it until later, he used this to help me deal with the loss of my first soulmate.

I came to Ash Wolves a broken man but ended up as my Alpha's righthand man. I found a family and future I thought I'd never have again.

Back then, I made friends with the dark, the shadows hiding the heartache ripping me in half. Once more, this familiar place resurrects hard memories, but in my mind, it will always be where I found solace and purpose. It's why I sometimes stay alone in the room we're heading to, so I can remember what I've lost and how I found reconciliation when my memories threaten to swallow me.

Coming here now with Meira brings it to a round-about closure. I first came here with a shattered heart. Now I return with love flooding every pore in my body.

Footfalls echo from the three following me, and

their presence alone confirms that I'll fight for the three of them. For our futures to the end.

"Hey, Bardhyl, what did you and the northern Alpha talk about back in the woods? You were talking in Danish, right? It's like you made a joke or something," Meira asks.

I glance over my shoulder to see Bardhyl smirk to himself. Even Dušan, who remains in the rear just in case anyone sneaks up on us, leans in, curious to hear the conversation.

"He asked me what region I came from, and when I told him, he said he thought I looked familiar, then made a joke that one of my distant relatives is marrying someone in his pack, and she's just as big as me. Her fated mate is not. But you know what this means? I have some blood family alive." He chuckles to himself, and it warms my heart to hear Bardhyl found a connection back to his roots. After his past, he accepted that he'd lost his blood family, so to know there are some family members remaining must be a godsend for him.

"That's amazing," Meira says. "If you go back, I want to join you and meet your relatives. I've always wanted to travel and visit other countries."

Bardhyl chuckles before saying, "If I do go, you're all coming with me. But let's see how things turn out."

"You haven't returned since leaving?" Meira asks.

"No." Bardhyl swallows loudly because what he went through when he lost control of his wolf is a hard burden for anyone to carry. Even for a huge bear like him. I shake my head. I fucking love him as a brother and this is fantastic news.

Dušan doesn't say anything, but what we all need now is rest after everything we've gone through. And thankfully, I stock up on supplies in this room regularly.

Rounding a corner deep in the tunnels where it smells heavily of earth, I reach out and my fingers graze a wooden door, just as I expected. Lowering my hand to the metal handle, I swing open the door.

A sliver of light comes from thin cracks in the ceiling.

I scope out the small room, taking it in one sweep of the empty space. It's safe.

The place is just as I left it. Two medium beds against the back wall, a table near the slits of light coming in, and a cupboard in the far corner. I plastered the walls with wooden panels long ago, and now they've faded to a pale brown. Simple, but what else is needed?

"Whoa. This is so cozy." Meira steps inside, as do the other two, and I shut the door, locking it behind them. Just in case anyone tries to sneak in.

Meira darts around the room, inspecting the beds, and the pantry cupboard filled with food.

Her smile brightens any day.

The feeling never gets old. Floating on her joy is a thing of amazement and it helps me deal with the shitty situation we've found ourselves in.

"We stay here for the night, rest, and then take the next steps," I suggest as Bardhyl moves over to the cupboard. He grabs blankets, while I take the bottle of water and metal containers I've filled with dried food. Then I begin to make a small feast on the table.

Whispers draw my attention to Meira and Dušan

making themselves comfortable on the bed, her curled in his arms. Bardhyl gives them space and sits at the table helping himself to dried meats, lost in his own thoughts. I unwrap a large piece of cheese and cut it into chunks with the knife. Down here, the temperature remains cool enough that food doesn't spoil quickly.

Before I know it, I'm joining Bardhyl, slumped in my seat, both of us still naked, eating cheese and meats on crackers. "Didn't realize how starved I was," I murmur.

"I could eat everything here and still be hungry." He smiles lopsidedly, and his gaze sails over to the pair on the bed. They need some alone time after everything.

"So, thoughts on how we destroy Mad?" I ask.

Bardhyl stuffs a big slice of cheese into his mouth before reaching for more crackers. When he swallows his food, he says, "Element of surprise. We need something he isn't expecting to give us time to reach him."

I scratch my head. "Great idea. We just don't *have* the element of surprise. Mad's surely expecting us."

His lips thin. "That's the part I haven't worked out yet."

MEIRA

*D*ušan wipes away the loose tear threading from the corner of my eye. "No more crying, gorgeous. We made it out alive and now we're the ones Mad should be scared of."

The determination in his voice, the belief he holds, is reason enough that I straighten my back and chase away the fear of what could have happened. I've always been one to put the past behind me and move forward. But with my growing feelings for these three Ash Wolves, something within me has shifted. A trepidation, a gut feeling weighing me down that I may lose them.

"You're right," I say. I wipe my cheeks clean as I pull a leg under me and twist to face Dušan on the bed. "I'm holding on to fear, and that's stupid."

He cradles the sides of my face with his large palms, and I beam under his gaze. He always makes me feel like nothing can touch me. "You are the strongest person I know. We are going to defeat Mad, and then the four of us can be together how we were meant to."

I try to ignore the shiver gripping my spine and avoid asking the obvious question of how in the world we're going to achieve that. This isn't the time for those thoughts. After being battered and deflated, this is a time to recharge.

"I'm ready to destroy Mad."

He laughs softly, and the way he looks at me, I almost expect him to say I'm not going to be facing Mad. But instead, his mouth suddenly grazes mine, gentle at first, then he kisses me intensely. It's scorching hot, thunderous. I melt against him. After everything, this is exactly what I desire. To have him against me, to hear the hunger in his growls, to feel his desperate arousal.

Whatever we have going is so much more than animal and physical attraction. This is a deep passion that sweeps through me like an inferno, and I stand no chance of driving it aside.

When he pushes his tongue past the seam of my lips, I moan with need, and I glide my hand along his rock-hard chest, my fingers pulling at his top. I draw him closer and kiss him with the built-up emotions that have me knotted up.

Eagerly, we kiss like chaotic teenagers, lips bruising, teeth clicking, and I want so much more. We may be in a small, icy cold grotto of a room that smells like stale bread, but a sense of comfort and safety encases me.

It's been too long since I had all my men with me, and now I intend to make the most of everything I've missed.

He groans against my mouth before dragging his lips over my chin and to the curve of my neck, where he nibbles on my skin. I tilt my head back, my eyes shut, and only focus on the heaviness of his breath, the warmth of his mouth, the hunger at which he takes mock bites out of my shoulder.

Greedy fingers tug on the sleeve of my coat, finding more skin to smother in kisses.

His hands fall between us and unbutton my coat hastily. He nudges the fabric open, exposing me completely naked underneath. Sliding the coat over my arms, he makes quick work of scrunching the material halfway down my arms. With my arms trapped in the sleeves, he tucks them behind my back.

"I'm caught," I whisper, breathing heavily, trying to pry free my arms.

His smile is devious and it sends shivers of exhilaration up my spine. "No, you are exactly where I want you. I've dreamed of you every moment we were apart, my wolf going mad with the need to connect. And I'm going to claim that sweet pussy I've missed so much."

Just hearing him talk this way has me practically on the edge of a climax. I suck in each breath, my hands tucked under my back.

Lucien and Bardhyl close in on either side of Dušan, their cocks erect as they have no doubt been watching us from across the room.

Dušan doesn't even seem to notice, but if he does, he doesn't bat an eye. His attention never leaves me as he slides his fingers over my knees and lower, then he grabs my ankles. He brings them up, my knees bending, as he props my heels up on the edge of the bed. With two hands, he pries them wide open.

There is no denial that having three men staring at my most intimate of places does something extraordinary to my confidence.

I feel like a queen, like someone so precious that everything I'd suffered in the past dissolves. And I adore that sensation so much.

"Cupcake, you are stunning," Bardhyl says in his deep voice, his hand on his large cock.

Lucien's eyes have already glazed over, lost in his thoughts.

Dušan strips down in seconds and before me stand my Alphas.

"Please…" I implore them.

That small demand has Dušan running his hands along the inside of my thighs, spreading me wider.

His thumb brushes over my clit so lightly, it sends me into small shudders.

"Is this what you want?" he asks.

"Fuck!" Lucien claims, his hand also palming his thick cock in slow strokes.

The edge of Dušan's erection dances over my entrance.

I'm drenched, and I crane my head forward to reach him, anything to make him take me.

Gripping the sides of my legs, he pushes into me. The other two watch like nothing in the world can rip them away from the sight.

I moan the deeper he plunges, spreading me, filling me. Energy skitters down my body as he thrusts so hard and fast, my whole body jerks on the bed.

I arch my back, crying out with the arousal burning through me. The sounds and the smells are hypnotic.

"Never stop," I murmur.

His fingers find my hardened nipples and he plucks them, flicks them, all while riding me. Our bodies grind together, his gaze never leaving mine. We stare into each other's eyes as he fucks me madly.

I belong to him, to Lucien, to Bardhyl. Months ago, I would have laughed hysterically at the thought of belonging to anyone, let alone three Alphas. Now I can't imagine my life without them.

And just as much I am theirs, they belong to me as well.

Dušan shoves into me, and my entire body jolts, my breasts bouncing. Lucien and Bardhyl stroke themselves quickly now, their gazes devouring me.

Adrenaline charges across my body, and already, there's the familiar sensation of Dušan swelling inside me. There's nothing that compares to the euphoria of him enlarging, his cock knotting. Pushing and nudging and hooking himself to remain locked within me.

Arousal rockets through me. Hastily, he loops an arm under my back and lifts me up and off the bed. I wrap my legs around his hips as he loosens my hands from the coat.

I throw my arms around his neck and bury my face against his chest as he ruts into me.

I'm gasping for air when my climax bursts from deep within me. I cry out, but he kisses me, stealing my scream as I convulse in his arms. My body is wracked with shudders.

"Fuck!" Lucien growls in the background.

Bardhyl snarls like a lion, while a primal animalistic roar rolls through Dušan's chest.

Nothing even comes close to the warmth pulsing through me, at my inner walls clenching Dušan's cock. I'm wrapped around him, and I feel his thickness thrumming within me. He grunts against my mouth suddenly, and that warmth spreading inside is him flooding me with his seed. He pumps into me, claiming me, laying his stake over me.

And it's everything I want.

We're both sweating, perspiration running down my back.

"That was fucking hot!" Lucien mumbles from the corner of the room, where he's grabbed tissues and is now cleaning himself up.

Bardhyl has his shirt pressed up against his erection, his eyes fluttering upward, as he's clearly still floating from his arousal.

When I meet Dušan's gaze, he kisses me once, gentler than before, and murmurs, "Now I feel like I'm at home."

CHAPTER 18

BARDHYL

I lie awake, on the floor on blankets while war plays on my mind, and my heart clenches at what is at risk. I consider the idea of us four just leaving everything behind, not endangering our lives. It won't be easy, but it's a direction forward. It's safer.

Except leaving behind the rest of the Ash Pack is not feasible option. We have friends we consider family, and there is no way Dušan will walk away. Which brings me back to how in the world we overcome Mad when we are outnumbered. Not to mention, Meira's at risk, and the woman is so stubborn, she won't remain behind if I command her.

I grind my teeth, exhaling loudly at the thought. No matter how I look at this, I don't know how to keep her safe. There are no guarantees we'll win this battle, but I can't bring her down with us. So, once Dušan wakes, he and I need to talk. We have a fucking problem and I need it to be resolved before we take on Mad.

"Can't sleep?" Meira's soft voice finds me in the early morning light barely illuminating the room.

I glance over at the bed, where she stares down at me, smiling. Sleep still clings to her eyes, her dark hair a mess, and she's yawning. When I look at her, I see everything I'm not, everything I wish I could be. I'm no fool. I lost my innocence long ago. Killing does that to you, but Meira is different. So how the fuck am I meant to risk her life?

"Not really," I answer.

Carefully, she climbs out of bed trying not to disturb the other two snoring away. She doesn't bother covering herself, coming to me naked, like a beautiful apparition. Those gorgeous curves undo me. *Shit!* My gaze trails over perfect tits, her tiny waist, the small thatch of hair between her legs. She's everything I desire in a woman... soft curves and swells, her scent intoxicating, and a damn temper to match my own. Everything about her is tempting. She's smart and quick-witted, rushes headfirst to protect those she's loyal to. I adore everything about her.

She kneels beside me.

With her naked and my erection hardening, the problem is keeping my head on straight. Last night after Dušan claimed her, she fell asleep in his arms from exhaustion. I finished off the food, by which time Lucien and Dušan had gone to bed with her.

Now, she leans in close and kisses me, the softness of her breasts on my chest. My breath catches in my throat. The enticement to lift her and place her over my hips suffocates the air out of my lungs. I long to bury myself deep inside her, to have her ride me.

I'm only a male, for fuck's sake. A horny bastard who can't get enough.

"Morning," she whispers, her breath warm on my ear, sending blood rushing down to my cock. "I need to go to the toilet," she says.

I almost burst out laughing. Here I am getting a hard-on, and my girl is bursting. "Of course, angel legs. Let's get dressed and I'll go outside with you. There are some old clothes in the cupboard."

What should have happened never does, though now I have more purpose to make this a quick trip and return to claim her while the other two remain asleep.

It doesn't take long before we're out in the tunnels. Meira's hand is in mine and my ears are alert, and even though I am still horny as hell, just being around her gives me a sense of peace.

It's deadly silent. Only the sound of wind whistling through the passage, and the scents reveal no intruders. By the time we reach the main tunnel, the faint trickle of light from the opening in the distance guides us forward.

"If you were a gambling man, what are our odds of defeating Mad?" Meira asks, which makes me wonder if I wasn't the only person unable to sleep last night.

"My confident self says there's no doubt we'll eradicate him."

"But…" She glances over at me, her hand stiffening in my grasp. She's worried, and how can I blame her when we still don't have a proper plan that goes beyond sneaking in and trying to get Mad alone? A plan riddled with holes that might get us killed.

"Nothing ever goes as smoothly," I admit. In truth, that's where my head is at, unable to see a clear path to end this quickly.

Meira takes my response as doom and gloom, and she looks ahead, shadows gathering under her worried gaze.

"Hey," I say, turning her to face me. "You will get out of this if I have anything to do with it."

"Just me?" She's quick to catch my mistake.

"I'm not going to mince my words, angel legs. I fear for your safety, and I would feel a damn lot more comfortable if I knew you were somewhere safe while the three of us went in for Mad."

She stares at me blankly, and I expect an explosion, but having her say nothing is worse. I can handle a verbal spar, but what do I do with silence? I know she'll keep her vow if I can get her to agree, but she's so stubborn.

"Say something," I prod.

She shrugs. "There's nothing to say. That's your opinion. It's not going to happen in this lifetime, but nice wish."

Her mocking tone... is more of what I expect. Still, I find myself grinding my teeth at her headstrong determination. The fault is mine in telling her about my thoughts, and now she'll suspect any plans I put into place will leave her behind.

"We'll see," I respond, guiding her back to the exit of the tunnel. Her hand tightens against mine, and she may infuriate me, but I don't expect anything less from her.

What I want is to claim her in every possible way right here, remind her I'm her Alpha, that she *is* staying behind. I want to protect her so nothing ever touches her again. I pray the moon goddess helps me, and I want to lock her up to know with confidence she will remain away from danger.

"What *is* the plan?" she asks.

"We need to work it out," I reply truthfully. "A big distraction might do the trick, though the hard part is how to get close enough to Mad without being attacked by his guards."

Her brows pull together, like she's pondering the answer. "Maybe we need to lure him out of the compound somehow?"

"Possibly." I squeeze out of the gap between the rocks blocking the entrance with a bit of grunting force. Surveying the forest for movement and sniff the air, I come back with the morning dew on the grass in my nostrils. It's clear.

When I turn to notify Meira, I practically step on her as she stands right behind me.

"All safe?" She arches an eyebrow.

"Let's make this quick," I say, my muscles clenching at how she puts herself in danger without thought.

Outside, the orange sun peeks over the horizon in the distance, tinting the woodlands in strokes of fiery colors. Meira hurries near the trees to my right, and I take the chance to relieve myself too on a huge shrub located in a spot that still lets me keep an eye on her.

A sudden snap of a twig has me stiffening, my feet glued to the ground. I jerk my head up in the direction of the sound from deeper in the woods.

The stale wind brings no scents. Panic rises through me, and I quickly tuck my cock in, retreating.

I give a thin whistle and glance over at Meira, who's standing, looking at me. She heard it too.

I point into the woods, in the direction the sound came from, then cock my head for her to join me.

Fast steps bring her to me just as the scent of death finds me, floods my nostrils, and stirs sickness in my gut. Undead have tracked us.

Before I step back into the cave, four shapes stumble out of the woods farther to my left, exactly where Meira stood barely moments ago.

She pauses, staring at them, while I snatch her arm to drag her inside. Once these fuckers get a whiff of me, they'll be crawling all over these woods.

"Wait." She bats my hand away and turns back toward the zombies.

"Meira, this isn't the time—" But my words flatline when I sweep my gaze over the deathly monsters.

Familiar faces I've seen before. "Hang on. Are they—"

"Yes. They followed us before and never attacked." She suddenly heads toward them and unease curls in my gut. I don't want to be anywhere near those filthy things.

They roam around her like she's a magnet and completely disregard the fact that I'm even standing here. She takes steps toward me, and the creatures lurch after her.

I back up, standing in the cave's entrance, as I'm too damn close to these things. One twitch, and they'll come at me.

"That's close enough," I command.

Meira stops about five feet away, and again, the zombies pause as well.

"Sit," she orders them.

Instantly, all four fall to the ground, sitting.

My mouth drops open with utter shock. "How the fuck are you doing that?"

Meira twists her head in my direction, smiling like she's just discovered a treasure chest. "I think I have an idea for how to take down Mad."

CHAPTER 19

MEIRA

I burst into the bunker, Bardhyl on my heels. "Wake up! I have incredible news!"

Just as the words leave my mouth, I notice they aren't needed. Both Lucien and Dušan are up and about, dressed and staring my way. Lucien lowers the bottle of water from his lips, while Dušan takes a bite from a large cracker.

"What's going on?" he asks, crumbs dusting down his top, a black sweater with a few tears around the neckline.

Bardhyl shuts the door behind us. "What I just saw outside might hold the answer to everything we need," he says, excitement teeming through his voice. "It seems our girl is a lot more special than we first thought."

"Out with it," Lucien insists, his attention completely on us.

"I think I can control those undead that have been following me around," I say in a strong voice. "I probably need to try again to make sure, but I just told them to sit and they obeyed me." Adrenaline zips through my veins, and I'm bouncing on my toes at what this means for us. "It just never occurred to me until now to understand why those four zombies followed me."

Dušan and Lucien blink at me like I've gone mad.

"She's telling the truth," Bardhyl adds. "If I hadn't seen it with my own eyes, I'd be as bug-eyed as you two are right now."

"You can control the four undead that were following you around?" Dušan repeats my words as though shocked, scratching his head. "What makes them so special? What about other zombies?"

I pinch my lips together, running through all my encounters with these specific Shadow Monsters, all the way back to when I first saw them. Then it hits me like a lightning bolt.

"I might know why. I don't understand the reason, but—"

"What is it?" Lucien asks, his voice taut and impatient.

"When I was helping Jae escape from Mad's attack in the woods, I fought several undead to stop them from reaching her. And the four outside, I think I bit during our scuffle."

Bardhyl's gasp draws my attention. "You infected them?"

"I think… maybe I did." My voice comes out unsure. "Whatever makes me still immune to the undead seems to have the opposite effect on them."

"Sweet fuck!" Lucien runs his hand through his hair, pacing, his gaze miles away. "This changes so much. Here Mad thinks you are the key to immunity. Except you're a million times better." He pauses in front of me, taking my hands and kisses the back of them. "You, my little one, can whip the zombies to your command. They are your slaves. You could rule sectors with this ability alone."

"Let's not get ahead of ourselves." I almost choke on my response. His enthusiasm is a bit scary. Ruling over zombies has never been my lifelong ambition, and this is a means to the end to get rid of Mad and gain the Ash Pack back.

"I was right," Bardhyl declares, the corners of his mouth curling upward. "You are our gorgeous little Zombie Queen."

I cringe on the inside at the title, but it's not like I can even rebuke it now.

"The question is," Dušan, who's been quiet, says, "how do you get more zombies under your control so we have an army against Mad? Do you need to bite each one?"

"Most likely. But what if it was something else... Me giving them a scratch?" I don't know why I'm tossing out random ideas... Maybe it's the whole idea of me going around biting zombies for a living to convert them. Doesn't that make me one of them but in reverse? And it was disgusting the first time I tasted their blood... I sure as hell don't look forward to doing it again.

"Only one way to find out. We're going zombie hunting," Dušan commands.

My mouth is suddenly dry, but I'm nodding. As much as the notion is strange, he has a point. And if this is the way to eradicate the world of Mad, I'm ready. Not like I have much of a choice if I intend to help my men. I straighten my spine and summon my bravery. "Let's do this."

Lucien claps like an excited kid while Bardhyl grins, and Dušan draws me toward him. "Are you sure you're okay with doing this?"

"Not really, but what are our other options?" I hold on to his hands a bit too tightly.

"I can see the fear in your eyes." His expression softens, but there's strength behind his gaze, like he's ready to catch me if I fall from this mission. "What are you scared of?"

"That I'll fail and somehow this is a huge misunderstanding that will get you three killed." My arms tremble.

Concern worries his brow. "If you have several zombies out there following your lead, we're already one step ahead of Mad." His hands squeeze mine lightly as his words reassure me.

"What's the plan?" Lucien looks at me, wearing the same painted expression of dread. "We track down a zombie, then we stay close as you do your thing in case we need to come help you?"

As much as dread fills me, I know pulling back now isn't going to help us. I swallow my trepidation and suggest, "It's still morning, so hopefully Ash Wolves aren't roaming the woods. So we should do it now." I hate my suggestion, but it's for the best. This isn't about me, but the pack's safety.

"Agreed," the three of them say in unison, which should make me laugh, but I'm too worried about having missed anything in our plan that might come back to haunt us. Mostly, I need to calm my jumping nerves that I have to change into a wolf again, and I still struggle to control her.

We are heading down the tunnels in no time, and the thought that so much relies on me making this work strikes me. It's one thing to make the undead sit down, but I have no clue how I'm meant to get an army to attack just Mad without hurting innocents.

I push those doubts aside. For now, let's just make sure they listen to me. It isn't like we're swimming in easy options, so I need to make this work.

Once we're outside, my ears prick for sounds and my gaze falls on the four Shadow Monsters still sitting on the ground exactly where I left them. Each of them look my way, not seeming to notice my men.

"Well, fuck me!" Lucien growls. "Never thought I'd ever see anything like this."

Bardhyl stands close by my side, and Dušan steps closer to the undead. He pauses within arm's reach, but none of them even seem to observe him.

Bardhyl murmurs, "I can hardly believe this. It's like they're hypnotized or under a spell of something. They're loyal to you, listening to your orders and all but completely ignoring us. This is insane."

"I want to get this done," I say, cracking my knuckles. The moment I emerge from the cave's entrance, I say, "Stand." The undead climb to their feet.

Dušan retreats instantly in panic, as do the other two men.

"I don't think they're going to attack you," I say. The four creatures stand there, staring at me. "Maybe it's best I do this alone."

When I meet my men's gazes, their eyes fill with the fire to argue, but I don't give them the chance. "I'm quieter on my own. The zombies can't trap me, and I can be faster this way."

"I said, *no more separation.*" Dušan raises his voice, and it takes me off guard.

He comes from a place of caring, but my hackles rise too. "I'm doing this my way, and you know it makes sense. It's not like I'm going to go far."

He's shaking his head. "I'm going with you, and as soon as we find zombies, I'll retreat."

It's not something I want to keep arguing over when I know he won't back down.

"Fine." I unbutton the shirt and pull down my pants, then step out of them.

Their eyes are on me... I feel them like a lover's caress. The cool morning breeze curls around my body, rousing goosebumps over my skin. My heart bangs in my chest as I remember Lucien's instructions to bring out my wolf. I can do this.

It still terrifies me how much she fights against me when I'm in wolf form, so what happens that one day when I lose control of her? What then? She'll kill everyone in sight?

As if sensing my uncertainty, Dušan whispers, "Deep breaths in and out, then let her flow out of you."

If only it were that simple.

Swallowing hard, I close my eyes and fill my lungs with oxygen. On my exhale, I call my wolf.

This time, she spills forward and out of me fast, like rushing water. I tense all over as I groan and fall to my knees, the stinging like the pain of a hundred blades slashing across my body.

Moments later, I'm breathing heavily, standing there as a wolf in my tawny red fur, the agony melting away. I embrace the sharpness of sights, the crispness of pine smells. And even before I take a step from where I am, the pungent scent of undead finds me from up ahead in the woods.

She half-howls, half-growls. The buzz of adrenaline soars through me as my wolf shoves me forward. I mentally push her aside, so it's not just her in the driver's seat.

Energy flares down my body and I teeter on the spot.

"You okay, angel legs?" Bardhyl asks.

The four undead watch me, waiting for a command, while my men stand alongside me. I suddenly burst into the woods, the fresh air splashing through my fur.

A quick glance back shows Dušan trailing behind, but so are the four undead.

I dart forward, past trees and over logs, when two silhouettes linger straight ahead.

But I keep running, my wolf refusing to pause. The inner battle inside me is like two animals fighting for control. Next thing I know, I'm veering directly into a pine tree, bumping into it. I can't even walk straight with both of us fighting for control.

My wolf silences, and I use that moment to sniff the air. The pungent reek confirms the creatures are Shadow Monsters.

Ruffling myself, savagery plays through my veins, and I lunge toward the newcomers.

Foliage crunches under the feet of two undead lurching forward, their heads suddenly jerking upward like something's caught their attention. Something behind me.

Dušan.

My heart pounds just as my wolf unleashes a dangerous snarl.

I fly past a dense bank of trees and charge for the first creature. Crashing into it, I bring it down with a thud to the ground. The sharp snap of my teeth crunching bones in its shoulder cuts through the silent woods. Tainted, stale, putrid blood coats my tongue, and I release my grip. Even my wolf agrees and backs off.

The breeze whips around me, and I coil around, throwing myself into a sprint after the second Shadow Monster.

I glance at the four other undead standing in the woods, watching like spectators at an arena.

I close the distance between me and the new fiend, then I slam into its back, flattening it in a heartbeat. I lash out, sinking my teeth into the back of its neck. I'm certain biting them will be more reliable than scratching. His flesh is tight and hard. Like before, I lurch off him right afterward, and shake my head to get the taste out of my mouth.

Wrenching my gaze over my shoulder, I watch the first Shadow Monster stagger to its feet. The shoulder I've bitten into slopes lower than the other, dark blood oozing from the wound down its gaunt, bare chest.

I've done my deed, and while my wolf is still coping with the putrid taste in our mouth, I shove her deep within me. The flare of energy clamps around me, and I suck in rapid breaths, calling to my human side.

Darkness rises in my mind as she fights the transformation, her hunger spilling through me like a river breaking its banks. Panic grips me, but I won't give in, won't let her take control, won't let her win.

The air pulses. I clench my whole body and shove her aside.

A warning growl cracks past my throat, shuddering me right to my bones.

No, you don't. I stiffen, holding myself strong... She is mine and I won't let an animal take me. I shove her energy as far as possible within me. Grasping that moment of reprieve, I fling myself out.

My change tears through me. I wince at the agony, at the drumming of my heart. I stumble upright on two feet, falling into the arms of a tree.

That was too damn close. She's getting harder and harder to control.

I turn to the encroaching undead, watching every-thing, waiting to see its behavior.

The second one is climbing to its feet as well.

There's no sign of Dušan, but if the Shadow Monsters gained his scent earlier, they'll keep following him.

"Please stop," I whisper. Holding myself tightly, I glance from one fiend to the next.

In unison, they both come to an abrupt halt a couple of feet in front of me. They stare at me with blank, dead eyes.

A hulking outline emerges from the shadows from the direction of the cave. Dušan steps forward, and his eyes are wide, shock palpable on his face. What is he thinking? What a freak I am?

"Fuck, you did it!" he says, and his words soften the hardness in my chest.

"Where there were four, now we have six." I grin at him.

He closes in to my side, and none of the monsters are going for him. They literally don't sense him. "This is incredible."

I look over and search his eyes. "Maybe this is going to work. I think six will be plenty. Easy for me to command and we can go do this now. Sneak into the compound. Right?"

The corner of his mouth twitches with tightness. "We only get one chance to take him by surprise with the zombies. So we need more of them, as Mad's guards know how to take out the undead."

I take a step backward. "I think we're fine like this," I answer.

He studies me for a long pause. "What's going on, Meira?" he asks.

I shake my head and look away from him, studying the undead watching us. Like statues, they stand as still as the trunks surrounding us. Getting more of them to follow me isn't the problem. It's the process of me doing it and not losing control of my wolf. Each time I transform, I worry this will be the last time before she claims me completely.

"Let's go see what the others think about how many undead we need," I suggest and I turn to move, but Dušan steps in my path.

"Meira." His stern voice carves through me.

"It's nothing." Just when I think I finally succeeded by transforming, by keeping my men, the universe refuses to give me a clean break. Not only am I still immune to the zombies, which makes me worry that I'm still sick, but my wolf refuses to kneel.

"Talk to me," he persists, his eyes narrowing. "Something's wrong, isn't it?"

His question wrenches me from my thoughts, and I blink at Dušan. There's a silence between us, and I don't know why I struggle to tell him about this. Or why it scares me to reveal the truth with the others too.

"We can help," he suggests, his concern swimming behind his eyes.

"I-I d-don't think I'm fully healed," I admit, my voice low. It's only when I see the reaction flaring over his face that I realize why I kept from talking to my men about this. His lips tighten and the color in his face drops a few shades. Fear darkens his gaze. That terror right there is like a knife in my gut, twisting and twisting.

"Because you're still immune to the undead? We're going to fix this, Meira, as soon as we deal with Mad. I promise."

"No, it's not just that." My arms shake by my side. I lick my lips and let the words roll free. "I can't control my wolf. When I change, she tries to take over, every single time. All she wants is to attack and hunt."

He takes my hands into his. "Oh, Meira, that's normal. The first time I shifted, my wolf took over and ate all the neighbor's chickens."

"And what about your next change and the one after?"

"It gets easier once you assert your dominance. You don't need to worry about this."

"No." I push his hands away. "You don't get it. It's not getting easier. Each time I've shifted, my wolf is stronger. It takes everything to fight her back."

I hug my middle and glance over to the undead, who haven't moved, just watching. I doubt they really understand what's going on. They resemble something robotic needing activation.

Dušan reaches over and takes my arm, holding me firmly. His finger brushes the inside of my arm, the touch coaxing a calmness racing up my arm. "Have you allowed your wolf to be in control at least once during your transformations?"

"Of course not. Are you crazy? If I do that, what if I never gain command over it again?"

"You will," he says sternly.

"You don't know that. Something is wrong with me and the normal wolf rules don't apply here, Dušan. You're not listening to me. What if when I let her have free rein, she becomes the monster you feared would tear out of me all along? What if I'm then forever lost while she goes on a rampage and kills everyone? What if she comes for you?" I'm shaking my head, my chin quivering at the thought.

Dušan drags me into his arms and holds me in his strong embrace. I sense the quickening of his heartbeat, and there's no denial I've touched a nerve.

"You're letting fear control you," he explains.

His words infuriate me because he's not listening to me. "That's not true." I shove my hand against his chest to get away from him, but his arms are like iron and he holds me in place.

"Listen to me," he says in a deep, authoritative voice. "Our wolves are part of us. They are our other halves. And I know it's terrifying, but to complete your connection with her, you need to let go of the reins on at least one transformation."

He's insane! The thought alone terrifies me.

Unease twinges in my gut. How can he think I can ever do this? I tense up just thinking about it, let alone going through with it.

"I can't," I say, shaking my head again.

"You have no choice. The only way your wolf will

become submissive to you is by showing her how much you trust her."

I wrinkle my nose with confusion. "That makes no sense."

"Yes, it does. And we're going to do it this morning, as soon as we find a big enough herd of zombies."

Fury blinds me, and I wrench free from his grip. "Don't tell me what to do!" I stand toe to toe with him, a cocktail of dread and anger coiling in my chest until I can't breathe.

His jawline clenches, and I expect him to lash out to grab me, force me into this. But that never comes. Only words. "We get one chance at the element of surprise. To save the families and innocents like Kinley and help them escape the shackles my stepbrother will impose on them. A few zombies will be taken out quickly against a pack. We need an army of them. I'm sorry you don't like having the responsibility placed on your shoulders. Fuck, if I could, I'd take it from you in a heartbeat and bear it myself." He leans in closer, still not touching me. "But I offer you the next best thing. Me by your side every step of the way."

Hurt rages to the surface of my thoughts. What he says is true, but worse yet, I can't shake the guilt that I'm too terrified to give my wolf full control.

A drop of sweat runs down my spine.

"You know I'm right," he reminds me.

"Yeah, but that doesn't mean I like it."

He laughs, and I hate how easily he breaks through my barriers. My insides are a battleground, emotions rising in me like a storm.

"Shall we do this?" He stretches out his hand, palm side up.

I huff, exasperated. "I'll try."

"That's all I ask." He grabs my wrists and yanks me to his side. Before I can protest, his lips are on mine, and he whisks me away to another world, where I forget my worries.

It's so unfair that he affects me this easily. I cling to him, loving the feeling that I can't escape. Fire ignites between us when he whispers against my mouth, "Never stop believing in yourself."

DUŠAN

*M*y heart hurts.

Meira is terrified, and it kills me to push her so hard. In truth, unleashing control of our wolf happens naturally when we transform the first time. But Meira isn't exactly a role model for following the normal wolf rules. She has a human parent. She has... or had leukemia. Her wolf refused to come out for most of her life. And then a damn tranquilizer from Mad forced her first change. Nothing here is normal.

My beautiful wolf needs to believe she can do this. And not just for the sake of the Ash Wolves pack, but for herself. If she doesn't relent power to her wolf soon, she will never gain its trust. So her whole life she'll battle for power during her changes rather than taking charge of her wild side.

She holds my hand as we traipse back to the cave,

and I study the six undead wandering in our direction behind us. It's incredible to see the aggression in their eyes now replaced with a haziness.

I am beyond proud of Meira and what she's able to accomplish.

Once we emerge from the woods, Lucien and Bardhyl jerk their attention our way. They stand in the cave's entrance. Their attention flips to the small tribe behind us.

"Fuck yes, you did it!" Lucien cheers.

Bardhyl rushes down to take Meira in his arms, lifting her off the ground. Her laughs are a song of promise as she radiates the beauty of a warrior still yet to unleash her wings.

"What's next?" Lucien asks.

"We find a herd of undead," Meira answers as her feet touch the ground. She stands tall and glances over at me with determination and I couldn't be prouder of her at this moment.

Lucien rubs his hands together gleefully. "We're making a zombie army."

The three of us surround Meira. The wind blows her dark hair over her face and she struggles to push it behind her ears. She's naked and isn't shying away. Whether she knows it or not, she has come so much further than she realizes.

Bardhyl kisses the top of her head. "Are we all going?"

"Only if you promise me to stay in the trees when we find the herd so you don't get trapped by them," she says, her voice suddenly serious and stern.

"Agreed," I answer, followed by Bardhyl and Lucien doing the same.

She looks up at me, sincerity deep in her gaze, and her expression screams terror. It kills me to see her still scared, but if I don't push her, she'll lose that opportunity to bond with her wolf. She may hate me for it, though I would rather live with that than have her suffer her whole life.

She jerks away from me, her shoulders curving forward.

My fingers tingle with the urgency to reach over and tell her she isn't alone. But a surge of electricity dances down my arms. She groans with pain before falling to the ground, transforming.

We watch over her, and each one of us would do anything to keep her protected. She means everything to me, and if she's going to be what Bardhyl coined, the Zombie Queen, then I'll adore her even more.

Seconds later, she's in her stunning tawny fur, her ears pointy, and her long tail behind her. Pain rages behind those beautiful eyes, and I hope she listens to me and releases her wolf once we find the herd.

She lifts her head, inhaling the air, then she nudges past Lucien and trots into the woods.

"We stay close," I say, and we're off. Meira takes the lead, and we three watch her back. The six zombies trail behind us. I won't deny it still unnerves me to have them so close.

We travel deeper into the woods, farther from the Ash Wolves compound, which puts me at ease. This area is less likely to be occupied by wolves hunting us down. But it doesn't take us long before the moaning sound of the undead finds us.

Enormous fir and oak trees surround us, trees exploding with green leaves. The place would be beautiful, if it weren't for the lurching shadows amid the trees. Disfigured silhouettes in the distance are exactly what we're here for, yet a shiver crawls up my spine.

Meira hurries forward, and we're running to keep up.

When the first zombie emerges, a barrel of a man with a shirt hanging off his body and ripped jeans, his eyes lock on to us.

A guttural growl shatters the air, and suddenly, the thumping of feet on the ground grows louder... closer.

Meira wastes no time and jumps at the hulking man, taking him down quickly, tearing half his arm off. Blood gushes from the wound staining the Earth.

"We need to hide now," Lucien whispers, his hand on my back.

That's when I spot the wave of the soulless emerging from the shadows. Several dozen at least. Fright shakes me to the core to be out here with so many of them.

I turn and follow Lucien's choice of a tree with low-hanging branches. Bardhyl is already up there. I jump up and snatch one, then swing myself up. Hastily, I make my way to a thick, sturdy branch to easily take my weight. Close to fifteen feet off the ground, I sit close to the trunk with a clear vantage point of the grounds below.

Lucien is above me, while Bardhyl is on a branch facing me.

"If this works, how do we get all the zombies into the compound?" Bardhyl asks. "It's not like we can ask Kinley to not mind us while we drag dozens of zombies through her home. She'll die of fright."

"Plus," Lucien adds, "it might cause a bottleneck once others spot zombies coming out of her house and start shooting at them."

The thoughts plague my mind. "The only option I see is getting them through one of the main entries to the compound."

I turn my attention to Meira. She's already taken down three creatures, but as I watch her calculate every move on whom to attack next, worry creeps across my mind. She hesitates as she looks around, and I sigh. She's still holding on to her wolf, instead of giving it free rein. *Dammit, Meira.*

This makes her slower to kill these while battling her own chaotic war in her mind.

Coldness seeps into my bones at the thought that I didn't realize earlier how much she struggled with her wolf. She will forever lose the ability to control her wolf if she keeps pushing it away.

"I'm sure she'll be fine," Lucien tries to reassure me. "The zombies won't touch her."

"That's not what I'm worried about. It's her not relinquishing control of her wolf yet. She hasn't yet given her wolf full trust yet."

"Oh, fuck!"

I tense, fingers clenching the branch beneath me, and I pray to the moon the damage she's done to herself so far isn't too far gone.

But as those thoughts tumble through my mind, a tsunami of zombies breach the shadows of the forest.

Next thing I know, there are close to a hundred of them pouring out.

My heart slams into my ribcage as I wrench my gaze from them and to Meira, who leaves a bloody trail in her path.

Fuck! Please don't let me have made a mistake by letting her handle this alone.

CHAPTER 20

LUCIEN

"Go to the right," Dušan bellows in my direction. "She's coming your way." He's in human form, hoping Meira seeing him this way will help her fight harder and gain power over her wolf.

Bardhyl and I run in our wolf forms to cover ground faster.

My heart pounding wildly, I careen around a tree and pivot to go back the other way. We've been chasing down Meira for the last twenty minutes at least. Since she butchered every last zombie from the herd, she's gone wild. My chest squeezes to see her frantically darting right and left in the woods, lost and confused.

No matter what we do, we can't seem to catch a break. And more than anything, Meira is our priority.

Stop her, then bring her back.

My insides clench with dread that her wolf is too far gone to be controlled again. It tears me apart to know she'll live with that her entire life. I just pray by some miracle it's not too late.

I charge faster, leaping over logs, darting after her.

MEIRA

I'm falling.

That's how it feels. Darkness pounds across my mind while my wolf takes charge. She's running wildly, so out of control, I sense her fear, her confusion. I'd lost her with the attack on the Shadow Monsters, her hunger too hard to tame. Even now, I taste the putrid blood at the back of my throat, while my adrenaline is on fire.

I shake off the heaviness trying to drown me. Once again, I push up against her, to steal back control.

With every last reserve, I drive her aside. My paws hit the ground, and my men surround us.

Her panic is palpable, while I scream in my head to slow down so they can catch me. They'll find a way to help. They have to.

Because I can't live like this.

Trapped.

Forgotten.

Ruled by a wild creature.

She veers right, and kicks me out of her way, and darkness comes for me once more.

I scream.

LUCIEN

*B*ardhyl steamrolls up ahead of her, but she's too busy glancing back at me closing in, Dušan flanking in from the right.

She swings left, like I knew she would, and I leap diagonally to meet her, to cut her off.

Fast paws carry me over the ground, and I scramble toward her, spearing through the forest.

She lunges over a log as I reach her, and I use that moment to throw myself at her from the edge.

I crash my shoulder into her, knocking her over.

Her desperate snarls slice through the air. We both slam down to the foliage-covered ground. With the momentum, we roll, tangled together in a furious mess of growls and kicking up dirt.

My head spins. The ground is hard and unforgiving, but it's her I'm worried about.

The moment we come to a pause, I scramble up to my feet, as does Meira, a growl rolling over her throat.

She backs away from me, her lips peeled back, ears flat against her head. I search for my mate in her eyes, but all I see is a feral wolf.

A phantom hand grips my heart, squeezing it.

Bardhyl suddenly leaps out of the shadows. He's in his human form already. He lands on her other side.

She bolts from him, but I'm on her in seconds when Bardhyl runs and jumps across her back.

His weight brings her down fast. She growls a warning to back away, a desperate and terrified sound that rips me apart on the inside.

Bardhyl doesn't wait a second, still straddling her, grabbing hold of her head, pressing her cheek to the ground so she doesn't bite him.

I call to my swift change as Dušan bursts past the shrubs and joins us. He throws himself to his knees so she can see him. I'm at her rear in seconds, grabbing her kicking back legs, holding her down as Bardhyl shuffles to kneel behind her, his large hands pushing down on her torso.

As cruel as this seems, it's the only way. If she escapes, Meira will struggle to come out. And by the time her wolf is exhausted and she does emerge, who knows where her wolf will have taken her?

But the more I look at her body bucking, hearing her distress, the more my heart shatters at the thought that maybe we're too late to have saved her wolf. Her strength is extraordinary. She attacked over a hundred zombies and the three of us still wrestle to keep her down, but what good is that if she can't bond with her animal?

"Meira," Dušan begins. "Listen to my voice. Focus on me, and pull yourself out. You are in charge. You are the wolf." He never stops encouraging her, letting her hear his voice.

She's been alone so long in her life that it makes me wonder if her wolf has assumed a lone wolf approach. I've heard it said that while our wolves may not emerge until we hit puberty, they can sense and experience the emotions we do.

Meira bucks harder against us, and I glance up. "It's not working. You need to dominate her," I demand.

"He's right," Bardhyl adds. "It's the only way if she hasn't calmed down yet. Her wolf is too wild."

Dušan is grief-stricken, and I don't blame him. He pushed her to do this. But in truth, we're all just as responsible. Each one of us owes her for putting her in this position. Salvation of the pack drove her to the edge and never once did we ask if she was really ready.

I grind my back teeth, fury lashing through me.

Dušan gives a single nod, and instantly, a charge of electricity threads through the air with his change.

His thunderous growl rises through him and covers even me in goosebumps from the power he exudes. Some wolves are born to be leaders; their wolves carry tremendous power. Their presence alone can drive other wolves into submission, and Dušan is one such Alpha.

With a sudden shake of his head, his lips peel back, and he unleashes a deep, gravelly growl. The corded muscles in his neck flex, the sound earthy, carrying a deadly warning.

Meira falls still. Her chest rises and falls rapidly with her fear. Still, a rumble rolls past her throat.

Bardhyl half-grins, but I can tell it's a struggle. "She's a fighter, my angel legs."

Dušan suddenly jerks forward, his mouth and teeth instantly latching on to the side of Meira's neck. He bites down. Not to kill her, but to hold her to the ground of his own force. To assert dominance, to get the wolf to back the fuck down.

Bardhyl and I release her. This is something that is

done by Alpha and Omega. If Meira can't control her wolf, then Dušan will take charge for now.

Threatening growls punch through the silence.

Meira doesn't move, her wolf well aware that such a bite could kill her, so she sits in silence.

And Dušan will force her down for as long as it takes for her to submit.

Bardhyl clenches his jaw, watching them.

Waiting.

Come on, little one. Just give in.

A brutal wind rushes past, rustling the branches, chilling my skin. All I can think about is the hardship Meira has been through her entire life. Losing her family. Surviving alone in the woods. Not understanding why she was different. And now to see her on her side on the ground like this makes me sick to my stomach.

I don't know how long we've waited, but when Meira finally quiets down, relief washes over me.

Moments later, her body morphs and stretches. Dušan pulls back, sitting on his heels.

Bardhyl and I approach her. All of us are on our knees around her as she transforms.

In a heartbeat, our soulmate lies on the ground between us, curled in on herself, naked, bruised from her earlier assault on the undead.

She cranes her head up and looks at each of us, the wolf still in her eyes.

I've never seen her this frightened, and her reaction carves through my heart.

"I-I t-thought, I'd never…" Her words fade and tears

stream down her face. The terror of knowing she was stuck in the wolf would have been petrifying.

Dušan swoops her into his embrace, an arm cradled under her knees, the other at her back, and she curls against his chest. Her soft cries are blades to my throat.

"I'm so sorry," Dušan whispers to her.

I've never heard him apologize, but the heartbreak in his voice has me choking up.

Bardhyl is just as lost in his thoughts, in his misery of what we almost lost today.

On the way back to the cave leading to the tunnels, the herd of zombies from the earlier massacre wander through the woods. There are so many of them, it leaves me uneasy. My pulse spikes because in truth, I can't tell if they're under Meira's control or wild creatures.

Regardless, the four of us keep a quick pace to our cave without a sound. As we enter, I glance back.

At least three dozen zombies thread through the woods, trailing after us, moaning, lurching, leaving blood in their wake.

Bardhyl's face blanches. "You think they're the safe ones?"

"I fucking hope so," I reply. Then we waste no time rushing to the bunker in the tunnels.

MEIRA

*D*arkness still clings to my mind like cobwebs. Even lying in bed in the underground room with my three wolves, I can't shake off the sensation of being swallowed by the dark, falling deeper and deeper. That's how it felt being under my wolf's strength.

The terror rose through me so jagged and fast, I swore that would be the last of me. All I pictured was the wolf running into the woods and I'd forever be trapped in my own mind.

I shiver while Dušan wipes my brow with a damp cloth. He sits on the edge of the bed while Lucien covers me with a blanket and Bardhyl sticks another pillow at my back.

"I'm sorry," Dušan says.

It's strange to hear those words from a powerful Alpha. He forced my wolf into submission to help me emerge, and I owe him everything. But there's pain etched over his face, and he's thinking of our conversation in the woods before I transformed. It's in his eyes, the burden that carries the weight of the world. It's been on my mind, too.

I reach over and take his hand in mine, bringing it to my chest. "What happened is not on any of you."

He's shaking his head. "The blame is on no one but me, as I knew better." The grief in his voice splinters my resolve.

"You don't get to say that when everything is chaotic outside. When we barely get two moments to think things through." I lift his hand to my lips. "We can't succeed if you're going to start hating yourself."

Lucien and Bardhyl sit on the bed too, moving closer, but keeping quiet for now.

"Meira, do you understand what happened today?" Dušan explains, his voice thin.

I lick my dry lips and nod. "I have zero control over my wolf, basically." My voice cracks.

He leans in, sliding loose strands of hair from my brow. "When you push your wolf away too often without establishing trust, you lose the ability to control your animal forever."

I stare at him. "What do you mean by *forever?*" Already, my stomach twists in on itself. For so long, I craved to release my wolf, and now that I have, I'm about to lose her once again. All because of my fear.

My throat chokes.

The corners of his mouth pinch. "It means that you can shift of your own free will, but when you do, the wolf will control you in animal form. You will struggle to change back, just as you did today. I'm sorry." He pauses, breathing heavily. "In our eyes, you're still a wolf, still one of us."

I blink away the tears threatening to spill and glance from one Alpha to the next, each staring at me with pity. And I hate myself for wanting the world to open up so I can drown in my tears. I've always been strong, always come through any adversity.

I'm a survivor.

But no matter how many times I tell myself that, I can't stop the tears. Dušan reaches over and catches one as it rolls over my jaw.

"So I can't really transform again, can I?" I ask in a faint voice.

He lowers his gaze and nods. "It's safer if you don't."

"That's not great news," I croak, and my attempt at smiling to push away the dread feels forced and lopsided. Before I know it, I'm sobbing in my hands. Deep, heart-wrenching crying, like my chest is cracking wide open.

My three men close in around me, holding me while I cry for the loss of something I only gained recently. I feel stupid for letting this upset me so much when I grew up without my wolf. Except the first couple of times I did transform awakened something inside me. A primal side, and for the first time in my life, I felt complete. Now it's been ripped away, and what's left is me.

The broken girl with no wolf.

My sobs grow louder as reality settles in. I'll no longer be able to trust my wolf. And I loathe myself for making such a horrible mistake that has cost me so much. For letting fear restrain me.

I don't know how long we stay huddled close, but when I finally lift my head and wipe away the tears, I'm determined to make a difference with what I have.

Glancing up at my three Alphas, I say, "Let's focus on getting our pack back, then we can deal with all this crap. I didn't go through all that with my last transformation to have it wasted. There are over a hundred undead out there under my control. And I'm fucking angry, and I want to destroy something... or *someone* called Mad." My voice trembles.

"I'm ready," Lucien confirms, his hand on my leg squeezing. "I know how it feels to lose so much, but like Dušan helped me get back on my feet, we will be here for you. First, let's kick some ass."

Bardhyl is on my other side. "I should've known

there was a reason I fell for you so fast. You're a survivor. We all are, and that makes us the most dangerous wolves out there." He steals a kiss, and I soften against him. "I'm ready to start ripping out spines."

During moments where so much goes to shit, having my three wolves by my side makes all the difference in the world.

Dušan sits back, smiling at me.

"What are you thinking about?" I ask.

"I'm ready to save my pack and finally give you the home where you'll always be loved and protected."

I want to cry all over again at all of their heartfelt words, but the time to shed tears is over.

Mad wants to fight. So I'll bring him a war.

CHAPTER 21

MEIRA

"*I*s everyone ready?" Dušan asks, standing tall and strong. The wind rustles through his dark hair, a contrast to those hypnotizing blue eyes. They shine brightly today, more than they have before, and behind them is a warrior who's had enough of running.

"I'm ready," I answer, as do Lucien and Bardhyl, though both are preoccupied with staring at the army of Shadow Monsters fanning outward in the woods behind Dušan. The creatures look our way, and even I'll admit there's an eeriness in having so many of them peppering the woods. Each as gross as the next, they're just instruments, I tell myself. There's no soul inside them, no emotion. They're only empty shells carrying a virus.

"I still think one of us should join Meira," Lucien says, his voice clipped, and the way he looks at me, his hands sliding into mine, softens me. He's worried...hell, we all are. After what I just went through earlier today on top of all the other shit, I don't blame him.

"Agreed," Bardhyl states.

I swing my gaze over to him standing on my other side, and I lean against him so he knows how much he means to me. "You're all incredible, but we already agreed. You three are breaking into the compound through the tunnels and I'm waiting near the rear door with this mismatched group of undead, so you can open the back door."

"As much as I hate leaving her too, it makes sense," Dušan adds. "If she's surrounded by over a hundred zombies, no wolf will get close to her. Plus, she'll be waiting for us in the woods, up a tree, so even if the Ash guards are near, she won't be spotted. And if us three are together in the compound, it's easier to fight off anyone if we're found."

I nod. "It's the only way to get all of the creatures into the settlement. And if I can get close enough to Mad and get him and his loyal men away from the innocents, then I'll unleash the zombies on them." I'm hoping with every fiber of my being that the sight of the creatures alone will be Mad's undoing. His men will panic, and Dušan, Lucien, and Bardhyl can take him out.

Well, that's the plan, at least.

Lucien and Bardhyl's misgivings are written all over their faces. "Really hate splitting up again," Bardhyl says, with Lucien nodding.

"I know," I say, "but you may need more of you in there if guards find you."

"Let's move," Dušan commands. He glances at me as his hand reaches for mine. "We'll take you near the compound, then the three of us are heading into the tunnels."

Straightening my posture, I step forward, the harsh wind tugging at my black baggy pants and a T-shirt that hangs off my shoulder. I never pictured myself going to war dressed so casually, but armor is not easy to come by in the stash of clothes in an underground room. Plus, my protection comes from the dozens of undead bodies following me.

Slipping my hand in Dušan's, the four of us hurry into the woods. We maneuver around the standing dead, and it's hard not to know they're there. I can't shake the shivers snaking up my arms at how close the monsters are to my men. The moment we pass them, they turn and proceed to follow. Soon enough, we have a long tail in our wake, with Lucien and Bardhyl extremely close at our backs.

"This is kinda freaky," Lucien murmurs.

"If I ever come back as one of those things," Bardhyl says with a soft voice, "chop off my head. I don't want to lurch randomly searching for food like a creep."

"Bruh, you'll be dead and won't have a brain to think beyond eating."

"What if we've all been wrong this whole time about them? They clearly must have some ability. How else do they understand Meira's commands?"

I glance over my shoulder at them, the men's conversation making me curious about the answer. "Maybe it's just a muscle memory. A few words they recognize and their meaning? Whatever's in my blood that I infect them with has to connects us to an extent, so it could be a combo of things." I shrug, though the thought that my influence may not last forever does cross my mind.

"It's one theory," Lucien responds, while Bardhyl nods.

Dušan says, "What matters is that right now they want to do your bidding."

"Absolutely." I squeeze his hand lightly.

We remain silent for the rest of the trip through the woods, and soon slow down as we approach the rear of the settlement.

When the compound finally comes into view beyond the trees that surround us, my stomach clenches.

Shuffling feet on the ground closes in behind us, and most of the Shadow Monsters have paused, staring my way. Dense trees, and shadows, are the perfect place to hide.

"This spot should work," I say.

"And this is your tree, cupcake," Bardhyl says, standing near an enormous fir bursting with heavily ladened branches that span outward at the base and cinch in the higher it reaches for the sky. I can't help but be reminded of a Christmas tree. Something I've seen a few times in old books. A tradition humans used to celebrate. The reason for the festivities wasn't clear, but it clearly always involved lots of food, gifts, and a tree like this one decorated in the most spectacular colors. It must have been beautiful.

"This will do." Lucien heads over to the tree, dodging several zombies standing in his path, and we follow him.

Dušan's grip pulls me to him. "Stay hidden no matter what until we come for you. We'll be quick to open the rear door from the inside. Just remember how much I love you."

Before I can respond, his lips are on mine. I lean against him, my hands on his chest, and kiss him back, not ready to part ways. His arms let go of mine and they slide around my back. Breathless and hot, I fist his shirt, needing more of these soft, cushioned lips, and the way his tongue explores my mouth.

Someone clears his throat. "Careful you don't give the zombies any ideas." The mirth in Lucien's voice has us breaking apart, and I roll my eyes at him.

Lucien takes the chance to close the distance between us, drawing me by my waist to his body. His kiss is instant, those wicked lips rolling against mine, his grip digging into my hips with need.

Fingers crawl up my back, when I realize it's a third hand and not Lucien's. Breaking from our kiss, I whisper to him, "Please take care of them."

"Love you, babe. We got this."

When I turn to Bardhyl, he grabs my waist and has me off my feet in seconds. I gasp and grip his shoulders as I snap my legs around his hips. His lips are on fire. And we kiss like this is our last day on Earth, ravenous and desperate. I adore how he's always rougher with me, and I'm left with bruised lips afterward.

In moments, he pulls from my mouth, and with

strong hands, he lifts me higher as he turns us toward the lowest-hanging branch. "Grab hold and I'll give you a boost."

I snatch a branch that is rough under my fingers.

Bardhyl's hands run down my legs and he grabs the back of my thighs, then pushes me higher.

In haste, I throw a leg over the branch and shuffle up until I'm sitting. I glance down and blow Bardhyl a kiss.

"Love you. Behave and stay up there," he commands.

"I promise," I say.

One last look my way with heartfelt smiles, and the three of them slide into the woods amid the undead, vanishing from view. The density of pine needles on this tree makes it difficult to see too much. Slowly, I get to my feet, grasping on to the trunk, reminded of my days living in trees. A time that feels so long ago.

I climb up to the next branch, which offers a better vantage point. And right there in the distance stands the lofty, metal fence of the compound with a small view of the back door. Nerves tangle inside me that Ash Wolves will ambush my men. I chew on my lower lip and just need to shove those thoughts aside or they will drive me crazy.

Settling down, I get comfortable and straddle the thick branch, my back to the trunk.

Now I stare out and wait, hoping that everything goes according to plan.

BARDHYL

I suck in every rapid breath, filling my lungs. We ran the whole fucking way back to the cave and through the tunnels. Now we're catching our breath inside Kinley's house at the back door.

Lucien peers out the window through a gap in the thick curtains, while Dušan has the door slightly ajar, staring out into the backyard that flows into the woodlands inside the settlement.

"Is it clear?" I ask, glancing back into the empty living room. We helped Kinley into her bedroom, and she shut the door, closing herself in to stay safe until this is over in case the fight breaks near her home. We told her the bare minimum but enough to know what's going to be happening outside.

Dušan's plan is simple, but the best ones usually are. Going for Mad directly exposes us easily to his guards. We'd be overpowered. So a massive breach in the settlement will make him less protected by his guards as panic spreads. And that is when we strike.

I've known the dickhead long enough to not expect Mad to get his hands dirty. He sends his men out to search for us in the woods while he sits back in the compound, taking it easy. *Sonofabitch.* His little rise to the top is going to be short-lived.

"Area's clear," Dušan whispers. "We make a break into the cluster of trees leading up to the rear entry of the compound. We'll be less likely to be spotted this way, then we can open the gate for Meira."

The door to the house swings open, and we're on the run.

A strong wind collides into us. My gut tightens and I hold my head low, stealing looks from either side of me. No one to see the three of us cut across the wide grounds and burst into the cluster of trees running along the edge of the settlement. It's not enough to conceal us completely, but the shadows are a cloak should anyone glance this way.

I can't stop thinking about Meira and praying she's safe. She's surrounded by zombies, but Ash Wolves are in the woods, and I hope to hell and back she remains up in that tree.

We pound the Earth, rushing up the slope, staying close to the trees. I remain behind Dušan and Lucien, and I keep checking over my shoulder. My skin crawls being out here; I feel damn exposed. I loathe how I feel anything but safe in my own home. And this is why I want to murder Mad slowly, make him squirm and cry. And, well, those worms who follow him blindly will also feel my wrath. I've taken down a mental list of names. None of them have escaped my attention. I don't forget.

Dušan glances back, and with two fingers, signals we're heading left and toward the rear door, where the woodland inside the compound spreads, offering us better coverage.

We move swiftly, and I scan the rolling landscape that leads back down to the fortress... the home we will reclaim.

About a dozen pack members roam near the back of

the building, and I can only assume they're guards. Since Mad's forced takeover, most of the pack seem to remain hidden in their homes. It's better this way, as they'll stay out of danger.

Lucien swings right sharply, along with Dušan, just as the hairs on my nape start lifting. The air thickens, and I sense someone near. I snatch the back of Lucien's top, just as a group of figures emerge from up ahead where the woods are thicker, darker. Dušan pauses with us.

Guards, maybe twenty of them, come at us so suddenly, I retreat.

A hum carries on the wind, closely followed by thundering steps racing up behind us as well. My nerves wound tight, I snap around just as a fist crunches right in the middle of my face.

I groan, the pain zigzagging across the bridge of my nose, and stars dance in my vision. "The fuck?!"

Fury blasts through me, and I'm already lunging at the enemy before I can clearly see who it is. Who gives a fuck when I'm tearing him down?

Punch after punch, I finish him, my anger a blinding bull pushing and pushing me. If our war has begun, I won't back down.

Someone smashes into my side, throwing me to the ground. I roar and leap up to my feet when a wall of guards rush toward me. Lucien and Dušan are fighting their own battles, but they're outnumbered.

This isn't part of the plan... we made a grave mistake. We assumed that Mad would leave this entrance manned with the usual number of guards.

I recoil, my legs slipping out from under me down the slope. My wolf shoves forward when the siren abruptly goes off, right as more guards emerge from the direction of the back entrance. Except the alarm has nothing to do with a breach. It's to announce to Mad that we've been caught. This was a damn trap.

Fuck!

Lucien and Dušan both look at me, and dread sweeps over their eyes. With guards coming at us from every side, the realization that we've walked into a trap sinks in. There's no way we can fight our way out of this, and I see it painted over their faces as well. I grind my teeth, fury bleeding into every fibre of my being.

Two guards leap onto Lucien, and he tosses one aside, the other clipping his face with a swinging fist. Another three guards circle Dušan. I dart toward them when more men came at me, and I'm knocked backward from their sheer force. Fire lashes over my back from the hard, rocky ground while I lose sight of Lucien and Dušan.

Instinct has me scrambling back up, recoiling, searching for a rock or something as a weapon.

Sucking in hard breaths, I meet each of my attackers' eyes. Asshole Alphas and Betas at the bottom of the pack hierarchy. I will destroy every last one of them.

Then they charge toward me.

Fists, knees, knuckles. They find me. Pummel into me. I lash out as ferociously as possible, needing a few seconds to transform, but more pile on top.

I snatch one by the neck and squeeze, his lips curling upward with a snarl. All the while, I deliver a punch to someone else's face. A hard whack comes to the back of my head, and yellow stars glint in my vision.

I snap around, my stomach tightening from the pain spearing over my skull. Before I can even kick the shit out of the brute, two others slam into my back, shoving me the ground. Rage rises through me like an inferno.

I buck and throw myself against him, hissing each time they belt into me. More and more of them come, giving me no chance to even get to my feet.

Blood drips from my mouth and nose, and for the first time in too long, fear creeps over me at the realization that maybe we've chewed off more than we can handle.

CHAPTER 22

MEIRA

A sharp, siren wails through the air. Sudden and loud.

I flinch at first, not expecting it. *Please don't let that be about my men.* Last time I heard that sound, Dušan had been tied up outside the settlement and left as food for the undead.

Blinking toward the compound through the gaps in the tree I'm perched in, I don't notice any commotion. But beyond the fence might be a different story.

My fingers tremble as I grip on to the branch, and a deep pain bites into my chest.

What if they're caught? And I'm waiting for them and they'll never come?

I chew on my lower lip, gnawing it, unsure what to do. They said to remain up here, and I toy with the notion back and forth.

Stay.

Go and check on them.

Fuck!

The siren wears on me like a mosquito refusing to leave me alone. And well, this mosquito is screaming for me to run to the compound.

Determination flares over me. There is a growing need to find them, to help them.

I grasp the thick branch I'm straddling, fingers digging into the timber. Down below, there's no sign of anything but the undead, who are near the tree, waiting for me.

Urgency furiously clings to me. While my throat tightens at the thought that I'm sending my wolves to their deaths by doing nothing.

Darkness feathers at the edges of my mind, coming at me in waves.

I'm shaking, fidgeting, anxiety knotting in my gut.

Choking on my breaths, I start descending, unable to stop myself if I tried. I will never be able to live with myself if I don't check. And I have enough regrets to live with already.

I jump down and my feet kiss the ground.

The surrounding Shadow Monsters flick their heads up, eyes on me, suddenly attentive. Turning away from them, I sprint through the woods as quietly as possible in the direction of the compound, keeping to the shadows.

Please, let them be all right. Please.

Behind me, the undead move slowly, so I'm hoping if I'm quick enough, any guards at the gate won't see the hoard of zombies coming their way.

I remember there were several trees not too far from the fence. If I climb one of those, it should give me a better look into the compound. The farther I move, the more sparse the trees become.

My skin crawls with the thought of being so easily exposed, but I'm not going to sit back if my wolves are in danger. As Dušan said, we have one chance to create the element of surprise… and that comes down to me. If Mad did capture them, then our plans change.

I duck under a branch and swerve around a large fir when a shadow falls over me. A shudder races down to my bones.

I turn and come face to face with a huge brute, with close-cropped, shaved hair and a crooked nose. A Beta, by his bitter scent, and definitely belonging to Mad, seeing as he's this close to the settlement. Omegas and Betas aren't made for each other, so to me, they don't smell appealing.

Recoiling, I glance quickly to where the Shadow Monsters are… They're still just shadows in the distance in the woods, making their way too slowly.

Shit!

I throw my hands up as he approaches. He grins, covering me in shivers, then I kick him in the knee hard.

A split second is all he gives me, but it's enough. I whip around and jolt away, right for the edge of the woods. And my anxiety goes off… If there's one guard, there are more and me bursting into the clearing will grab their attention. I keep looking back and the undead are still too damn far away, blended in among the shadows in the woods.

I swerve left and right to ditch the dickhead coming for me now.

The siren ends abruptly, and a deafening silence settles over the land. My ears pulse, my heart banging loudly in them.

The bastard snatches my top and yanks me backward. I stumble on my heels and slam into his chest. Despair floods me, along with images of him beating me until I'm unconscious. Then I'm no use to anyone.

His hot breath brushes over my cheek. "You're not escaping this time, Omega bitch."

Rage burns me, and I slam my heel into his foot, shoving myself away from him. Iron fingers snap over my wrist too fast for me to escape. Panic swallows me.

I swing back around, my fist crashing into the side of his head. Just as he snarls and wrenches me closer, I drive my knee deep into his balls, loving every moment of his fallen expression.

"Don't fucking touch me!" I shove my fists into his chest and he falls over, curling in on himself, moaning.

I snap around to escape, but I charge right into someone solid. Bouncing back, I teeter to catch my balance.

The new asshole snatches my hair and yanks me to him, sneering. "You dare raise a hand to us, you pathetic, plague-ridden filth?"

Pain roars over my scalp, and tears fill my eyes. I'm scratching his hand to get him to release me. Every inch of me trembles.

I grind my jaw, refusing to give in to them.

He's suddenly hauling me by my hair across the land

and right out of the woods. Desperately, I run to keep up with his long strides. I'm half-bent forward from his grip, so I can't even look back to see how far the undead are.

Hell, if there was ever a time I needed them by my side, it's freaking now.

The ass holding on to me pauses, growling. "Open the fucking door." He bangs a fist against the door, and I crane my head up to see there are no guards on patrol on the fence.

Though from inside, the faint sounds of shouting reaches us. My stomach locks at the thought that maybe I'd been right all along and my men are captured.

Loathing for Mad burns all the way down to my gut. I want to make him suffer so much.

When the man goes to bang on the door once more, I drive a fist into his ribs, then another.

He sneers, his grasp tightening, wrenching me by my hair.

I cry out and twist around just enough to glance behind us.

The undead are emerging from the woods like a great wave, and I've never been happier in my whole life to see them.

A creak sounds from the door to the compound opening, stealing my attention.

"Get the fuck in here," another guard bellows from inside. "We've got them."

I yell and punch my captor's arm, digging my heels in the ground to slow him. Anything.

I twist my head as the Shadow Monsters approach, closer and closer.

Just a bit more time.

"Well, look what I found." He wrenches me toward his friend, whose eyes bulge out of his head. His gaze is locked on something over my shoulder.

"Zombies!"

I feel the man holding me shake against me as he whips around.

"Goddammit, where'd they come from?" His voice trembles.

I'm kicking and shoving against him to escape as he drags me into the compound. I drop to my knees, and his grasp slackens.

In desperation, I scramble over and push myself off the ground.

Thick arms loop around my middle as he yanks me into his arms. "No, you don't."

I scream, my hands reaching out for the undead.

"Run to me!" I screech.

In seconds, they descend upon us like a storm, running awkwardly, lopsided, but they thunder onward regardless. Thin, ragged things that today have become my saviors.

Aggressively, the brute manhandles me, shoving me over his shoulder, and darts past the enormous metal door and into the settlement.

The guard from the door drives it shut, just as several undead slam into the entrance.

He growls, pushing his hands against the metal door, his feet pressing into the earth. "Help me!" he roars.

But there are no other guards in this area.

The man shoving a shoulder into the door is driven backward, his feet skidding over the soil. As I watch through the gap, wave after wave of them pushing to get to me. He stands no chance.

And then the sudden thumping against the nearby fence comes, over and over, I know exactly what's happening.

They're breaking it down.

I want them to tear it down and get in here.

The brute holding me shoves me to the ground as though I'm nothing but a sack. I collapse hard on my hip, but I scramble to my feet, when the back of his hand collides with the side of my face. His knuckles feel like I'd been whacked by a bag of rocks.

"Stay down!" he sneers.

Stars dance in my vision, and I fall flat onto my back. Fiery pain spears over my face. I cry out, clasping my cheek, as my head feels like it's cracking in half. *Damn idiot.*

Around me, the sounds of moaning escalate, and suddenly, the siren blares again.

This time, it's for a real breach.

My face throbs with a sharp ache. The world tilts for a few seconds, then settles.

I blink to clear my eyes as the two guards dart in my direction, panic-stricken. One bolts down the hill toward the fortress, while the other comes for me.

He goes to grab me, but I frantically roll away from him and rush to my feet.

He's too busy glancing over his shoulder when I

quickly sidestep him to reach the creatures, but his hand seizes my arm. His grasp squeezes until it hurts.

I spin and bash my fist into his grip. "Leave me alone," I cry out.

His face is as white as a sheet, yet he still drags me behind him.

I lose my footing and drop to my knees as he lugs me by my arm.

The undead are upon us, careening right alongside us now.

The idiot holding me glances back. He does a double take, his eyes bulging out of his head at how close he is to them.

Then he does what any frightened person does... He releases me and runs like mad down the hill.

Shadow Monsters gather on either side of me, behind me, and with the siren blaring, I guess I've made one hell of an entrance that won't go unnoticed.

CHAPTER 23

LUCIEN

A kick to the back of my legs has my knees hitting the ground right near the fortress. My stomach lurches, and I tense with fury. Dušan and Bardhyl are on either side of me, their deep, guttural growls matching my own. Mad's men had ambushed us, and now, I burn to know that he fooled us.

Abruptly, the sirens of a breach screech through the air. I jerk my head toward the rear entrance. There, shadows flit about in the woodlands within the settlement, moving erratically. What the hell is that?

Did they find Meira?

I glance over to Dušan and Bardhyl, their gazes locked on the movement up on the hill.

My adrenaline spikes as I picture the guards tracking her down, dragging her in here. How did they find her? I grind my teeth, knowing for a fact she would have willingly gotten down from the tree.

"What the fuck is going on?" Mad roars, marching in front of us, staring up the huge hill at the frenzy of shadows amid the cluster of trees. All I can imagine is how easily I can attack him right now, kill him in a heartbeat. Well, easy if there weren't a gun muzzle pointed to the back of our heads.

"Jack," Mad barks. "Get up there now! Find out what's going on." Then he turns on us. "There was never any doubt you would end on your knees before me," he gloats.

There is something so repulsive about a man whose ego exudes from every pore in his body, and he's proud of it. His attention homes in on Dušan. "You're not so great now. Only two men follow you, while the rest stay loyal by my side." He pats his own chest, a sneer of arrogance on the corner of his lips.

I see it now… This petty man has spent his whole life trying to prove to others he's greater and better. His desperation to be praised and seen as successful in ascending to the pack leader position has been nagging him his whole life.

It's why he stares at Dušan with vicious hatred. Jealousy can make someone horrendously vile and vindictive.

"Stefan," Dušan snaps, using Mad's real name. Something I rarely hear him use, and the few times he has have been when he's fucking pissed at him. "This isn't who you are. Most of the pack are in their homes terrified. You can't rule a pack on fear alone. You know this. Your father told us this all the time."

Mad spits on the ground, inches from us. "Fuck you. Easy to say when you claimed what was rightfully mine. He was my father by blood, not yours, but you still forced yourself to be Alpha of the pack, didn't you?"

"Could have something to do with you being too weak-assed to fight the previous Alpha to claim the Ash Wolves," Bardhyl snarls. "So you take the pack like all gutless pigs. By cheating."

The guard behind him whacks him in the back of his head. The thump has me cringing as Bardhyl falls face-first to the ground from the impact. He groans but pushes himself to his knees. Blood drips down his neck from the hit.

I clench my fists. My blood races with vengeance. The need to destroy all these bastards swallows me. Staring past Mad, I see Jack and two others heading up the hill, and there's no sign of what's causing the commotion farther up there.

"Today will be my happiest day. To see you three finally fucking killed." Mad's upper lip curls.

He lifts his head to the guards behind us, looking ready to give the order.

I stiffen, bending my arms, prepared to attack the prick behind me first.

A sudden scream, dark and terrifying, definitely belonging to a man, spears through the air from nearby on the hill.

We all glance in that direction.

Two guards are sprinting down, Jack and his followers, suddenly doing the same, darting like death chases them.

Near the edge of the trees, a cluster of undead lurch forward, dozens of them pouring out of the shadows.

Their moans are lost beneath the siren. I want to shout from the rooftops. *Fuck yes!* About damn time, and that's when I know it's Meira who must be there. I adore that little wolf.

"Who the fuck let them in?" Mad bellows. "Shoot them!" He's shuddering, his face red with rage.

My heart leaps, thundering as more of these filthy creatures that are the best sight in the world shuffle forward.

Someone stands from the ground in front of the zombies. Dark, long hair flowing over her shoulder, she's like a goddess rising out of the underworld with her followers crowding around her. As morbid as that sounds, there's something spectacular about seeing her wield such power.

"Meira," Bardhyl whispers, and Dušan's breath catches. While others fear her, we love her to hell and back.

The gun from the back of my head falls away, and panicked voices burst around us. I curl my fingers as Dušan climbs to his feet. Bardhyl and I follow suit.

Mad whips around to us, his eyes bulging. "Shoot these three now!" he shouts at the guards behind us.

My stomach tightens, squeezing the terror right up to my throat.

When I glance over my shoulder, the guards have recoiled, the guns in their hands trembling. It's one thing to shoot zombies from the safety of a fence, but to be in front of them brings out a raw, primal fear.

An explosive shot sounds, and my attention turns to

a guard aiming for the monsters running down toward us.

Meira. I can't see her. Has she given the monsters a command? Where the hell is she if Mad's men are firing? The terror of something happening to her grips me.

The wave of undead is like a tsunami, relentless, and it sends a shudder down my back.

"We need to move and find her," I suggest. "We don't know what order she gave them."

Dušan swings around and runs up behind Mad, who's distracted.

Bardhyl charges toward a guard who has his back turned to him and takes him down.

And suddenly, the walls of chaos close in around us. All I can think about is finding Meira, then finishing Mad, and I pivot toward the undead.

A sudden slamming into my side so hard, it has me hissing, my spine arching inward.

I whip around to the guard pointing his gun directly at my chest, and a dull, cold ache fills me. My feet are glued to the ground while the commotion around me fades and only the pounding of my heart sounds that this is it.

BARDHYL

*Z*ombies rush toward us while guards with weapons are running to stop them, shooting wildly.

Pop. Pop. Pop.

I frantically scan the area for Meira. One moment she stood at the top of the hill with the zombies, then she merged into their mass and vanished.

Fury skids across my mind as the siren in the distance howls like a wolf. Where the hell is she? With bullets flying, my insides clench at the thought that she'll get shot.

A hard punch comes to my shoulder "Get the fuck to the ground!"

I grunt with pain and swing around, my fist swinging. Clipping the bastard in the head, I follow his fall, delivering two more blows into his face.

Someone shoves a foot into my back, driving me flat on top of the guard. Rapidly, I roll off the first guy, seeing the other culprit stumbling to catch his step from being pushed by a zombie. But he's now lifting his gun toward me. So I kick out my leg, my heel striking him in the groin. He stumbles backward, crying like a baby, and I get up.

Several feet away, I spot Lucien iced over, looking at the man pointing a gun at his chest. I swallow hard.

Acid spills into my veins, scorching my insides. I don't even remember moving, but I sprint over to them, slamming into the guard, coming in from his side like an avalanche.

He hits the ground as his gun goes off, shooting into the air.

My ears ring with a tremendous buzz.

Frantically, I snatch the man's wrist and squeeze it until he drops the gun. I headbutt him in the face for good measure. My head spins, but it's damn worth it. He cries out, blood spilling from his nose.

Lucien is there in seconds, punching the shit out of him as I climb to my feet.

"Always saving your ass." I groan, smirking at my friend. He turns to me, a slash of blood across his cheek from the guy he just beat up. Looks like war paint, and it suits him.

"I had him right where I wanted him," he answers, but he smiles his thanks. "Where's Dušan? Last I saw, he was dashing for Mad."

I scan the yard.

There's madness all around, but there's no sign of him. Did Mad take him? "We gotta find them and Meira."

The zombies are closing in. They fan out, covering the slopes like locusts coming in for a feed. The three or so dozen guards don't even bother with us anymore, not when they're anticipating being eaten alive.

"Maybe it's not a bad idea to stay out of the zombies' way until we know they aren't going to eat us," I suggest. "And let's take out these disloyal motherfuckers working for Mad in the process."

"Hell yeah." Lucien rips his top up and over his head, undressing so fast, he's already half-transformed by the time his pants hit the ground. He bounds out as his gray wolf, and I call mine just as quickly, the sharp pain of transforming deep and agonizing, but I embrace it as I ready for war.

The moment I leap forward, the first wave of zombies reaches us. They scramble onward, not attacking, but slamming into whoever stands in their way.

Everyone is screaming as pandemonium strikes.

Lucien and I make a mad rush to the side and out of their way. From my perspective, not one undead has attacked anyone. They're stopping once they reach the fortress, so that must have been Meira's command.

Those terrified guards don't seem to notice and deliriously shout, shoving against the creatures spreading around the yard, shooting them. But there's no way they have enough ammunition for the whole herd.

And this is our moment. I exchange a glance with Lucien, then I crash into the masses, him doing the same. It's a strange feeling to be pressing against the undead… monsters I feared my whole life, and now look at me. Rubbing shoulders with them.

It's ridiculous.

But I also wonder if this is how Meira feels being immune around them.

Like she's untouchable.

A squeal comes from my left from a guy shuddering, trying to avoid touching the monsters all around him.

Darkness slips over me and I have no regrets. It's time to bring these dickheads their long overdue punishment.

CHAPTER 24

MEIRA

I sprint away from the zombies, cutting across the grounds and hurrying toward the side of the fortress. Moments ago, I rode the wave of the undead, using them as a shield against the bullets. My pulse is still in my throat. And now it beats frantically after I had spotted Dušan darting after Mad. They headed down this wide path between the building and lofty fence. Several of his guards followed, and that worries the hell out of me.

I desperately bolt after them because I want Mad dead, and I don't trust anything about him, let alone him not trapping Dušan.

The main yard is exploding with combat. There are so many Shadow Monsters that it's difficult to discern who is who down there. I instructed the undead to run down to the building, hoping that was enough to drive fear into the guards and get them to back away. It seems to have worked with them desperately trying to get away from the zombies.

My feet punch the ground, and with my head low, I sprint down the slope and toward the passage alongside the fortress.

Up ahead, two wolves are spiraling in a wild battle. Fur and fangs are all I see in the vicious fight. Dušan against Mad by his wolf size. Thunderous roars spill around us, primal and explosive. The way they tumble and bite into each other in violent motions has me shivering. Two guards still in human form watch them, and I don't miss that one is holding a rifle.

Ice fills my veins.

Will he shoot Dušan?

My legs explode in rapid movement just as the gray wolf with black ears who has to be Mad is tossed aside from the fight. He rolls and lands on his side with a huff. Blood mats his fur, peppering his body, and he scrambles upright.

My Alpha stands tall, heaving for each breath, blood running down the side of his wolf face. But he remains strong, head high and a growl erupting from his throat, his teeth exposed. The image is terrifying. Yet seeing him this powerful, this brutal, warms my heart. I love every inch of him even more when he's this dominant.

I duck behind several trees against the fortress. Everyone is too occupied with the fight to notice me, and I don't intend to get shot, either.

Dušan doesn't spare Mad a second. He charges him, headbutting him in the side, throwing him off his paws. But in that same moment, the two guards snarl and drop to their hands and knees. A heartbeat is all it takes for their clothes to shred and fall away as their bodies enlarge, giving way to an explosion of charcoal fur. The snap of bones fills the air.

It happens so fast that terror sinks through me. My wolf rises in me at my heightened anxiety. She pushes to escape, to deal with this for me. Except that would be suicidal. If I let her loose, I can never shift back.

"Dušan, watch out!" I scream, throwing myself out from behind the tree.

The two guards are already on him, the fight suddenly three against one.

Anger flares over me, my body heating with the rage of them all turning on him. Of course they wouldn't make this a fair fight.

I rush toward them and snatch the first rock I lay my sights on, something the size of my fist, then I grab a short, thick branch.

My brain is numb from the horrendous, cruel sounds of their barbaric brawl. My head spins, but they all leap as one after another, taking bites at Dušan. They move with tremendous speed.

The sight of my soulmate butchered will haunt me forever. I suck in shaky breaths and with all my strength, I hurl a rock at one of the guard wolves.

Thump.

It smacks right into his head, just below his ear, hard enough that it knocks him off Dušan. He teeters on his feet, then shakes his head. But I don't waste a second and sprint toward him.

My knees tremble as I rush to him. Before he reacts, I jab the pointy end of my stick right at his ribs. With all my weight behind me, I drive the branch into him, piercing skin. It sinks deeper than I expect.

He yelps and flinches away from me, sucking the branch right out of my hands, still jabbed between his ribs. His cries add to the chaotic sounds flooding the air. He collapses and starts transforming back into his human form, already passed out.

I turn to the fight, where I notice now it's only Dušan on top of the guard, but Mad has slipped from the fight. My heart speeds up. Where the hell is he?

A sudden, loud whistle carves through the sounds. My head swings toward the back of the fortress.

Mad stands about fifteen feet away, naked, his body covered in bitemarks and bruises. He's now holding the rifle the other guard carried. The butt is tucked into the pocket against his shoulder, one hand gripping the stock, and the other on the trigger. He's aiming at Dušan.

Darkness sweeps over me, stealing all my thoughts… taking everything but the ringing of the gun firing.

I scream, catapulting myself toward Dušan. "Run!"

My heart thunders as my world dissolves and moves too fucking slow for me to ever reach him in time.

The bullet strikes Dušan right in the chest with such force, it throws him backward. He hits the ground with a heavy thump. The guard next to him throws himself to the ground, barely missed by the bullet.

My insides shatter like glass, and I'm at his side in a flash. Dropping to my knees, I cry out, "Dušan, please tell me you're okay! *Please*."

So much blood pours from his chest where he got

shot. I can't even see the bullet in the tangle of blood and fur.

His eyes are glassy and he's looking up at me.

Tears run down my cheeks. I'm breaking apart. "Y-You h-have to heal." I hiccup my breaths, hating the feeling coming over me. I'll lose him. And the emptiness I lived with all my life rushes forward.

The hurt, the agonizing despair, the constant battle to make it through another day. All those feelings are tangled in a knot, swelling inside me.

He's still breathing, drawing in rugged, hissing breaths.

I'm sobbing uncontrollably as his body changes back to his human form.

Lying before me is my Dušan, trembling, curled on his side. Deep gash wounds cover his body, just as they did on Mad. I press my hands to his chest to stop the bleeding. His mouth moves, but no words come out.

"Just hold on. You'll heal. It's what wolves do. Please don't leave me. Don't you dare, Dušan."

Blood seeps between my fingers, dribbling down my hand and splattering into the soil.

He needs help.

"Hold on." My pleading slips past my lips as more tears fall.

Suddenly, someone grabs my hair and yanks me backward.

I cry out, reaching back to free my hair, my feet moving with the motion, all the while, my heart thundering.

"It's over. He's dead and you are mine." Mad's hoarse words tear over me.

I can't breathe from the anger crashing into me. My lungs tighten, as do my muscles. And I can't stop looking at Dušan, but I don't know if his ability can heal a bullet wound. He's on the ground, in a pool of blood.

This is too fucking much. I scream and shake violently.

I've lost everything once already, and I won't let someone take it from me again. I thrust and buck against Mad, my hands clawing at his grip on my hair. But on the inside, I'm dying at Dušan being left to suffer.

My entire body pulses with adrenaline.

With it comes a hatred that rages inside me, beating through me.

I'm broken. I've always been this way, and there's only one way to really finish this.

My monster lingers just beneath the surface, nudging me to come out, to be free.

She is my salvation, always has been, I see this now. And without her, I can't stop Mad.

And in an abrupt moment of desperation, I open my floodgates to my wolf.

She doesn't need coaxing and rushes out of me, coming so fast, her brutal growl startles even me. She's a tempest of vengeance, and I set her free, well aware of the consequences she brings to me. And I don't have a single regret.

I can't live with myself if I don't do everything in my

power to finish this fucking bastard who should have died long ago.

His grip slackens as my transformation rocks through me, ripping me apart like someone's taken a blade to my body, and then stitched me back together. The world sharpens, and for the first time, I ease my grasp over my wolf.

You are free, I tell her. *This is all you now.* I shudder, my thoughts constantly on Dušan. While the other half of me drowns in violent fury.

My wolf whips around without any encouragement from me.

Mad's raising his rifle, his lips twisted when he looks at me, but my wolf pounces on him, shoving him backward. The gun drops from his grip as he shouts for backup.

A large form slams into my side so abruptly, the world tilts around me.

With a snap, my wolf bites right into the side of the guard's face while bent over me. The ferociousness is stark and animalistic.

He screeches with terror, clutching the side of his head, batting me away with his other hand. I taste his blood, the metallic, coppery tang drowning me. My wolf spits out the man's ear on the ground, and that grosses me out.

As I get to my feet, a snarl soars from my mouth, and my wolf's bloodthirsty hunger floods me. For the first time, a new sense of confidence flares over me.

Lifting my gaze, I meet Mad's eyes.

He's backing away, his eyes locked on the rifle he had dropped several feet away.

And I dare him with my sneer alone to collect it.

My wolf freezes, watching him, my ears flat, breaths shallow.

Go for it, asshole.

He makes his call, and it's just as I hoped.

Mad scrambles desperately for the weapon.

My wolf takes off.

We crash into him before he takes another step. Adrenaline races through my veins. Sharp teeth bite into his neck, my wolf savagely shaking him, and she rips free with a chunk of him dangling from her mouth... my mouth. It's hard to tell when I feel and taste everything, like it's me moving.

There's no stopping her now. She goes back and rips him to shreds. Breaks bones, tears flesh. His terrifying gurgling sounds are too fast a death for him. Yet he doesn't deserve another moment to be alive. He's a pitiful excuse for a life.

After he took my Dušan, he needs to suffer.

My grip on my wolf hardens suddenly as blind fury burns me. And before I know it, it's me there with my wolf, greedily stealing Mad's last breaths away, stealing everything from him, as he's done to me and so many others.

Coppery blood fills my senses, and warm blood drips down my face.

Anger burns me. I'm screaming in my head for what I lost, for how hard I fought to finally have a fair life. Now it's gone.

I glance down at Mad. His eyes are wide and frozen with shock, staring into the sky. Gone from this world but not soon enough.

Stars dance in my vision, and I blink them away. Instead, my wolf presses forward once more and tilts her head up. She unleashes an ear-shattering howl.

Darkness comes at me, curling around me.

My wolf darts back toward Dušan, who hasn't moved. Then she recoils within me. I feel her pulling back until it's only me left.

The ache in my heart deepens to the point where it hurts like hell each time I stare down at him gasping for each breath. I need to get him help. It may not be too late.

I turn to fetch someone, when the agony, the exhaustion, the grief swallows me. My legs buckle out from under me, and I'm falling into a darkness that sweeps in and carries me away.

CHAPTER 25

DUŠAN

I startle awake, sitting upright so damn fast that the room spins. An excruciating ache burrows through my chest. I cry out with the pain and clutch my chest as I fall onto my back. Eyes shut, I inhale each deep breath, wading through the pain that comes and goes, but slowly, it eases.

Wait… Room?

I peel open one eye and then the other and stare up to a white ceiling with a single lightbulb. Turning my head, I take in the door and wardrobe in my bedroom.

Memories rush at me.

The zombies in the settlement.

Mad shooting me, and well, I'd have expected him to throw me into a prison if I'd survived. He sure as hell wouldn't take the time to try and fix me. I finger the bandages wrapped around my chest, confused as to how I survived that. When I really look at myself, I notice most of my bruises and bites from the fight have healed. But a bullet wound is something else.

And Meira's sweet face was the last thing I remember before... I thought I'd died.

Soft snoring sounds come from the end of my bed, and I wrinkle my brow, leaning forward, which only sends a shot of pain up my chest.

I clench my teeth, riding the wave of slashing pain, then I push my legs out of the bed. They touch the cold floorboards, and I get up, groaning. I don't remember the last time I ached so much.

With slow, agonizing steps, I come around the end of the bed to find a tawny red wolf fast asleep on the plush rug.

My heart twists with the sight of her in wolf form, curling in on herself, sleeping by my bed. And things are starting to make sense. She must have saved me by transforming and letting her wolf take care of Mad... but at what cost? To be forever locked in her wolf?

A pang of guilt seizes me. Because of me, she sacrificed everything. A desperate, ugly feeling grabs me, and my knees wobble.

What have I done?

Inch by inch, the cold, hard truth hits me over and over.

This was never the future I wanted for her. I'd give up mine instantly for her to have everything.

Never this.

I crumble and fall to my knees, the thumping sound rousing her awake. Her head jerks up, and she looks over at me with sleepy eyes, her fur all flat on the side she slept on.

My eyes prick as I stare into those beautiful pale

bronze irises. I reach over and hug her as my throat thickens with an overwhelming emotion that chokes me. "Oh, Meira, what did you do? I'm not worth it."

I hold her, close my eyes, and pretend she's with me like before, where she laughs in a way that brightens my darkest days. To feel her lips against mine. I try not to overthink everything I'll miss because it will destroy me. She is still with me, but the sting in my heart hurts more than the bullet wound.

A sudden charge of electricity runs up my arms. I snap open my eyes just as Meira begins to tremble violently in my arms. Her body stretches, and she's literally morphing into her human form.

I have no words, because one moment my heart is ripping out, and now I'm bursting with an unfathomable joy.

It isn't long before I'm holding a gorgeous, naked Meira, who's grinning at me. "Are you really crying because you thought I'd be a wolf all my life? Lucien said you would, but Bardhyl bet you'd still love anyway."

I laugh that she's already making a joke. "Well, they'd be right on both fronts." I have so many questions, but the important thing is that we're still alive.

"How are you feeling?" she asks, glancing down at my bandage. "Someone was looking out for you." She leans in and kisses my lips, my cheeks, my chin. "The bullet went right through your torso, missing all organs and arteries completely. Can you believe that? I think you have an angel caring for you."

The news floats in my mind that somehow I managed to survive such a shot.

"And what about you and your wolf?" I ask. "Seems we all have surprises."

She smiles widely and snuggles against my side, avoiding the injury. "I did what you told me to and gave my wolf full control, and it seems she rewarded me by submitting. I don't know why I was so afraid for so long to just give her control."

"After everything you went through, it's understandable. The important thing is that you are here and mine."

She pulls up and finds my lips again. We kiss softly, full of love. Everything I feared I would lose.

When she pulls back, her lips curl upward, and while I want to just drown in her gaze, my question escapes past my mouth.

"What happened to Mad?" It's not him I want to talk about while I hold my soulmate in my arms, but I need to make sure this is over.

"We never have to worry about him again." She winks at me so adorably, unable to hide her huge grin.

"Did you—"

"Yes," she interrupts. "My wolf and I finished him. I just wish I could have done that long before everything fell into chaos."

"Sometimes things happen for a reason, and really, it should have been me who stopped him a long time ago. But it's done. Thank you for saving me out there."

She shrugs, almost bashful, which has me pulling her closer to me. "You would have done the same for me."

"In a heartbeat."

ONE WEEK LATER

MEIRA

"*How* much longer?" I ask, pacing in Dušan's office, looking away from Lucien and Bardhyl. I can't stop worrying about what my blood results will show. That I'm still sick and it'll slowly wear me down? I haven't coughed up blood since transforming, so I'm praying with everything that my immunity to the zombies is some freak anomaly.

I keep glancing outside the window, where the sun shines brilliantly. Down on the settlement grounds, Ash Wolves are preparing for tonight's celebrations. It'll be a blue moon, and with it being a week since Dušan reclaimed his pack, there is a lot to party about. Mad and his dead followers were burned to ensure they didn't return as the undead and buried deep in the woods. Plus, tonight, Dušan will assure his pack that we are safe, that there is no cure as Mad claimed, but there will be changes to protect them all better. Those survivors who betrayed Dušan fled into the woods already, knowing death was coming for them. And add to all that, Dušan finally returned the serum Mad stole to the X-Clan to keep the peace.

Slowly, all the parts are falling back into place.

Except still, my stomach twists in on itself as I wait for news on my bloodwork. Footfalls approach me, and I turn to find Lucien standing behind me. Today he reminds me so much of when we first met by the side of the road. He's wearing his long-sleeved button-down shirt and those sexy dark jeans that hang low on narrow hips, and let's not forget his cowboy boots. His deep brown hair is swept off his face, and his gray-steeled eyes gleam. Every inch of him is spectacular. And there's a reason I fell for him the moment we met. He is a walking god.

"Come and sit with us." He takes my hand. "The blood results should be ready soon."

"Your pacing is making me tense," Bardhyl states from the three-seater couch where he lounges at one end, legs parted, one arm on his lap, the other along the back of the sofa. Something about him looks bigger today, broader, stronger. The white shirt he wears lays open at his throat, enough that the muscles below his collarbone flex each time he shifts around on the couch. Long white-blond hair drapes over his shoulders. A shadow of growth covers his chiseled jawline, and when he looks at me, he pats his lap, calling me to sit on him.

The corners of my lips involuntary curl upward in response. My body responds automatically to my soul-mates it seems.

Lucien's fingers thread with mine, and he walks me around the table and over to the sofa.

I throw myself down on the middle cushion as Bardhyl hastily slips his arm around my back, and in a split second, I'm sitting on his lap sideways.

"My little Zombie Queen, don't even think you can get away from me," he says, keeping his gaze on me, while his fingers find my skin under my top.

"I'm totally okay to stay next to you," I answer, even if sitting in his lap has me burning up in moments, and already, I feel the bulge in his pants poking against my thigh.

Lucien makes little work of lifting my feet so he can slip in next to Bardhyl and hold on to my legs. Sneakily, he also raises my skirt for a peak.

"Hey." I slap his hand away. "I *am* wearing underwear."

He smirks devilishly. "Had to check just in case you were holding out on us."

I wrinkle my nose at him in confusion. "You think that I randomly decide to not wear underwear so I can surprise you?"

Both men look at me with an overzealous expression, the answer painted all over their horny faces. I shake my head at how transparent they are.

The door suddenly opens, and my gaze jerks upward.

Dušan strolls inside, and I glance behind him, half-expecting Mariana, the pack doctor, to be with him. Except he's alone, and my breath jams in my throat.

Does he have bad news and wants to deliver it to me on his own?

Bardhyl's grip around me tightens, like he senses my unease. But I push myself out of his arms and stand to meet my Alpha, my soulmate, my everything.

He greets me with smiling blue eyes, his black hair laying messily around his face like he's just run through the wind.

"Come here, gorgeous." He collects me into his arms.

I stare up at him, trembling. "Please don't make me wait. Just tell me. What did my blood results say?"

He cups the sides of my face and kisses me with a hunger like he's letting himself be rough with me once again. For the past week as we waited for the tests, we cleaned up the mess caused by Mad.

I push myself closer and kiss him back harder, hoping this means he has good news.

When I break away, breathless, I stare at him desperately.

"The result showed that you still have leukemia." His arms tighten around me.

A chill races down my spine and instantly, tears spring to my eyes. It's stupid how just a few words send a shudder right through me.

Lucien and Bardhyl are off the couch and move to stand on either side of me, their hands on me.

"Don't cry, beautiful," Dušan assures me. "You've always been special, and it seems that because you transformed so late, your first shift couldn't completely eradicate the disease. But it has made it dormant and inactive in your body."

I'm still processing his words, trying to come to terms with the results.

"It's why she's still immune to the zombies," Lucien adds, to which Dušan nods. "Is that how you're controlling them?"

I shake my head. "I don't really know. Guessing it's got to do with me biting them."

"Mariana seemed to think it's connected to your immunity and the bite where you exchange some of your saliva into their blood system. It changes their hunger to obedience to you," Dušan explains.

Bardhyl hugs me from behind, his whisper in my ears, "This is incredible."

"Are you sure?" I ask Dušan, so used to always hearing bad news that I now struggle to believe that in a roundabout way, everything turned out so well.

"Beautiful Meira. You have nothing to worry about." He grabs me and lifts me off my feet, and I'm laughing, my chest close to bursting with happiness. I don't remember ever feeling this way. Where I don't have to be constantly concerned about surviving. About someone wanting to kill me. About running away.

That's no longer who I am.

"I still can't believe how it's all turned out," I say as he lowers me to my feet. I'm surrounded by my three Alphas. "But I have one question."

"Go on," Dušan says.

"What happens if I have kids? Will they get sick too?" It's crazy to think this, but the notion popped into my head. But I don't need them to suffer like I did, and to have them safe from the zombies is what I really want.

No one responds at first, which has me blushing at the thought that I've somehow put them on the spot, talking about babies when we've only just found our freedom.

Dušan finally says, "Mariana told me it's not a hereditary disease, but it can happen. Except seeing as yours is dormant, it's very unlikely. And when the child transforms, which we will ensure they do, their wolf side will protect them as it has you."

I blink at him, and it makes sense, though I still worry. I exhale loudly. "It's so much to take in all at once. All these changes and what's going on with me. But you're saying I have no real cure for everyone against the zombies."

He shakes his head, and I didn't think it would be, but it's worth asking.

"You don't need to think about anything right now but settling into your new home, then helping us three run the pack. Plus, we have the Northern Wolves promising to return for a visit, and I want everything set up to give them no excuse to think we're weak in any way."

My eyes widen, and already a plan is forming in my mind. "I have an idea." I turn so I'm facing all three Alphas. "Let's position zombies around the settlement. I can command them to stay there. Anyone who dares come near our compound will be terrified to come any closer." I shrug. "I just think it's a great cautionary measure. Once they decay away, we replace them. Hell, there are enough of these things in the woods."

"I love that idea," Bardhyl states. "Back in Denmark, we'd do that with wild wolves. Keep them around our campsite. When they made a sound, we knew we had intruders, and most were scared away by them."

"Agreed," Dušan says.

I glance over to Lucien, who's been silent and staring at me strangely. "Are you okay?" I ask.

Sunlight from outside spills through the window, casting over him, giving him a glow. "I'm still back on our previous conversation." He clears his throat. "You're ready to have a baby with us?"

The softness in his voice, the tenderness in his eyes, undoes me because they aren't from someone scared, but someone dreaming of this day. I step toward him and hug him. "Maybe not right away, but yes, if that's okay with all of you."

His breath hitches. "It's everything I've always wanted."

He holds me against him, with Bardhyl and Dušan joining the hug. Me in the middle of these powerful men who love me, who want me in their future. But it turns out they're not the only strong ones. All along, I thought I lived with a monster inside me. But the real fiend was my own fear.

My new life is everything and I love them so much. For the first time, I have a purpose in life. And now, I have a family.

I will never be alone again, and my cheeks hurt from smiling so much that things are finally looking up for me.

"Who's up for practicing baby-making early?" Bardhyl asks out of the blue, which has me rolling my eyes.

Strong hands that I think belong to Dušan slide under my skirt, and I twist to face him. But the deviant is too fast. His fingers curl under the elastic of my underwear and in a violent tug, he rips them off me. I jerk from the movement, and suddenly, I have three sexually starved men staring at me.

"Are you ready?" he asks.

I back away from them, the heat between my legs already slick with arousal.

My breaths rush, and in an instant, I am craving them insatiably.

"Wait. I know we haven't had sex for a week, but—"

"Do you think she's trying to distract us?" Lucien asks.

"Definitely," Bardhyl answers, never lifting his gaze from me.

We've crossed the line from serious talk and into the heady need to release, and even I can't deny the desire igniting me from the inside out.

"Look, how about we all just talk about this first?" I say, trying to distract them.

As they sigh, I whip around and dart to the door, throwing over my shoulder, "Suckers."

The explosion of rapid movement has them charging after me, and I burst out of the room, unable to stop laughing as I sprint down the long corridor.

Everything I've ever dreamed of has come to life,

and it still feels surreal, but I'm willing to make this work.

And who would have thought that even the most broken girl in the world could eventually find her happily ever after?

LOST WOLF

SAVAGE SECTOR

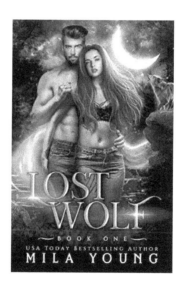

My fated mate sent me to my death

But I can't be killed easily.

Especially when four Viking Wolves awaken a passion within me that ignites fire through my veins and heat into my bones. They see my potential. See me despite my unique blend of darkness.

With me at their side, they want to conquer our broken wolf world.

But it's a deadly game, one I won't play without a few demands of my own--

Help me get revenge against my fated mate, no matter the cost.

START READING LOST WOLF TODAY

THANK YOU

Thank you for reading Shadowlands Sector Three

Reviews are super important to authors as it helps other reader make better decisions on books they will read. So if you have a moment, please do leave a review here, HERE.

Get your copy of Savage Sector 1 today!

Discover more books from Mila Young and find your Happily Ever After!

Start Reading.

NIGHT KISSED

I slay vampires... Then why does the master vamp insist I'm his?

When I'm called in to investigate a chain of suspicious deaths across Alaska, I meet three of the hottest, and most dangerous, monsters I've ever seen.

Just one problem.

They're the things that go bump in the night—a vampire, a fallen angel, and a demon. Enemies I must trust with my life if I'm to solve the dark trail of mysteries before more lives are lost.

But just as hard as solving the murders is denying my attraction to them all. And as things heat up in more ways than one, I know I'll never be the same again…

That is, if I survive the evil I'm sworn to kill... and the ones I've let into my heart.

Night Kissed is the first book in the Chosen Vampire Slayer series.

This is your kind of book if you love kick-ass heroines with sass to match, scorching hot monsters who take what they want, and is perfect for devourers of enemies to lovers books. Expect steam, action, and a supernatural world filled with vampires, demons, shifters, angels... and unhinged alphas who will do anything to protect their woman. Lovers of Anita Blake, Buffy the Vampire Slayer, and True Blood, this is your next addiction.

START READING NIGHT KISSED TODAY

ABOUT MILA YOUNG

Best-selling author, Mila Young tackles everything with the zeal and bravado of the fairytale heroes she grew up reading about. She slays monsters, real and imaginary, like there's no tomorrow. By day she rocks a keyboard as a marketing extraordinaire. At night she battles with her mighty pen-sword, creating fairytale retellings, and sexy ever after tales. In her spare time, she loves pretending she's a mighty warrior, walks on the beach with her dogs, cuddling up with her cats, and devouring every fantasy tale she can get her pinkies on.

Ready to read more and more from Mila Young?
Subscribe to her newsletter
www.subscribepage.com/milayoung

Join my Wicked Readers Group

facebook.com/groups/milayoungwickedreaders

For more information...
milayoungarc@gmail.com

Lightning Source UK Ltd.
Milton Keynes UK
UKHW040612121222
413785UK00003B/699